End Times Crossfire

Books by Stephen L. Thompson

The Crossfire Series

The SFO Series

End Times Crossfire

God says, *"Protect My Children"*

Stephen L. Thompson

End Times Crossfire

In *"End Times Crossfire"* The Crossfire Team becomes the target of a demon-controlled Army of the Anti-Christ, Marco Marino. The Revived Holy Roman Empire (RHONE) is massive and backed by billions of dollars. It is up to the Team to stop their assaults on Christians and Jews. Naturally this causes them to become the number one target for the RHONE's one hundred thousand troops.

- Stephen L. Thompson

End Times Crossfire

Copyright © 2013 Stephen L. Thompson
All rights reserved. This book may not be duplicated or reproduced in any form or manner whatsoever, except as allowed by the U.S. Copyright Act of 1989, as amended, without the prior and express written permission of the publisher.

Published by
Stephen L. Thompson
Facebook.com/CrossfireNovelSeries

Unless otherwise noted, Scripture quotations are taken from the HOLY BIBLE, NEW INTERNATIONAL VERSION®. Copyright© 1973, 1978, 1984 by International Bible Society. Used by permission of Zondervan Publishing House. All rights reserved.

ISBN- 978-1-943879-17-5

Published in the United States of America

Foreword

To my Christian readers –

The Crossfire continuing series of action-adventure novels include depictions of violence which are unusual in Christian literature. It would be nice if there were no conflict or violence in our world. But we live in a time when evil is increasing instead of diminishing, when some men seem to be controlled by selfishness, madness, or evil forces. When the enemies of decent mankind are bent on subjugation of other men and women, righteous men and women must stand against evil. The yoke of oppression is not lifted by prayer alone. God is our shepherd and we are his sheep. As long as there are wolves about, God will use some of us as sheep dogs to defend the rest of us. These stories are about people like that and the forces they fight against. The stories describe violence because it occurs in the real world and it is active in the lives of all people whether they recognize it or not.

To my non-Christian readers –

The Crossfire series include depictions of spiritual warfare and spiritual activity with which the non-Christian reader may not be familiar. These stories describe the realms and activities of both God and Satan because they're real and active in the lives of all people whether they recognize it or not.

Steve Thompson

All characters, incidents, and venues described in this book are entirely the product of the author's imagination and remain the property of the author. This book and all text are the copyrighted property of the author and may not be copied or reproduced in any form without express written permission by the author.

CHAPTER ONE

Jack Malone stood absolutely still. The only things that moved were his gray-green eyes. He felt there was someone near him but even with his night vision goggles or NVGs he couldn't see anything in the dim star light illuminating the desert. Jack slowly lowered his six-foot, four-inch tall body into a crouch, reducing his profile between the closely packed rocks and shrubs that covered this part of the desert.

To the west, the last twilight on the horizon was reduced to a soft glow at ground level. The temperature was on the cool side, somewhere around forty degrees Fahrenheit as the day's heat cooled down, and despite the exertion of the last few miles, he hadn't built up a sweat. The Syrian Desert smelled, well, like a desert. Soft, gritty aroma of warm sand, decaying shrubs and the fresh scent of new green growth. The sounds were normal ones of the wind and sliding sand noises. This part of Syria wasn't known for bears, mountain lions, or other large predators, except for man of course.

Jack remained still and let his senses reach out as he attempted to find the anomaly that had caused him to stop. As the wind died down briefly Jack heard a footstep quietly crush sand. The sound was coming from his left side and not too far behind him. He slowly pivoted in that direction and lowered himself from the crouch into a prone position with his silenced M-8 assault rifle pointed that way. As he waited to see who or what was there he realized that he had almost started to move again thinking he had only imagined the first sound. Whoever was following him was very good at his tracking. Jack prayed a quick prayer of gratitude to the Father for making him aware of the tracker and for the Lord's favor concerning the upcoming confrontation.

A dim figure appeared walking very carefully over the sand. Jack waited as his heart beat faster from the adrenalin in his blood stream. He prayed again inquiring of the Father if he should take this man's life. He felt no condemnation of that action. He didn't move a muscle. His face was coated with battle cosmetics and his fatigues, boots, and a desert hat which covered his blonde hair were in desert camo so that everything matched the sand and the shadows around him. Unless a person looked very carefully they would not see him because he matched his surroundings. Movement was the only real indication of his presence. So, he remained completely still as the tracker got closer.

As the man became clearer Jack determined it was probably one of the terrorists. Somehow the shadowy figure had detected his progress through the desert and was stalking him with an Uzi machine pistol. The little 9MM weapon didn't have much range but it could pour out a lot of bullets very quickly. Worse than the volume of bullets was the noise. The little Israeli weapon would announce itself loudly which could compromise the mission by alerting the terrorist camp.

Moving an inch at a time Jack brought his 6.8 caliber rifle into firing position and took careful aim. He slowly squeezed the trigger until the rifle bucked in his hands. The round was subsonic and the silencer only gave out a quiet cough. The terrorist's head snapped back as the round impacted in the middle of his forehead. The hydraulic shock of the round transiting his skull dropped him stone dead in an instant. It also instantaneously disconnected all brain activity. Soundlessly, the body of the dead man fell bonelessly backward to the desert floor.

Jack waited a full minute before moving, to make sure no one was flanking the dead man. Staying as low as possible Jack moved quickly and quietly to the corpse, When Jack reached the body it was evident that the man was dead He had totally voided his bladder and bowels. This was a normal result of sudden death and something that's not shown in movies and on TV because it was too distasteful for the viewers. Since Jack was wearing combat gloves he quickly broke down the Uzi and removed the firing pin to prevent anyone else from using it. He tossed the weapon into a small gully and shoved sand over it. He then risked several downward strobe flashes as he took several pictures with his phone camera. On a strange impulse, Jack took out the Ident kit from his battle pack and captured the man's finger prints and secured a DNA sample. Storing everything back in his pack he used his hands to scoop out a shallow grave and slid the body into it. He carefully covered the body with sand and policed the area as Mark had trained him. Getting his bearings, he took off for the target.

Checking his watch, he got back on track and sacrificed silence for speed for the next ten minutes. Then he saw the crest of the final dune between him and the reported position of the terrorist camp. He carefully approached the top of the dune and dropped into the prone position again. Creeping forward on his elbows and knees he slowly peered over the top of the sand using his NVGs.

The terrorist camp was there and what he saw made his blood run cold. Out of the twenty-three hostages this group of thugs had kidnapped off of a tour bus three days ago in Israel, six of the hostages lie dead in a row in an open grave. Using the magnification on his NVGs Jack could see that the three young men had been brutally beaten and probably tortured before being killed. Presuming from their lack of clothing the three young women had also been sexually assaulted before being killed.

Checking his watch he prayed that God would save their souls and would erase the horror that was still etched on their faces. The team contact time counted down to zero and he clicked his transmit button six times quickly. Immediately after that he heard, in order, five, four, three, two, and one click. That meant that Laura, Mark, Sarah, David, and Alexis were also in position, circled around the camp sixty degrees apart.

There was a shout in the camp and Jack ducked down thinking he had been seen. Risking a look, he saw a man run out of one of the three big tents and sprint for the rocks. The advanced electronics of Jack's NVGs handled the flare of light as the tent flap opened again. Men came out of all three tents to see what the ruckus was about. From the tent the man had run out of, a tall, tattooed man stepped out with a flashlight which highlighted the running man. The tall man raised his rifle with his other hand and fired one shot into the air. The running man came to a halt and raised his hands in the air over his head.

The tall terrorist shouted at the man in English to come back to the camp. The dejected man turned around and slowly plodded his way back to the man with the rifle. Jack could see that the runner was one of the teenage hostages.

The tall terrorist shook his head as the smaller man reached him. The tall man made a demand of the hostage. The hostage made some type of flippant comment and the tall terrorist calmly shot the smaller man in the stomach with his rifle.

Jack watched through the magnified NVGs as the impact slammed the smaller man to the ground where he rolled around in agony for several minutes until the tall man walked over to him and stomped on his stomach. The terrorist ground in his heel on the bullet wound. As the wounded man screamed from the pain the tall man laughed and shot him again, this time in the head.

The tall man shouted loud enough that even Jack could hear him. In rough tones he yelled, "This is what'll *@!! happen to any more of you trash that disobey me. Understand?" Then he went back inside ignoring the body of the hostage on the ground. The Australian accent convinced Jack that this man was Cordell Mansfife, the reported leader of the terrorist group.

Jack had seen enough. He rapidly tapped out four clicks on his transmitter three times. That signal meant "Save the hostages, give no quarter, take no prisoners".

As total darkness fell quickly on the desert, Jack pushed the GO button on his battle pack and headed down the slight grade towards the encampment. After the execution of the hostage Jack had watched as the majority of the terrorists had left the three sleeping tents and were sitting down to a meal under the canopy of the third big tent. Jack knew that these men were battle trained and were confident their three-tier guard system would keep them safe. Anyway, everyone knows that if a raid were planned it would happen in the early hours of the morning when everyone is less alert.

Which is exactly why Mark and Jack decided to hit the terrorists at dinner time. "Plus", Jack thought, "The terrorists wouldn't allow any hostages to eat with them. Jack pushed the second red button on the battle pack and almost five hundred miles away in an undersea base

Charlie Wu got the signal. Charlie was a muscular, compact man of Asian descent with the calm, undisturbed face of the Chinese race. He had been a top agent of the Chinese Internal Security Department until he met Christ and left China for the United States. He spoke to the team pilot, another Asian named Su Li, also from China, who was orbiting at 20,000 feet eight miles outside the terrorist encampment. Su Li fired a missile from the Shrew, the Crossfire Team's aircraft. Charlie guided the small missile as it drove for the Earth. The satellite video Charlie had been watching indicated the third tent as the mess hall and he put the crosshairs on that tent.

Jack watched as the missile arrived, coming straight down at over two hundred and sixty miles per hour went through the tent roof and detonated as it hit a table among the crew of terrorists. The precision ordinance-shaped-charge completely destroyed a circular space of fifty feet in diameter with the excess energy going straight upward. In the blink of an eye the bulk of the terrorists ceased to exist while leaving the rest of the base buffered, deafened, but essentially unharmed.

Jack reached the outer ring of security and took out two of the sentries with short bursts of his M-8. They were standing there with their mouths agape looking inward at the explosion in the camp. Since Jack's weapon was silenced the remaining two guards on his side of the camp weren't alerted to his attack from outside. The other two guards danced and died immediately after the two he had shot. Looking to his right Jack saw Laura as she moved in with her M-8 up and questing for more targets. She was ready to hunt for any more remaining terrorists so the team could begin the main event of tonight's festivities.

Jack and Laura came to the first closed tent and each of them sprayed a side of the tent with an accelerant. They both ignited the accelerant with a lighter. The entire fabric on both sides of the tent disappeared in a flash and Jack and Laura shot the first two hostage guards before they could react. Rushing into the tent from opposite sides, both of them covered their half of the tent and were ready to dispatch any remaining terrorists. There were only three more terrorists standing among the hostages who fell before they could determine where to fire.

Jack and Laura stayed on alert because their Intel had indicated everything these people did was by even numbers and they had only killed five. There was a sudden flurry of activity near the far corner of the tent and Laura found their remaining terrorist being beaten to death by the freed hostages. She didn't interfere with the action but made sure the man was dead when they finished beating him. She shot him through the head as insurance. God's directions had been explicit, no survivors among the terrorists.

Stepping back from the agitated people Jack checked his battle pack and saw green lights from the other two teams. Jack opened communications with the others. "We took out eight, what is your count?"

Mark's deep bass came back "We took down a total of twelve, six sentries and six hostage guards." This was quickly followed by David's count. "We eliminated ten, four sentries and five guards, and the leader, Cordell Mansfife."

Jack checked with Charlie back in Israel. "How many do you estimate the missile took out?"

Charlie responded immediately. "I've checked the videos three times. Thirty terrorists entered the mess tent and zero came out."

"Thanks", Jack told the ex-Chinese agent. That meant that they had eliminated sixty terrorists plus the one Jack took out in the desert outside the camp. Intel had numbered the gang at sixty. That was somewhat odd but Intel had been wrong before.

Jack made an open call to the team. "Form up on my location. Bring any hostages with you. Everyone move to your quadrant and stay alert. The terrorist contingent has been eliminated". Jack stared around his area as the others formed up. He watched as an additional sixteen hostages joined the ten in their tent. "This is where things get exciting." he thought.

CHAPTER TWO

Several minutes later, everyone except David had laid down their rifles and stood quietly between the hostages and the main open part of the tent. Laura was praying in her prayer language. The air quickly became charged with a violent energy which caused the lights in the tent to go out. Accompanied by an ominous cracking and creaking noise several dozen demons stepped out of their dimension and into the darkness of the human world. Laura stepped forward and her golden armor of God blazed into sight along with the gleaming chrome sword of the Word of God which lit up the area with the esteem of Yahveh streaming off of the blade.

Obviously expecting this reaction, four of the largest demons vectored in on the smaller woman with their large black swords. As they closed with Laura the other demons moved to destroy the remaining hostages and the other members of the team.

David used his M8 in full auto to fan bullets across the mass of demons. None of the demons were affected and David dropped his rifle.

Jack smiled a grim smile and said, "Now!"

Two more suits of golden armor and three of glowing silver armor appeared and each team member had a sword like Laura's. As the demons attacked, the team went into high speed mode and weaved their way among the slowly moving black blades and hideous demons. The swordsmanship of the team members was far superior to that of the age-old demons that, apparently, relied heavily on their appearance to frighten and freeze people in place.

Jack kept an eye on the hostages huddled together to make sure no demons appeared among them to wreak death among the unarmed civilians. He noticed several brief flashes of gold and white and knew then that the angel Rose was protecting them.

A monstrously large demon stepped out of their dimension into the battle. He was armed with a large club as well as a big sword. Jack saw Sarah move to intercept this new threat when she was stopped in place as a bright light appeared between her and the big demon. The Archangel Caleb appeared in pure white and a look of holy anger was on his face.

Caleb closed with the giant demon and deflected a blow of the huge club with his shield. Caleb jabbed and parried with the big demon and the sound of their blades colliding drowned out the other sounds of battle.

Jack continued to fight the other demons while he prayed for God's anointing to cover Caleb and empower him to victory.

The huge demon swung a mighty overhead smash with his club and Caleb sidestepped to the right avoiding the blow. Spinning quickly to his left as the demon smashed the club into the floor, Caleb swung his sword to his left, striking the demon in the back of the neck and beheading him. As the demon collapsed and evaporated into a smelly black cloud, Caleb turned his head, winked at Jack, and then disappeared.

By this time the first clash was over the demons had lost sixteen of their members. None of the hostages or on the Crossfire team had suffered any injuries or deaths.

The remaining demons now backpedaled, wanting to escape back into their dimension but couldn't because they couldn't disengage from the attacks of the humans. Since the demons had lost heart and now feared the humans the remainder of the battle was short.

Mark ducked a mighty crossbody swing from the last demon by squatting below the whistling blade and driving his glowing blade through the belly of the beast. As the demon and its sword dissolved with a snarl into ugly red and orange smoke, Mark stood up and walked away. His armor faded out of sight and he joined the other team members trying to reassure the hostages that they were safe. Most of the hostages were frantic teen-agers now almost frightened out of their wits; some of them had fainted from fear.

Jack smiled at Alexis and Sarah and nodded his satisfaction to David as he high fived with Mark. "Think they'll try again before we can get this group back to Tel Aviv?"

Mark shrugged his shoulders. "Who knows, we'll just have to stay alert."

There were no more attacks during the run to the pickup zone or on the nighttime helicopter flights back to Israel and Tel Aviv. The team and the hostages were debriefed by the Mossad. The hostages were sworn to not mention anything about the rescue or the team. They were clearly warned not to speak of the demons because they would be deemed unbalanced. If they had questions about that part of the rescue they had a number they could call that would put them in contact with the Crossfire Team.

Back in their hidden base that afternoon the team was cleaning their equipment and putting the restored body armor and their personal weapons in the lockers when Jack mentioned to Mark that they had taken out one more terrorist than they had expected.

Mark looked up with a questioning look. "Where did we end up with an extra terrorist? The count at the camp was right on the numbers."

Jack explained about his tracker in the desert and gave the pictures and DNA and fingerprints to Mark.

Mark looked at the pictures and got a grim look on his own face. Taking the samples and pictures he got Jack to go with him to Charlie Wu in the COMSEC group.

Jack always felt awed by the array of leading edge CRAY computers, cooled by liquid nitrogen that were the backbone of the communications and security operations of the team. The latest versions at the subsea base were the world's fastest supercomputer, the Cray SXT1, also known as Minitar. The Minitar can perform more than 100 quadrillion calculations per second. Charlie had over twenty SXT1s at his command.

Mark gave the samples and pictures to one of the techs who ran the prints and the DNA sample against all known data bases. Charlie was a computer spy and guru so they were looking at all the U.S., Russian, Chinese, EU, and Asian military and law enforcement data bases. That included the NSA, CIA, DIA, HLS, FBI, and every other "secure" data base in the world.

It only took thirty seconds to get a match. The tech printed everything out and gave the pages to Mark. Mark looked them over and shook his head. He handed the papers to Jack and waited to see his reaction.

Jack understood as soon as he read the first page. He thanked the tech and walked off to the elevator. When they were in the war room Jack keyed the recorder and linked all the other team members in the room which included all the people on the raid yesterday.

Jack looked around at the team. "People, we have to find a solution to these continued assassination attempts by this particular arm of the Russian Mafia. They succeeded in killing Stan and Debbie in the heart of Jerusalem and almost tagged me in the Syrian desert while we were on an operation no less. An offspring of Moscow's Solntsevskaya Bratva, known as the Organization, they trade in everything from stolen art to nuclear technology and leave rivals riddled with bullets in the streets of Moscow".

"From its base in Moscow, this syndicate runs rackets in extortion, drug trafficking, car theft, stolen art, money laundering, contract killings, arms dealing, trading nuclear material, prostitution and oil deals."

"The FBI believes that out of the hundreds of Russian Mafia groups around today the Organization is made up of some of the most dangerous people on the planet".

Jack scanned the other people. "As you are aware, the Organization backed Sam Sturgis and harbored him in one of their bases in Russia. Since he was attempting to destroy us, we hunted him down and killed him there. This gave the Organization a major black eye in their world of hate and death. To make things right from their perspective they have to eliminate everyone on this team."

"Part of this group makes up some the four hundred thousand members of the various Russian Mafia personnel outside Russia, including those in Israel. To kill the top members would only make new leaders with the same objectives. So, does anyone have an idea how to make them stop hunting us?"

David spoke up. "The only way to make an evil organization like this leave you alone is to make it too costly or embarrassing to continue their quest. I have an idea on how to do that."

Laura felt a presence in her spirit and quietly got up and left the war room. She went to her room and got down on her knees and inquired of the Lord as to the call she felt. While she waited for a response she quietly sang a song of praise to God the Father. Her heart felt lightened and she sank into the song, singing from her heart.

Sensing a presence, she opened her eyes to find that she was in a quiet setting she had seen before. Sitting across from her was the angel Hugo both of them sitting in overstuffed chairs facing each other. A being of great age yet still young in appearance, Hugo was quietly watching her. He smiled, "Hello Laura, how are you?"

Laura returned his smile, "I'm fine Hugo, and how can I be of service?"

Hugo smiled a bigger smile, almost a grin. "Actually, I am here to be of service to you. The Lord heard your prayer and honored me to give you some answers to that prayer."

Laura sat quietly because even though she hadn't actually spoken her needs in prayer, she knew the Father knew what she needed before she ever said anything. "It is I who am honored. Please enlighten me."

Hugo became more somber and said, "I bring you several answers, some guidance, and a message. The first answer is that, as of today, your team no longer has to worry about the group of Russian gangsters that have been seeking your lives. Their operations have achieved a large enough success that they have become known and detested by a far larger and more vicious group. As of daybreak in Israel today they have already lost over sixty percent of their members throughout the world and the remainder are attempting, in vain, to escape total destruction. Because they use terror and violence to rule as much of the world as they can, the Anti-Christ, Marco Marino, has ordered them utterly destroyed, immediately. Because Satan is behind both Marino and the group doomed for destruction, and the fact there are no believers in their group, there will be no escape for the Russians, at home or in other countries. They will be hunted down and destroyed by Marino in the name of the international good. This will be leaked to the public and will cause many to applaud his actions."

"The second answer is that the Most High is protecting your operation from Satan's attempts to interfere with your

11

business so that you can fulfill the Lord's plans. You will still be vilified and hated by the mass of remaining humanity because all Christians remaining on Earth or anyone known by that name will become the enemy of the state and therefore of all people. But not too much where you are because Israel, along with Russia and China will not join the one world order of Marco Marino. Although as the One World Leader Marco will set up his base of operations in Jerusalem after three years and some months. The rulers and administrators in Israel know who you are and they keep their friends close to their hearts. Be aware that they have partially compromised themselves when they signed the so called, "peace treaty" with the Anti-Christ"

"Thirdly, as the world darkens under the demonic efforts of Satan and his followers like the Anti-Christ and RHONE, your group will be tasked to accomplish many things for the Father in the time left to you. Most of these tasks will involve Israel and the remaining Christian believers worldwide who were not saved in the removal of Yahveh's church from the world in what you call the Rapture. Remember, that as the Anti-Christ tightens his grip as the ruler of the world he will demand total loyalty and homage to his person. Many that refuse will be executed or be imprisoned to be killed later. After the mid-point of the last seven years, any that will not revere and worship the Anti-Christ will die by beheading. This is a real trial of faith for the remaining Christians. For many, this is the only way to Heaven. If any take the sign willingly they are doomed to hell."

"Lastly, even though you are shielded from Satan directly, Marco Marino will be commanded by Satan to uncover your operations and begin to focus more resources and manpower to affect your elimination. Always be on your guard and maintain your secrecy and isolation as much as possible."

"As to my advice, pray in the spirit always. Keep your eyes and your faith on Yahshua and Yahveh at all times. You and the rest of the team's sacrifices to stay and battle are known in Heaven and there can be no greater reward than to lay down one's life for their friends. Listen carefully to the angels but especially to the Most High and to

Yahshua. The enemy will attempt to fool you in many ways. Stay in the word and stay in prayer for everything."

"The message I have from the Most High is this: "*My children, the whole world with a very few exceptions will hate you for my name and that of your Savior. Do not fear this, it was prophesied from times of old. You are unique and special to Me. You chose to serve rather than come to me when your Savior gathered His church. Your rewards will be great for that service. But know this, the assignments I have for you and the hard times that are coming are going to try your reserve and your nerve, and they will try to make you doubt your faith in me. I will be with you as Yahshua is with you until your time on Earth is done. Then we will be together forever. I have an everlasting love for each of you and it grows every day.*"

CHAPTER THREE

Laura quietly came back to the war room and took her seat. Jack looked at her and realized she had a peace about her that hadn't been there before. He raised an eyebrow in question and she smiled back. Jack tipped his head in understanding and asked the group to listen to his wife.

Laura quietly told the entire group what Hugo had revealed to her. Then she gave the meeting back to Jack. Jack thought for a few seconds and nodded. He looked at the others in the war room. "Thank you Laura. This changes the entire focus of the team from being concerned about the Russian Mafia to individually and corporately seeking Heaven for the direction we should go. I would like. . .."

Jack was interrupted by the entrance of Carol Moffet, a young woman who had come to the team to train them concerning the new world of geothermal power and was recruited by God to become a watchman on the wall for the team.

Carol had grown up being home schooled K-12 by her loving and considerate parents in Yuma, Arizona. After finishing high school, she found that she excelled at computers and physics and had gone to a private University. She was rated as one of the best software engineers in the world of geophysical research by the time she graduated with honors.

She had taken a premier position with the new GTherm Corporation and quickly established herself as a very young but brilliant theoretical physicist. When the Omicron Cartel had targeted her company in a quest to control geothermal power she had been saved by the Crossfire Team. As Omicron was apparently targeting another geothermal site, the team asked her to come to their Fortress in Colorado to train them in the science of geothermal engineering and installations.

During her training session the team responded to a demonic incident in Denver in which the enemy captured and tortured Jack and Laura for over two days in the demon dimension. Carol had been led to go along on the mission. In Earth time Jack and Laura returned to our dimension in less than ten minutes. Tended by the other team members they were headed back to the Fortress for medical care. Carol had been given a vision on the ride back to the Fortress that involved her in the prayers to heal the couple.

The Father healed Jack and Laura and then took the six core members and Carol to heaven so that they could instantly see and understand why God allowed the kidnapping and torture. He gave them the understanding of the function of many more dimensions that exist and operate outside of our physical three dimensions and time.

Carol was anointed by the Father to become the interface between the team and the matrix of dimensions to help counteract Satan's illegal advantage in opposing the Crossfire Team's operations by bringing his demons into the human world without permission. Carol had gone through several training sessions with Hugo, one that took ten minutes of Earth time and spanned several years of time in heaven. At the Earth age of twenty-three the young woman from Arizona was far wiser than many women far older than herself.

Carol stood in the doorway of the war room looking at Jack. Jack nodded his head and gestured with his hand toward the console in approval for her to address the group.

Carol stepped into the war room and walked up to the assembled warriors. There was an amazing amount of wisdom in her brown eyes that added a subtle aura of mystery to her young face. At five foot, seven inches she was towered over by most of the members of the team but her knowledge of the spiritual plane more than evened the playing field.

Carol's clear voice had grown more expressive as she grew in her ability to interpret the thousands of plans, schemes, false plots, and strategies she could see in the complex, multilayered and intermixed matrix. Jack remembered that Carol had once told him it was like playing chess in eleven dimensions except that it was with lives on the line.

Carol brought up her four-dimensional version of a small portion of the eleven dimensional matrix. She slowly scanned the faces around the war room. "If you all will look at this representation of events occurring over the next seven days, starting at six a.m. tomorrow morning, you will notice a convergence of six major time lines. I have highlighted the six in six different colors." She indicated the six with a laser pointer.

Jack noted that her enunciation was markedly more precise and professional than when she had joined the team nine months earlier.

Carol continued, "The anointing that the Father gave me concerning the matrix and the other dimensions only allows me to see plans and events that involve the Crossfire Team or their activities. That is why I am not privy to other matters, such as the return of Yahshua or the other plans of a person or group, such as the anti-Christ."

She looked directly at Jack. "The bright red timeline is the most probable for the team. It does involve combat with forces from the anti-Christ because you would have to go into his world to accomplish the Father's will. The complications are involved and intertwined with the Israeli Mossad and the IDF due to Middle East politics and a power play from a fundamentalist Arab terror group to gain control over the Palestine problem. My recommendation is to avoid this timeline since the enemy is aware of your probable involvement and may have, in fact, contributed to the creation of this action to possibly entrap and destroy you by bringing the Crossfire Team directly to the attention of the anti-Christ and therefore elevating his need to eliminate the team."

"The blue, green, orange, and pink lines are essentially wastes of time and again put the team directly in the sights of Marco Marino's operations to cleanse the world of possible threats to his control."

"That leaves the purple path as the only option." She amplified the view of the purple timeline and deleted the others. "If you agree to follow this path it will require the most preplanning and adherence to precise timing to accomplish the Father's will. As you can see in this detail there are very few possible alternative variations."

Mark was following her logic as he traced out the requirements but had a few questions. "Pardon me Carol. I get somewhat lost when the purple line seems to go into your design and disappears only to return at an earlier time. Can you clear this up for me?"

Carol smiled a wan smile. "There are three other dimensions involved at those points and none of the functions in those dimensions involve time as we know it. In our limited human view, it seems impossible that an operation can stop and then resume at an earlier time. But, it is possible to accomplish the operation in four dimensions by using different people to do the different parts of the path functioning simultaneously with each other."

Mark nodded, "Okay, I see why you said it will take a great deal of preplanning to have the right people at the right place at the right time without the preceding continuity of that part of the operation. We can do that as long as the parameters don't change between the various actions. But, why do you think this highly complex operation is the best path for the team?"

Carol liked the way Mark thought out the operation without having access to the eleven-dimension matrix. "Because it will accomplish what the Father wants done and will have the most impact on the demonic involvement while keeping the identity of the team hidden from the minions of the anti-Christ and therefore minimizing future impact between the forces of the anti-Christ and the team."

Jack liked the concept Carol was suggesting but had a question of his own. "Carol, does the Father agree with your assessment?"

Carol stared at the Crossfire Team leader for several seconds and the white diamonds at her forehead and throat glowed briefly. She nodded and quietly intoned, "Yes, He does."

Jack also prayed for confirmation and felt the leading in his spirit to accept the young woman's assessment of their future actions. "Okay, we will accept this challenge as the best path we can take. I assume we have until six a.m. local time to prepare before it starts?"

Carol nodded her head to concur with his understanding. She pushed a button on her remote and the scene on the monitors changed to display a row of pictures across the top of the large screen with profiles of two people and places beneath the individual pictures. "These represent the two major players, the demonic involvements and where the people are presently."

Carol turned off the projection. "The Father's goal is that the man and woman shown here be prevented from accomplishing their plan to totally eliminate peaceful relations between Israel and America. To alienate the two nations, this group, which I believe are called the RHONE, will create a major atrocity and manipulate the event in the world news to cast all the blame on the Israelis. While this is an old ploy it has a high rate of probable success because of the direct demonic involvement, their plan would not have worked before the Rapture due to the number of Christians around the world who would have prayed against the event after the fact and their prayers would have moved God to pre-emptively protect the Jews. Those praying people are no longer on Earth to come against the enemy. That is why the Crossfire Team needs to prevent the event from occurring in the first place."

CHAPTER FOUR

Carol lifted her hands, palms up. "That is all I have for you. If you pursue the purple line, I'll continue to watch it for new developments or major changes. If your plans change, let me know."

She cocked her head and looked at Laura. "I, of course, don't know what the event is or even when it could happen. Hopefully what I have gleaned will help the team in their pursuit of the Father's will. Keep me in touch as things develop and I'll do anything I can. Thanks for listening." She rose and turned to leave the war room.

Laura had one of those messages from God. She'd had them before. It was a complete concept which was instantly communicated and understood.

Laura laughed out loud. She realized that her laugh coming right on the heels of Carol's last words would seem out of place and she grinned at the thought.

Carol turned back to stare at Laura, trying to figure out what the laugh, and the grin meant.

Laura grinned even wider. "Carol, you seem a little discouraged by your role in the events we deal with every day. You know how important your part is in keeping us alive and aware of the enemy's plans. But, the Father knows your heart and how you yearn to be more involved. I just got a word from Him concerning you."

Carol's eyebrows rose slightly in curiosity, "And what, exactly, was that word?"

Laura's smile softened. "You need to understand that God puts the desires in your heart to begin with. You're going to get your heart's desire to be more directly involved in this effort. The Father feels you are ready to join us in the field as a fellow warrior. While this effort will consume a great deal of your waking day you need to know that it doesn't excuse you from your primary talent in any way. It will be a double duty. Does that work for you?"

Carol's eyes had grown wider as she listened. "Yes Ma'am. I understand. I won't let you or God down."

Laura looked at Jack, "Is she ready for field operations?"

Jack thought a bit, prayed a bit, and nodded. "Carol has become proficient in hand-to-hand combat and sword fighting during our training sessions. Mark, is she combat compliant?"

Mark had listened to the discussion and was ready with an answer. "Carol has excelled in all of the handgun, shotgun, and assault rifle training as well as heavier weapons such as the light anti-tank rocket system and the .50 caliber sniper rifle. She is also more than competent in knife fighting and the combat course. How has she responded to your training Sarah?"

Sarah had been praying for the correct answers. She knew Carol was competent in spy craft, and clandestine operations but she was not blooded by actual combat as yet. She looked directly at Carol. "I give her acceptable marks in spy craft and her other training but remind her and the rest of us that she has only had training and no real experience in the field as yet. I will concur that she has the tools to accompany us but only as a coordinated partner with an experienced member until she has proven to herself, and us, that she is capable in the real world of combat."

David coughed lightly to get everyone's attention. "My suggestion is that we give her a chance and protect and support her as she acquires real combat experience. Every one of us had to start out like her and I remind you that her potential has been approved by the Father since he told Laura she could go with us."

David looked around at the assembled crew. "Are there any objections or comments?"

Almost everyone offered to partner with Carol on her beginning ventures.

Jack nodded, "Okay, it is decided that Carol will join the field team on this venture. Laura, I want you to partner with her unless we assign another person due to the variations in our plan that requires you to do otherwise."

Jack turned to Mark and spoke aloud for Charlie Wu's sake. "Mark, Charlie, how do we find out what it is we need to stop?"

CHAPTER FIVE

Carol thanked everyone and said that she would pray for additional insight into the enemy's plans to assist the team in their efforts. She left the war room in a state of confusion and elation. She had been training hard so that she could fight alongside her friends. But, she had never said a word about her ambitions. Now the Father had laid bare her desires and the team had determined her qualified to do what she wanted to do.

But, now that she could do what she secretly hoped for, she was faced with actually doing it. Could she take a life? Should she? Would she freeze when actual combat happened?

Reaching her room, she fell back on her strengths and prayed to God about her concerns. Since she wasn't functioning as the interface the matrix didn't open up and the spiritual diamonds on her forehead and throat remained invisible. This was personal and she prayed to a loving God her concerns and it turned into a plea to the Lord to not let her fail, to not let these people down, to not give into anxiety about possible failure.

Carol felt the closeness of the Holy Spirit and felt reassured that she wasn't alone. The one reassurance she got was the truism that God was on her side and who could stand against God. He promised never to leave her nor abandon her. She knew the Lord and she had been training, at her own request, for the last year. She felt she was ready to go with the team into the conflict and would leave her performance anxiety to the Father.

At that point in her prayer she focused on using her unique talents to help plan the strategy to accomplish the mission. The white diamonds glowed and her spirit flew over the matrix seeking all the information she could understand and apply to this mission.

Momentarily alone with Laura in the war room, Jack discussed their actions to include the youngest member of the team to move into the field with his wife. "Did we do the right thing? Could combat distress Carol too much?"

Laura smiled at the varying confidence or knowledge Jack had in the Father. "Yes, we did the right thing because the word I got from the Father was to let Carol join us in the field. You know that the Father doesn't make mistakes nor is he surprised by anything. His word is true and complete. I didn't mention that he also wants Carol to train with Sarah to hone her skills as a sniper to replace Debbie Hargrove. Apparently she will become an accomplished warrior and assassin for the Father's purposes. Carol needs to feel confident in her combat capabilities before learning to be Debbie's replacement. The Father included in his word that she will become awesome in her abilities. She just doesn't know that yet."

Jack sat back and thought about that concept. Then he smiled ruefully, "Sorry, I keep sinning and falling back on my talents instead of seeking the Lord's will. I will seek His forgiveness for my sins of pride and ego in these matters. And I want to ask your forgiveness for doubting you."

Laura felt her love for Jack swell in her heart as she prayed for the Father to forgive him. She shook her head slightly. "I forgive you. Like you I have to continually ask Him for forgiveness for the silly human things I do instead of relying on His perfect word."

Just then Mark walked back into the war room accompanied by Charlie and Linda Wu. "Hey guys, I think we have come up with a basic strategy to determine what we are up against this time."

Charlie Wu smiled at Jack and Laura. He really enjoyed interfacing with people. That understanding made him realize that he needed to get out of the computer center more often. "Well", he thought, "This should give me more than enough time away."

Charlie sat down at one of the console seats and nodded to the leaders of the team. "Mark brought the information that Carol has discerned from the matrix to ComSec to figure out how to determine the "event" that we are supposed to prevent. Using the photos and profile information we were able to pinpoint the location of the apparent leaders of this operation. The first one, Brock Andrews, is a multimillionaire whose shady dealings in the oil industry have provided his wealth but alienated him from others in the industry. This is affecting his income and he is apparently willing to sink to new lows to recoup his losses."

Charlie brought up the picture of the man on the consoles. Jack studied the man. Blonde hair that was receding and a calculating look to his face. Anglo, probably about 180 pounds he looked to have a gym physique and tan. His face looked like it could easily drop into a sneer based on the lines beginning to form a permanent pattern around his mouth. A smug man, he thought he was far better than the people he associated with in his business dealings. Still, there was an undertone of hardness in his eyes that spoke of a fierce drive to succeed at all costs, especially other people's costs.

Charlie continued his profile on Brock Andrews. "Recently he acquired several smaller oil distribution companies in leveraged buyouts. He turned their customers to his company and then fired the workers, managers, and staff. Stripped the companies by selling anything of value and closed them. More than six hundred employees were let go without a pension or anything. Rather cruel treatment but not unheard of in that field. Where he gets rotten is his ability to sell the same oil to several nations and then manipulate the deliveries so that no one really catches on. This is sort of a reverse tactic of robbing Peter to pay Paul. He robs both Peter and Paul and trades on keeping ahead of the game by using future oil production to cover up his present larceny. "

Jack said, "In the finance industry I think it's called a Ponzi scheme."

Charlie nodded as he showed a scene of a court house. "Brock has been identified by the U.S. government as running an oil version of a Ponzi scheme but, he has enough high priced lawyers to stay out of jail for now. He really needs a mass infusion of capital to save him and that is apparently why he is involved with the other main character in this anti-Jewish action."

Charlie put another photo up on the monitor. "Meet Mrs. Judith Carlington. Contrary to her title, she acquired all the assets of the wealthy Mr. Carlington eight years ago after he died in a freak accident while hiking with his wife in the mountains of Wyoming. That was about the same time she came up on the FBI's radar by becoming involved with an underground group of anti-Israeli radicals. I first thought they were taking advantage of her. But, after looking at the CIA and FBI files on her it was probably the other way around. The FBI believes that she is now firmly in control of this group which is called the Rhone. My guess is that they need access to the oil industry, so she seduced the, less than reputable, Brock Andrews and then blackmailed him to give her the control she needs. According to the CIA the woman doesn't have an emotional bone in her body. She uses her body as a lever or as a weapon to achieve her goals. Therefore, I doubt that Brock Andrews will survive long after this "event" that she is engineering and that we have been tasked to prevent."

Laura considered the woman in the photo. She looked to be in her early thirties but her actual age was closer to fifty-five. In the photo she had a vain and superior look on her face. Very expensive and hard to detect cosmetic and shape surgery kept her body young looking but it couldn't hide the anger in her eyes. Laura's spirit recoiled from the look in the woman's eyes. Laura intuitively understood that the anger was demonic. "Oh", she thought, "Judith wasn't in control as much as she thinks after all."

Mark asked Charlie, "What does the acronym RHONE stand for?"

Charlie shook his head. "I believe it stands for Revived Highest Order Nazi Empire or some such nonsense."

CHAPTER SIX

Jack thought for a minute. "Charlie, why don't you get "Crayton" to brainstorm the possible scenarios Mrs. Carlington could use Brock Andrew's oil industry capabilities to create a major, world-shaking incident that would give Israel such a bad image with America and Israel's other national partners so as to alienate them.

"Crayton" was a computer program alter-ego that Charlie had developed two years ago, after he was given a group of CRAY computers to provide security and communications for the team. Charlie could task his alter-ego program to search the world's databases and extrapolate the most probable or possible scenarios. Crayton could deduce millions of possible paths in seconds. It then eliminated all but the most likely. It had become an extremely effective tool for the team.

The ex-Chinese spy smiled and headed back to his COMSEC office.

Mark had been speculating himself and decided to describe his idea. "I've been considering a possibility. One, with the advent of the Anti-Christ and the emerging one world order, the economies of the various nations are stabilizing because nobody will be allowed to gain too much. This would be one way to bring the ire of the world down on Israel. If this Carlington woman can engineer a coup, or at least a supposed coup, by Israel in the oil industry, everyone will turn against them. A quick way to do that would be to eliminate one or more competing nations oil resources and blame it on Israel."

Jack thought that was a really good possibility. "Okay, how will the Golems do that and how do we stop them?"

Mark had thought about that part of his suggestion. "They will want to hit some form of nexus like a major loading port or off-shore island terminal. That would damage both supertankers and the port terminal and interrupt oil shipments and sales for months if not for years. It would have to be where Israel has no interests or would suffer no loss. Mrs. Carlington could use one of Brock

Andrew's tankers and make it an air-fuel bomb big enough to destroy such a port. If he arranged it to sail from an Israeli port of record and put a phony Jewish crew on it to establish the culprit as the Jewish nation."

Jack nodded, "If this is a realistic plan that we can justify our actions against then we can have Crayton figure out which ship they would use based on the movements of Brock Andrew's fleet."

Mark held his hand up stopping Jack's assessment of the potential plan. "We are possibly falling into a trap because of the obviousness of the relationship to the plan. I think that this woman is smart enough to put out a really easily detectable plan that has nothing to do with their operation but would have us chasing our tails for no purpose."

Jack smiled, "It does seem very obvious but it probably has something to do with her plan or she wouldn't go to all the trouble to involve Andrews at all. But, it could easily be a wild hare to mislead any effort to stop their plan."

Charlie's urgent voice came out of thin air. "Jack, Mark, will you both come to COMSEC as soon as possible.

Mark and Jack hurried to Charlie's domain and into his office. Jack asked the Oriental man, "What do you have Charlie?"

Charlie pointed to the large monitor above his desk. "Crayton has extrapolated all possible facts about the two instigators in this affair. I, personally, favored the concept of Mrs. Carlington using Brock Andrew's fleet of oil tankers to destroy a major oil transshipment center and blaming it on the Israelis. But, Crayton has postulated a much more sinister plot.

Using time tables, loading manifests, crew emplacement lists and the two villains involved, Crayton gives a 99.9 percent probable rating to the use of an Andrew's vessel manned by a phony Israeli crew to deliver a stolen Israeli nuclear weapon right up to the steps of the U.S. Capital and detonating it. They are going to make it look like a violent Jewish response to a vehement speech by two liberal senators to immediately cut off all U.S. funding for Israel.

Jack asked, "Wasn't that anti-Israel speech given last week?"

Charlie nodded and pointed to his monitor. "That ship will dock on the Potomac River the day after tomorrow."

The look on Mark's face was grim. "I'd guess that the weapon is being shielded by demonic covering like the one that destroyed Houston, Texas last year, right?"

Charlie pointed to a smaller monitor. There were the tell-tale swirling radiation patterns at several points along the length of the small tanker. "The satellite surveillance shows heavy demonic activity all over the ship."

Jack pulled out his cell phone and auto-dialed their FBI contact in the U.S. Gary Rhodes answered somewhat groggily on the second ring. "Hello Jack, what can I do for you?"

Jack smiled at the memories of their shared history. "Sorry to wake you up Gary but we have another, very urgent, critical situation for the FBI".

Gary's voice sharpened considerably. The last two of the Crossfire Team warnings had been disasters that were in the making for the U.S. That included the warning about the nuclear bombing of Houston, Texas. "What have you got?"

Jack related the information they had been given by God and their analysis of the potential nuclear strike on Washington, D.C. within the next twenty-four hours. Gary thanked him and said he would be in contact soon.

As Jack disconnected the call, Mark shook his head. "Gary will do all he can but the administration doesn't like us and will probably tell Gary to ignore our input."

Jack sighed, "All too true. We know that the Father wants us to prevent this attack on His chosen people regardless what the FBI and the political administration in Washington plans to do with the information. Can we get there in time to stop the Carlington plan?"

Mark keyed in a phone number on his cell phone to Su Li and Mike White. "Hi guys. I need both Shrews ready for takeoff in thirty minutes or less and we need to be in the area of Washington, D.C. as quickly as possible." He closed the call and made a team call from his console. "Laura, Sarah, David, Alexis, Charlie, and Carol. Grab your gear and report to the hanger immediately for an eastern seaboard U.S. mission."

Jack had already headed out to get his gear when Laura came into the war room already geared up and lugging Jack's gear with her. Sarah was only a dozen yards behind her with Mark's gear.

Taking the elevator up to the subterranean "ground" level the team got to their two team air transportation assets. Mark had everyone load their gear and weapons onto Shrew number 1 and board the aircraft. Mark used the intercom radio to talk to Mike White as the pilot of Shrew number 2 and explained his plans. Both aircraft taxied out to the runway and one by one were given permission and lifted off the runway into the air in the undersea domain. The huge exhaust fans near the air field and the exit tunnel went into high speed to suck the fumes from the jet exhausts out of the undersea base.

Su Li reluctantly released control of her aircraft to the corridor flight computer and watched the walls of the subterranean corridor flash by in the landing lights. Within minutes she saw the rectangle of light that was the retractable wall opening in the base of the man-made island two thousand feet above their base. The plane shot through the exit like it was a video game. Su Li took control of the aircraft back from the computer, switched off the landing lights, and stayed within one hundred feet of the calm sea as she followed their clandestine protocols.

With the second Shrew on her right wingtip she got permission to climb to the eastern military air corridor above Israel at 40,000 feet. Both planes flew up and into the corridor and accelerated to Mach 2 in supercruise as they headed out over the Mediterranean Sea and the trip across the Atlantic Ocean towards the eastern seaboard of the U.S.

Mike White maneuvered the second shrew into a position directly above the first shrew and within fifty feet of Su Li's aircraft. He assumed contact with air traffic control and Mike and Su Li linked their autopilots to maintain the separation between the aircraft and monitored every other aircraft near them as the two aircraft winged their way west.

CHAPTER SEVEN

After two "unofficial" mid-air refuelings arranged by the Mossad, the two aircraft neared the east coast of the United States. As Mike maintained his approach to Andrews Air Force Base he momentarily dropped below the radar coverage. He immediately rose back to the correct glide path and verbally told the air traffic controller about the wind shear area and rate of drop. He continued to complete the approach and landed properly on runway 1L and taxied out toward the appointed military control portion of the air base.

During the momentary drop out of the radar coverage Su Li continued to lose altitude after the first Shrew rose back to the correct glide path. Su Li carefully brought the second Shrew into a landing at a small commercial field in Maryland. She completed the landing and roll out. She parked the aircraft next to an empty hanger. After she shut the aircraft down, she reconnected the transponder that showed ATC where her aircraft was, except when she didn't want them to know, like this time.

Jack walked over to the commercial tower which also served as the terminal. He rented a large SUV and drove back to their aircraft. Moving their gear to the SUV the team then helped cover the Shrew with an aircraft cover that secured the aircraft from sight and set up an alarm arrangement. Su Li locked the aircraft and joined the rest of the team in the SUV.

Jack drove the entire team into the Washington, D.C. area and ended up within sight of the dock where the small Andrew's registered freighter that was their target would dock. Charlie was in touch with Linda Wu back at their base in Israel and kept tabs on everything via satellite coverage. Jack made sure that he maintained sufficient distance from the freighter's location at the dock so as to not alert the demonic force covering the ship and its cargo of death. Laura continued to pray for the Lord's covering of their presence and intent so that the overall demonic covering over the Eastern Seaboard and the demonic "Prince" over the entire U.S. wasn't aware of them either.

As Laura and Carol were earnestly praying for God's concealment from the enemy and the Father's favor as they accomplished His will in this matter, Charlie spoke up. "Here comes the freighter."

The white diamonds on Carol's forehead and throat faded from sight as she left the multi-dimensional matrix. She looked at Laura and nodded. "There have been no significant changes to the timeline for this event. I don't think the enemy is aware of our proximity or our intentions."

Jack nodded his approval and watched the sun drop below the horizon on the far inland side of the city. As the darkness covered the area and to the West the lights of Washington filled the air with city glow, Sarah smiled and told Mark, "It's a beautiful evening for an illegal raid on a demonically guarded ship with a nuclear weapon set to go off in our faces, don't you think?"

Mark grunted his agreement as he waited for the next step in their planned raid.

Jack called Gary Rhodes and inquired as to the U.S. efforts in the matter.

Gary's voice on the phone seemed strained. "I've taken this warning to everyone I can and they are uninterested in the possibility. I can almost see the various secretaries of the Homeland Security, the FBI, the CIA, and NSA squirm under the pressure from the White House to disregard this warning because it came from you. I've been ordered to investigate possible criminal charges against the source of the warning but to ignore the content. I'm ready to tender my resignation over this."

Jack commiserated with his friend. "Gary, politics is a part of your position. You should know that none of this comes as a surprise to God. He will take care of the situation this time through His own agents rather than the garbage mill that is the present administration of the country. Even though God allowed them to come to power in this country, He can't rely on that source after what happened to Houston."

Gary sighed, "Is there anything I CAN do?"

Jack thought for a few minutes. "Pray for God to prevent the detonation of that bomb which would eliminate the administration that prefers to bury its head in the sand along with the majority of the city of Washington, D.C. I would also document everything and use it to change the attitudes after the situation is resolved."

Gary sighed again. "If there is anybody left to convince."

CHAPTER EIGHT

Jack watched the small freighter as it docked and set up its routine. After ten p.m. a bunch of the sailors left the ship and headed into town. Jack woke up David, Sarah, Mark, and Carol. The four warriors put on dock worker clothing. The only protection they carried was silenced and concealed hand guns. Leaving the van, they positioned themselves at the edge of the small boardwalk nearest to the entrance to the dock and waited into the early morning hours. The shops had all closed up and there were no activities on the small commercial strip leading into town.

Jack was waiting for a rating to come off the ship. He explained to Laura that a rating was a person who had some authority on the ship and should be able to answer their questions. Jack was pleased when an officer of the ship finally descended the passenger ramp by himself and started walking down the boardwalk. "Heads up, boys and girls. Your mark is just reaching the shore, alone. Officer's cap, uniform, about five feet, ten inches tall, Caucasian, brown hair and beard."

As the man passed one of the closed shops a shadow detached itself from the dark and grabbed the man with one hand over his mouth and an arm around his throat. The ship's officer was unceremoniously yanked off his feet and into the darkness.

As Mark held the struggling man in the back of the space between shops, David plunged a needle into the man's neck on his right side. His struggles lessened and finally stopped all together.

Mark moved the man behind one of the shops and the others moved their perimeter back with them. David lightly slapped the man and started asking him questions. Twenty minutes later Sarah opened the man's mouth and administered as much rum as the man could swallow. She then carefully spilled some on his shirt and hands. Dumping the rest of the contents into the water she carefully placed the unconscious man's right hand around the bottle and left him relaxing on the ground. The team then carefully melted into the darkness and back to the SUV.

As they climbed in David told Jack and the others, "We hit the mother lode. Marvin Lukens is the Executive Officer or XO of that ship and is very well informed on everything going on with it. He craftily warned me not to be anywhere nears it tomorrow around noontime just before he took his nap.

Jack shook his head. "Thank you guys. That means we have to strike tonight to have any surprise element. What else did the inebriated sailor have to offer?"

Mark summed it up. "The man has zero spiritual knowledge, doesn't realize that there are demons all over his ship, and has probably been told not to be there at noon because the explosion will probably be around 8 to 9 a.m. tomorrow morning and eliminate him in a nuclear stir-fry. That fits a demon's sense of humor and ethics very well."

Jack smiled, "Did he give up the location of the bomb?"

Mark made a face. "Maybe. Maybe not. He thinks that there are special passengers in stateroom 18. There's also a locked storage area in Hold #3 that no one gets to go in."

Looking at her cell phone Sarah added, "According to our plans of the ship, stateroom 18 has roughly 3500 square feet of space, and is above water and dock lines. Hold #3 is an equivalent amount of space but the storage area only shows to be 300 square feet and its fifteen feet below the water line. I'd go for the stateroom."

Jack agreed and assigned the members of the team to a predetermined pattern of attack to eliminate the bomb crew and disable the weapon, if possible.

Twenty-five minutes later the team came to the surface of the water just behind the ship and in the shadow of the ship from the dockside lights. One by one they went up one of the huge ropes tying the ship to the dock. Shaking the water from their equipment the team fanned out on the appropriately named, Fan Tail deck. Jack recorded the time they had reached the target as 0235 or two thirty-five in the morning.

Mark, Sarah, Carol, and David slipped quietly away and took off through the shadows toward the small passenger portion of the freighter.

Laura waited expectantly along with Alexis, Charlie, Su Li, and Jack. The heavenly cover for their activities would end as soon as the other part of the team did anything to change the outcome of the demon's plan to destroy Washington. Laura looked around and asked, "Where is the night watch on this ship?"

Jack scanned the part of the ship he could see with his Infrared goggles. "I don't have a heat signature anywhere. It's like they are all still asleep or they are being covered by the demons."

While Jack and Laura worried about the missing men from a normal deck watch, Sarah crept along the corridor on the passenger portion of the ship. Stopping, she knelt down and pointed at the closed doorway to her left. A large number 18 was affixed to the door frame. Sarah used her gloved hand to try the door handle. Nothing happened. Sarah pointed to her eyes and then to Mark and Carol and then the end of the corridor ahead of her and then repeated the signal to David to watch the other way. She pulled out her lock pick kit and worked on the door lock. In twenty seconds she had the door open and flicked her LED pen light into the dark room. She made an barely audible gasp and motioned David to her position.

David used his hi-intensity LED light and looked inside the room. He was awed somewhat by the gray nuclear containment vessel that took up most of the huge space. He stepped into the room and examined the control hook up. He used his combat microphone to summon Charlie Wu to the room. Charlie showed up in less than two minutes. David gestured for him to come into the room.

Charlie examined the setup and nodded. It was a fairly basic setup. But it had a huge computer twist. The bomb in the containment vessel was computer controlled in a serious way. Charlie whispered to Mark and David. "The only way we can prevent this thing from going off is to eliminate all control inputs at the same time."

David looked at the dozens of wiring groups going into the containment vessel. "How do we do that? Most likely anything we touch will cause the bomb to detonate."

Charlie smiled. "Like this". He turned and gathered all of the wiring bundles into one, three-foot long, twenty-inch-thick assembly. He used two long cable ties to hold the bundles together and then wrapped a three-foot long piece of detcord around the bundles.

Mark stopped him at that point. "The outer groups will separate hundredths of seconds before the inner ones. That could detonate the bomb by itself."

Charlie shook his head. "No, it won't. This detcord is a new version of a mobile shaped-charge with advanced technology. It will be like a super, super sharp blade of energy that cuts everything at once. I've used it before. Trust me."

Carol had been doing guard duty when the Lord summoned her to the matrix. The white diamonds on her head and throat glowed with the esteem of the Father and she was instantly hovering over the timeline for this incident. She carefully studied the event milestones and the small changes. She suddenly saw what God wanted her to see. She was suddenly back in stateroom 18. She whirled around and loudly whispered, "Don't cut the wires!"

Charlie carefully lifted his thumb off of the button with a concerned look on his face and he raised his eyebrows at Carol.

Carol said, "I don't believe this is the bomb! The timeline shows a continuation after our intervention. That means we aren't going to stop it this way."

Sarah went over to the containment vessel and used her miniaturized Geiger counter. She carefully checked all around the vessel, especially at the wiring interface. She turned to Mark. "Carol is right; this isn't the bomb. It all looks right and there is elevated background radiation in here. But, no energy indicating there is a nuclear weapon in the containment vessel." She indicated the door and the entire team snuck out of the room and headed back to the Fan Tail deck.

CHAPTER NINE

As the other half of the team appeared, Jack expected the demons to attack them. But nothing happened.

Mark quickly explained what they found to Jack. Jack nodded his head. He told everyone else to hide while he took Sarah with him and they went down to check the small storage area just in case.

They were back in less than six minutes. Jack shook his head, "There was nothing down there that indicated a bomb. I'm afraid that we've been faked out completely." Mark shook his head, "I knew it! This whole thing is just a red herring."

Charlie stood there and thought out the whole situation. He pulled out his cell and called his wife back at the base. When she answered, Charlie said, "I love you, I miss you and right now the team needs your help. Can you check the ship and tell me if those demonic indicators are still there?"

She confirmed it in less than a moment. "But, they are moving towards the back of the vessel as we speak."

Charlie said, "Thanks, see you soon." and hung up. "Guys! I'm not sure but my guess is that this whole ship is the bomb and the demons are gathering back here on the ship to stop us because we just figured it out."

Jack and Laura started praying out loud. Laura's golden armor and Jack's silver armor and their glowing swords appeared as they stood forth to do battle with the demons appearing on the Fan Tail deck.

Charlie caught Carol's eye and they took off to one side of the advancing demons. The demons had their complete attention on Jack and Laura and couldn't take time to stop the two humans.

But, after they reached the passenger area their way was blocked by an ugly demon with a sword. Charlie moved forward to attack the demon in his own strength of martial arts when Carol put her left hand against his chest to stop him. The demon moved forward toward them and Carol took a step forward and focused entirely on the demon. She spoke a single word in a language not heard on Earth.

When Carol spoke the unpronounceable word in a loud voice the demon looked surprised and then simply vanished. Charlie looked at Carol, "What was that you said?"

Carol made a little face and shrugged her shoulders. "I really don't know. It was something that Hugo taught me while I was training for my role as team advisor on heavenly events."

About that time, Jack and the others ran up to them. Jack shook his head, "Carol, I don't know what you said but it caused all the demons on the ship to disappear."

Mark smiled a grim smile. "That was great Carol, but, we really need to keep this ship from going boom, right now."

Charlie had continued to process his concepts about the bomb situation and he suddenly waved his hands to get everyone's attention. "Guys! I understand this setup now. The wiring in the stateroom really does control the bomb. But the bomb isn't present in the containment vessel. I'll bet you that it is integrated into the entire fabric of the ship and covered in lead. It just dawned on me that we saw one of the holds and there isn't anything there, but the ship is almost down to its deepest legal depth on the marks on the hull."

Looking around the ship Jack had a bad feeling. "I see a man at the window in the pilot house of this ship. He's grinning and that can't be a good thing."

Everyone looked up at the man in the pilot house of the freighter. He raised a control box and pointed at it.

Several things happened at the same time. Charlie's eyes widened while Mark drew and fired his silenced weapon in one smooth motion. The glass shattered and the man in the window staggered back from the impact of Mark's pistol but still held the control box up and pushed the button on it. There was a small rumble and the ship shook ever so slightly but that was all. The man's face turned angry and he pushed the button again. That resulted in the man's death. Not by explosion but by a second shot from Mark. The second round hit him in the forehead and he dropped the control box as he fell out of sight.

Laura looked around, "What was that little explosion? What happened?"

Charlie laughed out loud and pulled out his detcord control box. "Remember, we left the detcord on the wires when we left the stateroom? Well, I severed the wires to the bomb just before he tried to detonate the ship. That was the little rumble you heard."

The relief that was felt by the team was substantial. Everyone shook hands with Charlie or hugged him, or both. Jack stepped back and called Gary Rhodes.

When the federal officer answered, Jack told him what had just transpired in general terms with no names. There was subtle laughter in Gary's words as he solemnly informed the unknown person on the line that this call was sufficient cause for the FBI to impound and investigate the ship for weapons of mass destruction. Especially one that involved using the entire ship as a bomb. "Now, whoever you are, you need to stay right there on the ship until the FBI team can get there in about fifteen minutes and arrest you for not following the orders of our administration that strictly forbids unauthorized military operations on U.S. soil, especially those that save several hundred thousand American lives."

Jack grinned as he disconnected the call, "Okay folks, we need to be somewhere else, now!"

Fourteen minutes later the team watched from their van as a dozen FBI agents swarmed onto the small ship. They drove quietly away.

Fifty minutes later the Shrew lifted off of the small, private air field and headed east out over the Atlantic Ocean with all hands on board.

Meanwhile, at the Joint Base Andrews Naval Air Facility in Maryland outside of Washington, D.C., Mike White filed a flight plan and eventually followed the same flight path.

On Shrew Number One, Laura asked Carol, "Did you know that the Lord had given you the power to send demons packing with only one word if it was necessary?"

Carol shook her head, "No, I just assumed it was for my protection. How did Jack know I said anything? We were hundreds of feet away inside a corridor and you guys were in combat at the time."

Laura laughed a happy little laugh. "You haven't had much experience in the field so you don't realize that angelic commands in our dimension are very loud and your voice is very recognizable to the other members of the team. Oh yes, we knew it was you without a doubt and that command caused all the demons to vanish at one time."

Carol smiled and felt warmed by the camaraderie evident in Laura's voice.

CHAPTER TEN

The next morning Jack received a call from Gary Rhodes at their base in Israel.

"Jack, you probably can't believe the furious beehive you stirred up in wonderland yesterday. First, we, the FBI, were congratulated on preventing the detonation of the nuclear weapon which would have killed many thousands of Americans and destroyed a great deal of our national history, not to mention most of the administration, congress, and the Washington, D.C. infrastructure. Since that self-same administration doesn't want to admit the enemy got a bomb that close there will be no public notification of any kind for many years."

Jack snorted, "So, what's new about that?"

Gary laughed, "Touché, but, that's just the tip of the iceberg. Homeland Security had serious egg on their face since we gave the credit to an unknown source outside the U.S. alerting our department to the danger while they ignored your warnings about that particular action. They insisted that we divulge the source. While we didn't mention your involvement in stopping the operation, we did tell them that the Crossfire Team called us to warn us about the nuclear weapon. That really muddied the waters because the administration has demanded that all federal departments sever all ties with organizations like yours. The director of Homeland Security realizes that your input saved Washington, their lives, and incidental, all their jobs at the same time, but, they can't report the salvation as coming from you."

Jack laughed, "Sorry to put you in such a quandary, but it seems to me that the administration is doing everything they can to assist any and all of America's enemies."

Gary concurred. "True, but they are so good at spinning the news their followers believe that the administration is winning the terror war because of their great foreign diplomacy. Anyway, I'd lose my job if I was overheard saying that, so I am using a burn phone to make this call, which is also a dismissal offense. But, you haven't heard all of it yet. The FBI agents that raided the ship will not stir things up or discuss what they found on the ship even though they know they didn't stop the explosion. They don't know who did and that I made sure that part of the case is closed. The problem is that a rather powerful lobbyist is insisting that the ship wasn't a bomb, even though NRC scientists have investigated and proven that the metal of the hull was the radioactive material that made up the bomb. The lobbyist says that it the whole thing is one of several feeble attempts by the government to further blacken the image of the ship's owner, Brock Andrews."

Jack asked, "Would that lobbyist just happen to represent one Mrs. Judith Carlington?"

Gary looked at his files. "Why, yes. She's also apparently the largest contributor to that lobbyist."

Jack explained what their research had suggested about her and her association with Brock Andrews. Then he asked, "Can you leak enough about that association to the press that she has to hide for a while and it can prevent them from sending another bombship?"

Gary was silent for several seconds. "Will do. I've got just the blogger to bring that up without showing any connection with us. I'll have enough of the dirty exposed, as a supposition, that there will be ten investigations started by this afternoon. That will give Homeland Security enough facts to head in the right direction and allow them do a flash and dazzle on the public so that they won't look totally inept. The Homeland people are dedicated and professional but they have their hands tied by politics and political correctness that they get blindsided frequently. By the way, since the FBI can't publicly take the credit for preventing the explosion I have used our back room operations with the other alphabet organizations to "unofficially" notify them of your involvement in addition to your warning."

Jack asked, "Is that wise?"

Gary laughed, "Don't worry about them letting the cat out of the bag. It seems we have some video proof that there were supernatural elements on the ship that we wouldn't have been able to handle anyway. If anybody says anything about your involvement they have to admit there were demons involved, which no one would believe anyway. But, the directors are a closed mouth bunch anyway. They don't want their dirty little secrets exposed and therefore won't squeal about the FBI's "black" operations. One thing was interesting and probably rankled the Homeland people at the same time."

Gary continued, "It seems that the administration, in its efforts to prevent non-controlled "black ops", established a monetary reward to whoever prevents terroristic actions by telling them or one of the other law enforcement agencies about pending large-scale terroristic attacks. By their procedures, they had to send the reward to me so that their hands will be clean of giving a banned agency like yours the reward. The amount is based on what the information prevented. I guess they couldn't even come to a full accounting of all the damage that ship would have done. So they just gave me a check for twenty million dollars. I very carefully documented everything and wired it to your bank in Israel in your team's name."

Jack was impressed, "Thank you Gary. And to cover your miscellaneous expenses, like that burn phone, we are going to send you your agent's fee for your assistance. I will see that it is deposited in an anonymous bank account and will text you the necessary information to retrieve it without tripping the FBI or NSA alarms." Jack shook his head. "I'm glad you have the guts to work with us and still handle the Washington two-step with other organizations. Thanks for letting us know how things went down."

Gary was about to go when he stopped and casually asked Jack just how much the agent's fee was. Jack told him, "Just a small fee, let's say twenty percent."

There was a long silence and then Gary said, "I know a lot of people I can help with that much. I will just have to keep it off my income, inventory, and the tax rolls."

After letting Gary go back to his daytime job, Jack told the other members of the team the high points of his conversation.

Mark shook his head. "It's a wonder they get anything done right with all the politics they have to wade through." He raised an eyebrow. "Do I understand you're going to leave Mrs. Carlington to these impending Congressional investigations?"

Jack laughed a grim laugh. "Not at all. She can tap dance with the best of them and will probably pay enough to come out of the investigations clean by dumping everything on someone else, probably Brock Andrews. No, I kicked that off to distract her. We need to pray about it but I think the Lord will want us to bring her to justice in a much more effective way than a Congressional investigation."

CHAPTER ELEVEN

At five-thirty a.m. the next morning a strident alarm sounded throughout the underwater base. Pulled out of a sound sleep by the blare, Jack rubbed his face and ran barefoot to the control room in his suite. Keying in his authorization code he scanned the data and then called the ComSec group. He wasn't surprised to see Charlie and Linda Wu already at their consoles although Linda's hair was less than combed out. "Charlie, whose sub is it and does it have the capability to attack us if they are hostile?"

Charlie studied his monitor for a few more seconds. "It reads as a Russian Graney-class nuclear submarine which is interesting as the Russians had to cancel that development after the first one topped one billion U.S. dollars in development costs. The Graney was supposed to provide a platform that would allow them to launch a variety of long-range cruise missiles with a range of up to 3,100 miles, with conventional or nuclear warheads, and effectively engage submarines, surface warships and land-based targets.

The submarine's armament was originally designed to include 24 cruise missiles and eight torpedo launchers, as well as the ability to launch mines and anti-ship missiles. This is must be the original and only Graney-class nuclear sub that Russia has. The outfitting and launching of this design must have been a major "black" operation for the cash-strapped country. I don't have any idea what it is carrying in weapons. The sub has slowly moved into its present position less than a mile away from the entry to our flight corridor. It has maintained that position for the last hour.

Mark added a comment to the networked base. "Could the entire submarine be used as a nuclear bomb to remove this base? We've sort have run into that concept recently."

David keyed in to the conversation. "I think we need to be more concerned about its mission and whether it's after us, this base, or Israel itself."

Jack checked his monitor. Carol wasn't on the network which probably meant that she was checking the matrix to see what she could find on the situation. He keyed his talk button. "David, can you check with the Mossad and see if they have anything more definite? I don't think Israel is taking the presence of a nuclear submarine off its coast too well."

David concurred and broke off of the combat network.

Laura sat quietly beside Jack and continued to pray for understanding.

Less than twenty minutes later David came back on the combat network with a concerned voice. "Well, this is, as you, excuse me, *"we"* Americans say, when the rubber meets the road. The Prime Minister just concluded a hot line phone call to the Russian President demanding that Russia move their submarine out of Israeli waters within twenty minutes, which is about fifteen minutes from now or Israel will destroy it."

David sighed, "Russia denies having a submarine in Israeli waters and the claim that a Graney-class submarine even exists is ridiculous. The one they had constructed was torn down for parts a decade ago."

Mark added, "That is true. The CIA confirmed it both photographically and by eyes-on. The prototype was destroyed."

Jack thought for a few seconds. "Okay, if none of the possible explanations can be true then you need to consider the impossible. Comments? Suggestions? Ideas?"

Jack listened to the possibilities from the ridiculous to impossible and summed up the ones with any reasonable chance of being true in his view. "Most likely, Russia lied and there was more than one prototype created and only one destroyed. Next most likely, it was a different project with a similar design. Then we should also consider that the sub here isn't real but a projection of some type, it's a mass hallucination, and, someone, possibly China, created a copy of this submarine and is using it to start a war between the west and Russia."

David spoke up. "We may never know if any one of our suppositions is correct because one of Israel's diesel-electric, Dolphin-class submarines is in attack position near the enemy submarine and is probably going to fire on it in less than eight minutes."

Jack asked, "Who decides what action will be taken?"

"The IDF Chief of Staff will direct the firing of the torpedoes but the Knesset will have to give permission due to the political importance of firing on a foreign power in time of peace."

Laura sighed, "This could be a major change in the politics of the world and I wonder if Marco Marino is behind it."

Charlie spoke up. "Four minutes to the deadline."

CHAPTER TWELVE

Charlie called out, "The mystery sub is underway and headed away from the Israeli coast. It's moving quickly and will be out of the territorial twelve-mile limit in less than twenty minutes."

David heaved a sigh of relief. "That is good. It would not be to Israel's advantage to initiate hostilities with whoever controls that boat."

Jack agreed, "True, but that doesn't answer any of the questions like whose sub is it?

Mark added, "And, what was it doing here so close to the Israeli coast and coincidentally to our base."

Charlie deactivated the alert status and added, "I will do everything I can to track that sub regardless where it goes."

Jack shut down his combat console and headed back to the bedroom.

As he lay down he prayed that the Holy Spirit would give him knowledge and wisdom concerning their roles concerning both the mystery submarine and Mrs. Carlington.

He sensed a presence and looked to his left. The angel Hugo stood there quietly contemplating him. Jack smiled, "Hello Hugo, how are you doing?"

Hugo smiled back and stepped closer. "I'm fine Jack. You asked the Spirit of God to guide you and to give you wisdom. Hugo held up his hands, "and so, here I am to provide answers."

Right then Laura came out of the bathroom and yelped when she saw someone other than Jack. She stepped back into the bathroom and half closed the door. Looking around the door she recognized the angel. "I'm sorry Hugo, I'm not used to finding a strange person in this situation. I'm not dressed yet." She looked at Jack like he should have warned her but realized that angelic visitors can disrupt the normal flow of courtesies.

Jack focused back on Hugo, "What can you tell me about either of the subjects I was praying about?"

Hugo held up his hand to stop Jack. "In a moment. Let us adjourn to your sitting room and give Laura some privacy."

After leaving the bedroom and closing the door Jack mentioned a thought. "As angels you can look in on humans at any time, but I still appreciate your gesture for Laura's privacy."

Hugo laughed a quiet laugh. "I understand the concept of propriety although I don't understand the need for it. God gave human beings bodies for your time on this world. Ever since Adam and Eve sinned humans have been ashamed of their bodies. It's not of God to be ashamed of your bodies."

Jack's eyebrow lifted as he considered the long established concern over nudity and the effort that would be required to change that concern. He shook his head, "Not my department" he thought. Jack returned to the team's problems at hand. "Any help on the submarine or our role concerning Mrs. Carlington?"

Hugo nodded his head slowly. "As to the submarine, you will find that it is a vital part of the new One World Government. It was not seeking your team this morning but it was testing the Israeli resolve and willingness to defend their land. This submarine was demonically created and maintained and it is not presently a concern for you or your team."

Jack nodded his understanding.

Hugo continued, "As to Ms. Carlington, she has defied God from a young age and has finally, knowingly, and willingly given her soul over to the enemy of mankind. She has attempted to destroy many of His people and actively despises God. She has become the brute beast created to be destroyed."

She will be attempting to commit a small precision slaughter of the next generation of left behind believers of Yahshua, tomorrow at McKindred High School in Evanston, Illinois at two o'clock in the afternoon. These teenage children are the few left at this school after the Rapture. It seems that Ms. Carlington's demon has convinced her that the next great man of God will be in the thirty-three teenaged children graduating class. The Lord has chosen your team to stop her and to end her violence on humanity forever. Rose will be with you. Prayer will be necessary as there are going to be demons there to insure her plans are not derailed. You need to make an example of her evil so that all will know the truth. Go with God."

Hugo faded out of sight, leaving a thoughtful Jack to himself. He prayed his obedience and love for the Lord and the Father. He got up to round up the troops who were still recovering from their last transatlantic trip.

CHAPTER THIRTEEN

The rest of the day was devoted to prayer, travel, and planning.

Mark spread out the overhead view of the school from a Keyhole satellite. He pointed out the important aspects to the rest of the core team. "This building here is the main school building. The field directly behind it is the athletic field. The graduation ceremony will be held on the assembly yard between the building and the athletic field. This building and that one have line of sight to the assembly yard. The first building is the gymnasium and it has no doors or windows facing the target area. The second building is the science building that houses the labs for those classes. That building has fifteen windows and two double glass doors fronting onto the target area."

David held up his hand. "How do you know that Mrs. Carlington's forces will attempt to kill the special children on the assembly field? Couldn't they do it just as easily inside the main building as they get together to walk out?"

Mark shook his head. "I don't think so. The teenagers will only be grouped together on the field as time for the ceremony arrives. And, they will disperse immediately afterward. This is the most likely attack zone. Unless, if they decide to destroy the entire school site with a bomb of course."

Jack checked his spirit. "I believe they want to make a statement and they will surgically dispatch just the four or five teenagers Satan has pointed out. Otherwise it will just be a random terrorist action and not be thumbing their nose at God."

Carol nodded her agreement. "The matrix indicates that they will only kill the three or four teenagers if they can. There could be collateral damage of course."

Jack shook his head. "I don't like our unilateral action in this matter. But, I am sure if we try to convince the American authorities that such an attack will take place they will deny us any access."

Mark nodded, "And, then they will blame us when they can't stop the killing because of the demons."

Sarah had held her silence up until then. "Okay guys, how are we going to save all of the teenagers, make an example of her evil, and not be identified or captured?"

Jack looked at Mark. Mark nodded. "We have decided that this particular egomaniacal group will not just shoot or bomb these four or five teens but will want to be seen killing them up front and personally. This would be their way to create maximum impact and terror. Whatever means they plan to use has to be fairly quick and messy. Our best guess is that the attackers will quickly separate the targeted teens from their adults by force or show of arms and then deal with each young boy or girl, one at a time."

Laura was shaking her head. "How cruel and evil that is to let the other teens watch as each one of the four or five is slaughtered."

Jack's face was grim. "That's the mark of demons, both real and human."

Mark picked up the discussion again. "True, and Charlie and I believe they will allow one or more demons do the actual killings. Our challenge is to let it be seen what Mrs. Carlington and her allies, human and demon, are planning to do and still stop them before they do it."

David stared at Mark. "You want to let them "almost" kill these teens and then stop them? How?"

Mark smiled, "By being right there and challenging them after they have declared or shown their intent. Four of us will be standing there at the ceremony tomorrow ready to intervene instantly. I want those four to be Laura, Sarah, Alexis, and Su Li. Women don't get the same scrutiny that men do when you are dealing with teens. So, they should be able to get close enough to the action without raising any alarm on the part of the school. We're going to have Sarah and Su Li act as a news team recording the event."

David evaluated the concept and found it workable as long as the team members could perform without delay. He had seen all of these four in battle and wasn't concerned on that point. "And the rest of us?"

Mark indicated two positions behind the children. "You and Jack will be in the crowd but further away as backup for the women. Carol and I will be your high guard snipers and we will be in FBI-marked combat armor with darkened shields in the event a camera catches us or we are spotted by civilians. We won't appear until the ceremony starts. Since it takes less than a half hour to graduate all of the students we'll stay camouflaged until the terrorists show up. We will concentrate our fire on the human elements leaving the demons to the forces on the ground. Everyone understand their roles?"

Landing as a business jet at O'Hare airport at two a.m. the team loaded their weapons and equipment into a large rental van and drove to the area of the school. Aware that the attackers could have eyes on the area around the school they found a major chain motel and checked in for the few hours left before morning.

At eight in the morning Sarah, dressed in a trendy designer business suit walked into the school and identified herself and Su Li as a television crew that wanted to record the ceremony for publication on the evening news. The two women were shown where the ceremony would be held. They walked around looking at the site and attempted to decide where to set up to record the event. Actually they were scoping out the assembly field for lines of fire, potential redoubts, exit and entry paths, and all the other things one would look for in an ambush situation.

Thanking the Principal for being so cooperative they left the school and returned to the team in the van. After using their videos and determining all of the pertinent approaches and exits they geared up at one p.m. Mark and Carol left with their equipment to get into position without being seen. Everyone else left at one-thirty and got into position.

Su Li whispered to Sarah, "Which way are the attackers going to come from?"

Sarah looked around and muttered, "We don't know, so stay sharp." She picked up the TV microphone and had Su Li take some footage of her talking to the camera for anyone who was watching them.

The graduation ceremony started as the teenagers assembled into a double line across the assembly area.

They were all dressed in the same jackets and beret's done in gold with red trim. The youth were smiling and laughing as the school's principal walked up to the front of the group.

CHAPTER FOURTEEN

The actual assault started slowly and quietly. The team members were aware of the action but kept to their various innocuous roles, not seeming to notice the influx of eight new men who were all wearing long coats which were not in season at this time of year in Chicago.

Jack pulled out a small digital camera and moved up to the front of the on-looking parents and friends, supposedly to get a better shot of the kids. David shadowed him a few feet behind.

Jack watched as the Principal finished her comments and was about to call the first graduate when a tall woman in dark glasses and a large hat walked forward past the teenagers and forcefully shoved the Principal to the side. She grabbed the microphone and in a loud and grating voice announced, "I am "Lamia" a servant of the god Moloch, Moloch has demanded several of your children's lives and they are to be sacrificed now."

The eight late arrivals threw off their coats and displayed automatic weapons which they used to threaten the assembled adults. The teens were screaming and trying to run but were hemmed in by the men with weapons. Some of the people were yelling, others were crying, and most were screaming at the terrorists and attempting to reach their children.

Sarah and Su Li started quietly praying and when a demon appeared next to Mrs. Carlington their armor appeared along with their gleaming swords. They both advanced on the large and fairly ugly demon. Everyone moved away from the women in the gleaming armor.

One of the attackers fired his Mac-10 at the two shining women. The bullets bounced off of their armor but the impacts knocked Su Li down and made Sarah stumble backward several steps. A booming report indicated that Mark and Carol had weighed into the battle. The terrorist shooting at Sarah and Su Li flew backward against a brick wall of the main school building, dropping his weapon and sliding down the wall leaving a bright red trail of blood. A second terrorist also flew backward from the impact of another one of the huge .50 caliber rounds.

The demon stepped off the podium and headed towards the teens. The father of one of the children put himself between the demon and his daughter. The demon reached out and with one large hand knocked the man to the ground and raised a foot to stomp the man to death when Sarah's sword cut it into two pieces and it started to disappear in oily smoke of a sickly dark green color.

Mrs. Carlington was screaming into the microphone for her men to stop looking for the sniper and kill the kids themselves when two more rolling reports knocked over two more of the gunmen. Carol was getting real-time on-the-job training for her sniper studies.

Carol had already seen Mark in action before the ceremony. As they reached the roof of the building they saw two men with rifles lying on the roof as high cover for the enemy. Mark motioned for Carol to wait. He sat down his bag and quietly walked over to the two men. The man on the left sensed Mark's approach and rolled over to confront him. Mark used his silenced pistol and calmly shot both men in the head. The man on the right never knew what happened. Mark signaled Carol to join him and they pulled the bodies over to the other side of the roof. Mark looked over and carefully shoved the two bodies over the side. Three floors down there were two large garbage bins and both men landed in them.

On the Assembly Field two more large demons suddenly appeared and one slammed Sarah from the back and knocked her to the ground. The demon then smashed his large black sword into the fallen woman. Sarah raised her shield and deflected the blade but the impact slammed her back against the ground so hard it knocked her out. As Sarah passed out her armor and sword disappeared. The demon raised its sword for a killing blow to the unprotected woman when Alexis ran her sword through the demon from the back. With a surprised grunt the demon turned into black smoke.

The other demon ran at Su Li only to find Laura in her armor standing in its way. The demon backhanded Alexis from the rear as she finished off the demon attacking Sarah. Alexis was attempting to get her sword in position when the backhanded blow caused her to fly forward through the dissolving demon she had just killed. To clear Sarah's prone body, she executed a forward flip and landed on her feet. She turned back to the battle with a holy anger on her face.

Laura used her sword in a reverse slash at the demon that attacked Alexis and just missed its arm. This demon was very agile and avoided Laura's sword several times while battering at her shield and sword. It was the most proficient demonic combatant that Laura had ever faced. The demon swung a mighty slash from Laura's left to her right. Laura ducked the sword and slashed upward through the armpit of the demon. Leaking smoke, the demon attempted to grab its sword from its damaged hand but Laura reversed her motion and cut the creature in half from the top of its head to its middle with a powerful downward stroke of her sword.

Four more demons appeared out of thin air and attacked Laura. Jack began to pray and his silver armor appeared. Seeing Sarah on the ground and not moving filled his heart with a righteous anger and he prayed that the Lord would empower him to destroy the demons and to also put his angels around Sarah. He saw flashes of gold and white near Sarah and knew that the angel Rose was protecting her.

Jack waded into the new contingent of demons utilizing the high speed technique that Hugo had taught them. This time management technique was something this group of demons hadn't anticipated or apparently didn't understand. The demons were all slashing at places Jack had already moved out of. This concentration on Jack left the two remaining demons as easy targets for the three still functioning Crossfire women warriors.

In the background of the demonic battle two more of the human terrorists died from the fifty-caliber rounds fired by Mark and Carol.

In the melee and confusing combat the thirty-three teens were managing to escape the killing field by avoiding the live demons and slashing swords and running past dead men and dissolving demons to be taken by their anguished parents who fled the scene any way they could. Mrs. Carlington could see that this whole battle wasn't going her way so she quietly moved to one side of the combat and waited for her chance to slip away.

The two remaining terrorists had spotted Mark and Carol at the roof edge and were blasting away with their short range Mac-10s at the snipers. It wasn't much of an even match.

Mark and Carol finished off the last two terrorists and were leaving the rooftop when a demon appeared behind them. It was a smaller demon but had a large black sword which it swung at Carol who stood frozen in indecision. The black blade smashed against a brilliant blade and bounced back. Mark overpowered the smaller demon's blade and hacked the creature to death with two passes of his blade. He stopped praying and his armor and sword disappeared. He grabbed his rifle and Carol's arm and ran with her to the stairwell.

Running down the stairs and out onto the battleground, they stashed their weapons behind some bushes and ran onto the almost deserted assembly field.

They ran to where Jack was kneeling next to Sarah. Jack helped Sarah to sit up. She held her head in her hands.

As the Crossfire team quickly wrapped up the battle, Mrs. Carlington was finally able to slide around the last of the combat and quickly head for an exit. Suddenly she stopped in her tracks. David stood there with a Mac-10 he had picked up from one of the dead terrorists. He held it level and aimed at the woman. Imperiously she demanded, "Move out of my way NOW!"

David smiled, "Well, Lamia, give Moloch a message from me." In Hebrew he said, "The Lake of Fire is your fate so go there now and take this witch with you." He then triggered the remaining fifteen rounds directly into the woman and watched her body dance and jerk as the multiple rounds impacted her. David unemotionally watched as she died. As her dead body crashed to the ground David casually dropped the machine pistol. He turned and, removing his gloves, he walked back to the assembly field. As he went he checked his watch. He was not surprised to see that only eight minutes had elapsed since the first shots were fired.

Gathering with the rest of the team he helped Su Li, who had was somewhat banged up, as they left the field. Mark carried Sarah in his arms as everyone headed for the van. Carol ran back to the bushes and picked up the sniper rifles and then hurried after the others.

In the silent assembly area there were only the bloodied bodies of Mrs. Carlington and her terrorist cohorts and a bunch of ugly, smelly, smoky areas on the ground.

A man and woman stood near their path. Holding a young girl by her left arm the woman put out her other hand as Jack and Laura drew near. "Thank you, so much!" Jack nodded and smiled at the family. "Thank God. He sent us here. Sorry to rush off, but we've got to go now."

Running to the van they all piled in. Mark laid Sarah on the rear seat. Jack drove away carefully and slowly. They were less than a block away when four police cars converged on the school.

Looking in his rear view mirror he asked, "Is everyone alright?"

He got some groans and sighs but he also got affirmatives from each member as they drove quietly and carefully toward Chicago's O'Hare airport.

An hour later the Shrew winged it's way east away from the U.S. and back toward Israel with Mark as the pilot under the watchful eyes of Su Li who was sort of resting from her battering in the co-pilot's seat. Mark was in his own virtual heaven as he flew the advanced commercial/fighter aircraft.

CHAPTER FIFTEEN

By the time the aircraft was parked in its hanger at their base in Israel Sarah was feeling more like her old self. Some pain medicine and six hours' sleep had restored her equilibrium and eliminated the flashes of light she had been seeing after being knocked out.

Su Li had taken over the piloting chores halfway back with some muttered comments to Mark about rank amateurs flying her aircraft. But the comments were accompanied by a grin so Mark gladly gave up the pilot's seat. He did stay on in the co-pilot's seat in the event Su Li needed assistance. She proved to be resilient and healthy by the time they got back.

After a good night's sleep for everyone, things were getting back to normal. The base operator forwarded a call to Jack from the FBI. Jack answered casually, "Hi Gary, how are things going with you?"

Gary laughed, "You guys sure do get around, don't you?"

Jack smiled, "Whatever do you mean?"

"Your little war in Chicago two days ago. You can't deny it. Not only are there hundreds of videos of every one of your team battling something that didn't show up on the videos and human terrorists on You-Tube, but there are some almost professional videos of much of the battle. Are Sarah and Su Li doing alright?"

It was Jack's turn to laugh. "Yes sir, they survived to fight another day. What do you mean "almost professional" videos?"

Gary asked if Jack was near any computing equipment. He sent a copy of the professional quality video. From the angle of the video Jack realized that it was the video camera that Sarah and Su Li were using to stay near the kids. He had to admit it gave a very good account of a lot of the battle with the unseen demons. "That was a present for you so that the FBI could put together what happened there."

"Well, I appreciate it but it has raised another maelstrom in the capital. There's no sweeping it under the rug this time. Too many civilians involved with far too many digital cameras. The White House is demanding extradition of all parties involved for illegal entry into the U.S. for clandestine operations, illegal use of weapons on U.S. soil, for murder of nine people, and a bunch of other equally asinine charges."

"How stupid can they be? Your team saved a boatload of youth, parents, and school officials from certain death and all the cretin in the White House can do is bray about how you did something he doesn't allow. I suggest you go public with the real facts and show the world that their administration doesn't care about the public in any way. Put it to Congress to decide if what you did was right or wrong. There are good politicians in the House and Senate that will quash this nonsense in a minute. Heck, they may do that anyway without your help. We're losing it as a nation when the leader is more interested in his pride and ego than saving the lives of Americans."

Jack smiled to himself. "Wow! Gary. You're really upset by this aren't you?" I understand and agree with you. But, we have to let the country resolve what's important to them. God has not given us permission to clear our name for doing His work. I have to leave it in his hands. So do you, Okay?"

Gary was silent for a few seconds. "Okay, I agree that God is far more capable and I do need to trust Him rather than myself. I'm not sure how that defense will fly with the administration's spin doctors perverting everything to make you guys the villains."

"God is in control, Gary. We'll take it one day at a time. At least tell me that Mrs. Carlington was seen as the evil cause of the entire action."

"While there is no debate that she came to kill children and her death was the result of her actions along with her minions, the problem is that Washington doesn't like the fact that you and your team acted without their permission."

Jack snorted, "Gary, we both know that they will not talk to us or give us any permission. God told us through an angel to stop her from killing those teenagers. There was no mention of getting the administration's permission or seeking anybody else's help. It was an assignment from the Almighty and didn't involve man's okay. I would do it again to save children, wouldn't you?"

Gary agreed, "Look, I'll run all the interference I can and talk up the insanity to anyone who'll listen, but, I don't know if you won't be branded as terrorists by the government."

"Okay Gary, go with God and be blessed."

After Gary hung up Jack considered all the facts and decided that the team would trust in God and not worry about the U.S. administration.

He called the core team and updated them on the situation. Mark's comment summed up everyone's feelings. "So? What's new?"

That evening Laura found Jack reading reports and watching videos of actions that he felt might interest the team in their combat/office room of their apartment. "Jack, the Mossad director for the base wants a word with you. You want me to patch you in to him?"

Jack thought about it and said, "Sure, go ahead." He waited a second and heard Hiram's voice on the phone. "Jack, I have an American member of Congress in the waiting room. He would like to speak with you on an urgent matter. Can you come up here and meet with him?"

Jack laughed. "Sure Hiram, he probably wants to subpoena me. I'll be right up."

Jack told Laura where he was headed and took the tram to the topside base elevator and passed through several security checkpoints. He was well aware of the firepower and hi-tech defense systems arrayed at these checkpoints. He was glad they were there and manned by IDF Special Forces personnel.

Leaving the elevator, he walked down several halls until he entered the waiting room door. He immediately recognized the conservative Senator from Texas, Randall Powers. Jack liked the man and his stand for the truth and honesty. Two quantities frequently not found in American politics at his level. "Hello Senator Powers. To what grand purpose does the Crossfire Team owe such a distinguished visitor?"

The Senator was the image of a Texas rancher, or maybe a Texas Ranger. Even though he was in his fifties he still had a full head of black hair and a body like a full back in the NFL.

Randy Powers sized up the leader of the Crossfire Team and liked what he saw. Jack was a couple of inches taller than the Senator and radiated a power that his body looked like it could back up. Jack's blonde hair and gray-green eyes framed a face that looked very focused. The Senator decided he could like this man and addressed him as an equal. "Mr. Malone, I'm here representing a majority of conservative legislators and many of the liberal ones too. I need your assistance in preparing an article of impeachment of the acting President of the United States of America. This man has so degraded the ability of the U.S. to defend itself and given every terroristic supporting nation anything they want that we don't have time to try to retrain him. We needed a touchstone event to show his anti-U.S. bend and your battle to save those children the other day is the perfect one. My job is to make sure of everything we are going to charge him with is correct, verifiable, and indisputable so that he can't wiggle out of it this time."

Jack was somewhat taken aback by the Senator's declaration because he had expected to be served a paper as the first step in vilifying the team.

CHAPTER SIXTEEN

Jack prayed that he would speak the truth and do God's will in this matter.

"All right Senator Powers, what can we do for you?"

The Senator was obviously pleased with the straight forward manner in which Jack was handling the issue. "I need to understand exactly why you did what you did, even though you knew you'd catch hell from the current administration."

Jack told the man, in a conversational manner, about God's assignment, Hugo's visit and detail, their preparation, travel, and combat with Mrs. Carlington and her forces."

The Senator had asked if he could record Jack's comments and after getting the okay, he had recorded the whole conversation. He sat back and looked at his notes. "I understand God as I am a believer, but I don't know if the rest of the politicians will be that understanding."

Jack laughed, "There are many camera videos of our combat with demons during the battle. I realize many people want to deny that are such things as demons but surely you and the other believers can convince them of the reality of hell, Satan, and demons. Even if they don't appear on recordings or videos."

The Senator sighed, "Jack you've been doing this so long it probably doesn't seem weird or unusual but you and your team move in a higher plane of spiritual knowledge and understanding due to your lifestyle. I have never seen a demon or an angel and while I believe what the Bible says about them, that isn't experiential, simply brain knowledge and faith. The legislators that aren't spirit filled are even less positive and will be crying, "special effects" or "Photoshop". All I can do is tell them that I believe that they are real. That's not too convincing in the playground I work in."

Jack was praying that the Lord would give the Senator real conviction about angels and demons when one of the Mossad staff knocked on the door. When Jack told him to come in he entered and gave Jack a note. Jack scanned the note and both of his eyebrows went upward. Looking up he told the Senator; "Would you come with me for a few minutes?"

The Senator didn't want to break their progress but couldn't do anything without Jack anyway. So, he got up and accompanied Jack down the first hallway to a large door on the other side of the hallway.

The two men walked down a hallway and turned into the control room of a interrogation unit. Through the one-way glass they could see two men sitting across the table in the interrogation room. The man closer to the one-way glass had his back to the one-way mirror. He was upset and demanding information from the other man who simply stared at the first man and said nothing.

The control agent saw Jack and called him over to the control console. "We caught this guy coming through the sewer trying to sneak into this portion of the base. I'm not very spiritual but something about this character is what I would call "unworldly" and he scares me. Down deep somewhere inside I am very afraid of him."

Jack was fairly sure of the problem from the extremely heavy check in his spirit but he wanted confirmation. He started to pray and saw the large man on the other side of the table suddenly look up, directly at him. At that point Jack knew for certain that the "man" being interviewed wasn't human.

He asked the controller to call his man out of the room immediately. The controller sensed the power in Jack and the urgency of his request. He hit the comm button and told the interviewer to leave and come to control, now!

Jack asked the Senator to stay where he was as Jack walked out of the control room toward the interrogation room. The Senator said, "Nope, I'm going with you, I think I'm supposed to."

That fairly well convinced Jack that this event was for the Senator's enlightenment as he had guessed before.

The two men entered the large interrogation room and Jack locked eyes with the reptilian cold eyes of the demon. "Why are you sneaking around in the sewers instead of just crossing the barrier where you want to be?"

The gravelly voice of the man struck both Jack and the Senator as what a graveyard voice would sound like. "Because the master told me to do this."

Jack stared at the creature. "Well, you've been caught and must not only leave but return seven times over all that you've cost us as Yahshua demanded."

The anger and the pain that the name of the Son of God caused the beast was palatable. It jumped up and threw the interrogation table across the room smashing and cracking the one-way mirror. This was even more impressive since the table had been securely bolted to the floor. The demon seemed to shutter and blur, changing shape and color. It was a rock-solid large demon with a club it pulled out of its carryall on its right side. It approached Jack and the Senator with death in its eyes.

Jack started praying and his silver armor and the gleaming sword exploded into view. He went to a high guard position with his sword held by two hands above his right shoulder.

The demon was so incensed by its anger it kept coming. Jack tried to simply destroy the beast's club but it was fast and swung the club out of the way of Jack's sword.

Jack knew he was taking a chance by not just killing the demon with his first strike. Now he was vulnerable to a counterstrike from the demon. But, if he danced away he would leave the Senator defenseless and easy prey.

The demon was distracted by the choice of pursuing Jack or attacking the Senator. He decided that Jack was more important and he swung his club directly into Jack's exposed right side and back. The force of the impact threw Jack against the wall hard enough to shatter the remaining pieces of the one-way mirror.

Satisfied, the demon turned its baleful glare on Senator Powers. It took a step toward the man and raised its club to smash him to death. Jack was trying to regroup and protect the Senator. Even as he turned away from the wall he knew he would never make it in time.

A bright flash of fierce white appeared between the demon and the Senator and resolved itself into the angel Rose. From high guard position she threatened the demon who backed up. Jack saw his chance and ran the demon through from its right side. With a horrific scream of frustration, the demon collapsed onto the floor and melted into putrid green and yellow smoke, which quickly dissipated.

Jack's armor faded from view along with his sword and he dropped to his knees to prevent falling on his face. His armor had prevented any direct damage but the wall wasn't soft and fluffy either. It would take him a while to recuperate from the beating he'd taken.

Rose stepped over and lifted Jack by one hand and Jack felt the pain and dizziness fade away completely. Rose looked at him and said, in her beautiful contralto voice, "Never, never give a demon a chance like that. They are brute beasts created to be killed. Don't forget that in the future." She turned around, winked at the Senator and whirled into a gold and white glow that just disappeared.

CHAPTER SEVENTEEN

Back in the conference room Jack dropped heavily into his chair as he worked off the tension of combat. He shook his head and smiled at the Senator. "Okay, now you've also been moved to a higher spiritual level. Do you think you could convince your fellow legislators of the reality of angels and demons?"

The Senator sat without speaking and staring into the distance. Jack realized the man was still in shock. "Senator? Are you all right?"

Senator Powers looked at Jack and sat quietly for a few minutes and then abstractly said to Jack. "You know that demon was totally going to take my life because it hated my existence. I've never seen such pure, concentrated evil in my life. And, I am a twice-decorated Marine while I was in Iraq during the invasion. Sadam's Iraqis hated us but it was a human hatred not a hatred of humanity."

Jack shook his head, "True, they hate humanity. But, they hate the light of Christ you carry far more."

The politician sat there thinking about what had just happened. "I'm not sure how, but, I will convince the right people that these things are not only real but pure evil, you can count on that. But, I need to know, how do you keep your sanity dealing with these "things" so much?"

Jack nodded his head. "I know what you mean Senator. I know it may sound corny but I stand against those things because the Father asked me to do it. I focus on Yahveh and Yahshua and ask them for strength and cleansing. If not for my walk with the Lord, I couldn't have faced the least of them at one time not too long ago. You have the tools to endure their enmity. Now that you know what is real, focus more on Yahshua and the Father and pray that they will protect you and yours. There is a real probability, with you being as important as you are that the devil will pay more attention to trying to use you or to destroy you now that you've come up on his radar during this little set to."

Jack leaned back and thought about the sales job the Senator would have in the next few days. Making up his mind, Jack stood up. "Why don't you come with me Senator." He stopped as he saw the sharp look on the Senator's face.

"Oh", said Jack with a laugh, "Don't worry. It will be less dramatic than the last time, I assure you."

Jack got the clearance for the Senator to enter the undersea base and took him down on the elevator. His electric cart was waiting for them right where he had left it.

After Jack passed through three more security portals he drove the cart out into the base proper. When the Senator saw the blue sky, the clouds, birds in the air and the air strip he turned to Jack. Why the secrecy? We could have just driven over here couldn't we?"

Jack smiled, "Senator, the reason that we couldn't drive directly over here is because we are a half mile below the surface of the sea off the coast of Israel."

It took the Senator a few minutes to absorb the new concept. The panoramic view of the Crossfire base was more than amazing. and fairly breathtaking.

Jack waved his hand to encompass the field level of the base. "This, Senator, is a masterwork by Major Gary Danning. First, this location is a geological bubble in the earth's crust that is over one-half mile below the sea bed surface which is actually granite bed-rock with an additional three hundred feet of water above the sea bed directly over the base. This location is very secret from all but trusted friends, of which you are now the newest one. The base is within the legal three-mile limit of Israel."

Jack continued his description as he drove toward the Crossfire quarters. "Using the terra forming science that the U.S. has been developing for future Moon and Mars colonies they were able to create a small world for us to operate from. While we do use wave-power machines to generate electricity for the base, the majority of the working power is from three fifty-thousand Megawatt nuclear reactors which drive generators located near the base but remote enough to protect the base from radiation or melt downs."

Jack drove by an immense park with grass and trees and a river wandering through the park. It looked like a beautiful day anywhere in the world with the sun shining and some far-away clouds in the sky.

Jack pointed up at the sky as he said to the Senator. "Notice that this is a fresh air open park. You're probably wondering how we can do that over a half of mile below the surface of the sea. Well, it is a prototype but it seems to work very well. The "sun" emits all the correct wavelengths and sufficient heat to keep the vegetation happy and growing. They transplanted the vegetation from the surface."

"The "sun" is nuclear powered, just as the real sun is a nuclear furnace. The "sun" in the base rises in the east and travels over a precise path to set in the west at the appropriate time of the year. It is based on the time in Israel so that it isn't jarring to one who goes out or comes in. If the real Sun is at high noon over Israel, then the base "sun" is also at high noon. It is almost as if you went indoors and had a huge atrium. There are also some major air handling centers to keep everything fresh and breathable."

"The physical dimensions of the base are four miles in length, one-half mile in height at the base location and one and one-half miles in width, not including the power stations outside of that. It's that big because we have to have a one-mile runway for the combat and experimental aircraft to land and take off."

Jack parked the cart in its assigned place at their headquarters. As he got out he checked his watch. He took the Senator back to the vehicle entry and said "Watch this."

The light over the base darkened somewhat and thunder could be heard growing in volume. A light rain started to fall and it got a bit heavier. With the light level reduced and a brisk breeze blowing the rain fell and splattered and one could easily feel that it was normal rain storm on the surface.

Jack turned and motioned the Senator to accompany him.

The Senator asked "How long does the rain fall?"

Jack looked at his watch. "For another thirty-five minutes. It rains for exactly forty-five minutes each day varied by one hour each week, one hour forward, then two hours back. It waters the greenery and adds humidity to the air. It also seems to be something that people need as a break from a system of continual sunshine during the days."

The Senator asked, "Doesn't it ever rain at night down here?"

Jack nodded, "Actually, it does rain in the evening and during the morning hours. Sometimes it is a gentle mist and sometimes it is a downpour. The model is unpredictable similar to the patterns on the surface. It is controlled by the CRAY computer array in our Communication and Security or "ComSec" division."

Jack walked into their headquarters and got a visitor's badge for the Senator. The badge included a temporary guardian disk that would identify him to the NOVASTAR2 defense system throughout the Sea Base.

Jack took the Senator up to the ComSec section and introduced him to Charlie Wu. Senator Powers looked around at the leading edge electronics, computer screens, and liquid-hydrogen cooled CRAY computers and then whistled. "Boy, this must have cost a lot."

Charlie smiled and nodded, "Almost a billion dollars."

Jack added, "Totally self-funded without a cent of taxpayer dollars. Charlie, can you play that satellite record of the battle at the school yard two days ago for us please?"

CHAPTER EIGHTEEN

Charlie played all three versions of the battle as he had recorded it during the battle. Each recording was ten minutes long. Afterward, he asked the Senator, "Were you able to understand our symbology for the demonic forces?"

Senator Powers frowned, "Yes, but why don't any of your recordings show the demons?"

Jack replied, "For the same reason you can't get a photograph of God, or an angel. Demons are spiritual beings and while they can enter our dimension and affect us physically, they don't really exist in this dimension and normally they can't be recorded. What Charlie has done is create a computer program that identifies their unique energy output so that we can locate them. The human mind is designed to respond to the spirit inside of us which allows us to see, spiritual beings and, like the one you saw upstairs, it is real to you, but not to a mechanical recording device or a camera lens. That's why it takes direct human interface to experience them."

The Senator nodded his head, "I see. That's why so many people deny their existence, because they've never run into a manifesting demon. But, what did you mean, normally they can't be recorded?"

Charlie said, "There are images recorded on thermal recordings of ghosts, which are really just demons. But they are usually not very clear." He waved his hand to include the CRAY computers behind them. "I could create an image at the locations represented by our symbols, but then that would be simply computer graphics and therefore not acceptable."

Senator Powers thought for a few seconds. "Could you generate images or accurate representations of demons your team has encountered to use as a training aide?"

Charlie typed in several keystrokes and four representative demons appeared on the main screens. "These are four that I have personally run into over the last two years. I could generate more like this but people could call it all mass hallucinations, or an overactive imagination."

The Senator grinned. "I recognize the third type because I saw it in action with Jack a little while ago. I don't want these to try and convince people that they are real. I want them for their innate shock value."

Charlie nodded. "I'll give the computer direction to create more of the representations from the detailed action reports each member files after an encounter. I can have them to you before you leave."

The Senator smiled. "Can you make several of the really gross or ugly ones animated to show their violence?"

Charlie laughed. "Do you want me to create a whole new action set of demons? You know, action figures and such?"

"No, just convincing enough to scare the wits out of naysayers."

Jack took the Senator on a guided tour of their facility. When he was done he had the Senator sign the standard form agreeing not to disclose the location or operational capabilities of the base to anyone.

Charlie showed up at the end of the tour and gave the Senator three DVDs. "You should have what you want on here. I would suggest that you preview the material and select the best ones so that they can appear or come to life as you want them to." Charlie then pulled out a small device about the size of a laptop computer. He looked at the Senator. "Would you look to your right, down that aisle?"

The Senator did as he was told. Charlie pushed two buttons on the device and suddenly the grotesque demon the Senator had seen in the interrogation room appeared and ran down the aisle directly at him.

The Senator jerked back and the demon disappeared. Charlie handed him the device. "Just to make it seem real for you, I programmed this holographic generator I built, to show any one, or several of the demons I have on the disc to sort of come to life for you. Was it effective?"

The Senator shook his head. "Effective! You just about literally scared the water out of me." He took the holographic projector from Charlie and tried it himself. He quickly shut it off. "How did you get the demon so real? I mean, I could sense the vile hatred that beast had for me."

Charlie laughed. "It doesn't generate feelings like that. You're still reacting to the real thing you just met upstairs. Still I thank you for your wholehearted appreciation of my work." Charlie shook the Senator's hand and left for his office.

After Jack took the Senator with him and returned him to the real world in Tel Aviv the Senator shook hands with Jack and smiled. "It is refreshing to find a group and an operation like yours that is on the side of the Lord and trying to help humanity. Thank you, Jack. This has been most gratifying and enlightening. With these aids I'm pretty sure I can turn enough people around so that your group will be recognized as good for the country and not anti-American. It is a very real shame you had to leave Colorado and move here to Israel."

Jack shook his head slightly. "I appreciate your visit and your understanding Senator. Just remember, the Rapture has already happened, the Anti-Christ, in the person of Marco Marino is already active in the world and things will continue to get darker for truth, love, and fairness until Christ returns in less than seven years. Take care of yourself and your family and call on the name of the Lord for your protection."

After the Senator left Jack returned to the base and brought the rest of the team up to date on their newest sponsor.

CHAPTER NINETEEN

The following week Charlie reported that the Senator had turned enough of the Congress into believers that the government stopped trying to prosecute the Crossfire Team. Even though the President survived the attempt to have himself run out of office he had stopped his rhetoric and personal drive to have beneficial groups like the team eliminated.

Charlie also noted that the antichrist, Marco Marino, rejected this reasonable change in attitude by the government of the United States and started beating the international drums to vilify any group not under his control especially any that had military combat capability.

Laura noted Charlie's inputs and, as usual, went into prayer. She beseeched the Son of God to enlighten her as to the direction and operations God wanted the Crossfire Team to do. She waited while she continued her praise and worship of God. She finally went down to the training facility and joined Jack who was teaching sword practice.

She was well into her sword practice when she felt a burden to pray. She excused herself from the group and put her sword away. She went to one of the separate rooms set aside for personal reflection, prayer, and meditation. She praised God and then prayed for edification.

What she got concerned her enough to call an immediate Core Team meeting in the assembly hall. When everybody showed up she told them what she had learned.

"I was praying for direction and knowledge for future team actions. You're aware that the rapture removed hundreds of millions of adult Christians and children off of the Earth last month. The Lord showed me that the first major ramifications of that action are occurring now."

"First, the entire world, but especially the United States, has no hard assets to back up their economy. There are no gold supplies, diamonds, or any other form of tangible substance backing up all the funds, mortgages, bonds, stocks, etc. Everything is computerized paper, which by itself is worthless. There are still some assets such as oil, natural gas reserves, and things like that. But, the majority of liquidity is only backed up on computers. When the infrastructure starts to fail, the economy is doomed and there will be no money in banks that is worth anything."

"The disappearance of millions of people from America has resulted in trillions of dollars demanded from insurance companies as people claim their losses against life insurance policies. None of the insurance companies can cover this staggering number of claims which has resulted in the failure and closing of all major and minor insurers. This in turn has resulted in millions of law suits to recover the losses from the failed life insurance companies. There is no insurance company that hasn't gone belly up and the legal system is overwhelmingly crushed under the demands."

"For the last forty years, most major stock brokerages have monitored the world's financial markets by computer. After Yahshua called the church to heaven the drop of several hundred points triggered programmed selling, computers automatically issuing sell orders. The result has been the largest stock market crash ever, 1000-2000 points in the first day. The governments of the major financial powers had no choice but to suspend trading in all the major stock exchanges. Of course, this greatly increased the panic among the general population. "

"At the same time, as people realized that a major stock market crash was in progress, there was a run on banks, as there were in the 1930's and, to a lesser extent, in the mid-1980's. Once again, the world's major financial powers stepped in, freezing all banking transactions in the major nations. Credit cards and other kinds of bank credit were worthless. And again this greatly increased public panic."

"With employers and governments unable to access frozen bank accounts, people haven't been paid. This has resulted in bills not getting paid, etc. Unemployment has become pandemic. Meanwhile, throughout the world, hundreds of millions of people who worked for small businesses have shown up at work to find that the lawyer, the doctor, the CPA, the shop-keeper, or other business owner they worked for have closed their doors. These people are out of a job. Within two weeks after the Rapture the number of unemployment claims skyrocketed, bankrupting unemployment insurance programs in the major countries."

"Widespread anger and panic skyrocketed as people realized their wealth had evaporated and they are without their savings or their income. They can't feed their families. Panic hoarding of food, medical supplies, gasoline, heating oil, and similar commodities erupted starting three weeks ago."

"Runaway inflation, gas lines and rationing began two weeks after the Rapture. These events have created a domino effect in most communities. The panic and great uncertainty fostered by the sudden massive decline in most people's financial situations resulted in major social upheavals. We have been isolated from this by our location and self-sufficiency, not to mention the government clamp down on the news media's to prevent additional rioting and panic. According to the ten o'clock news everything is working out and the economy is staggered but working. Nothing can be farther from the truth. When the population discovers that the administration is controlling the news there will be even more discontent."

"The US has been the hardest hit because it had the largest economy, a large national debt, and as I said before, an economy that is largely cashless, an economy based on credit, and a population greatly divided by race and other cultural differences such as financial status. Also, many people in the U.S. have been so blessed by God over the years that many of the younger people have developed a mindset that they are entitled to jobs, good income and success without substantial effort to earn those things. That all came to a halt when the Rapture happened."

"In the Scriptures, in Isaiah chapter 2, verses 5 to 9 in the New International Version it says, *[5] Come, O house of Jacob, let us walk in the light of the Lord. [6] You have abandoned your people, the house of Jacob. They are full of superstitions from the East; they practice divination like the Philistines and clasp hands with pagans. [7] Their land is full of silver and gold; there is no end to their treasures. Their land is full of horses; there is no end to their chariots.*

[8] Their land is full of idols; they bow down to the work of their hands, to what their fingers have made. [9] So man will be brought low and mankind humbled -- do not forgive them. [10] Go into the rocks, hide in the ground from dread of the Lord and the splendor of his majesty! [11] The eyes of the arrogant man will be humbled and the pride of men brought low; the Lord alone will be exalted in that day. "

"Contrasted to the US economic system, there are a number of countries where wealth is stored less in the form of paper, and more in the form of tangible assets with intrinsic value. In particular, the Middle East states still sit on billions of barrels of crude oil, at a time when the financial markets of the major powers are crumbling. But this does those little good because the west, especially the United States has no money to buy the oil and their markets have disappeared. Also, there are several other major powers where very little wealth is stored "on paper", particularly Russia and China. In fact, these countries have seen an improvement in their quality of life, since their leading economic competitors, the US and the European Union are in the grip of a crippling depression and social distress."

"Needless to say, Marco Marino is advocating a complete takeover of the western world, incorporating their economies into his One World Government scheme. No one will refuse his offer because their societies are crumbling and anarchy is at their doorstep. They will have no choice but to become servants, really slaves, to the antichrist to survive."

CHAPTER TWENTY

Laura continued, "While God's people, through the Rapture, have avoided the individual pain of these failures of government and society we all know that over the next six years and nine months' things will be much worse for the remaining billions of people on the planet, culminating in the death of over half of the population by the time Yahshua returns."

Mark spoke up. "The remorse and fear of those left behind, the ones who knew about Yahshua but didn't know Him personally really tears at my heart. Also for the ones who refused to acknowledge God or His Son. I'm so sad for the ones I wasn't able to convince about Jesus or that this time would come."

Laura sighed, "I know, my youngest brother knew the Lord and he went in the Rapture. But, no matter how much I talked to my other brother, he wouldn't listen. But again, it isn't me that will lead them to the Lord but the unction of the Holy Spirit. I can plant seeds but the Holy Spirit is the one that has to make the desire grow. I still feel love for my brother, and I fear for him in that he has to go through the tribulation."

Jack nodded, "My families, including my brother were included in the Rapture. I never thought he would make it but my dad told me that Mike gave his life to Jesus and was baptized years ago in Texas. He backslid greatly but, he repented just three months ago and had begun to walk with the Lord."

Jack saw the look on Laura's face and knew there was more coming. "What does the Lord have for us to do?"

Laura sighed, "While the antichrist is gaining power and control over most of the world except for China, Russia, and Israel, the sudden absence of the Christian church has also empowered Satan to let loose the dogs. His demons are pushing the satanic groups to do their worst because there is no Godly prayer restraining evil disorder and little collective moral restraint. What the Lord showed me is that we are to defend the innocent, weak, and lost against the vile, hate-filled, and amoral criminals when they are guided by demons present in our dimension. Our commission and anointing has always been, and still is to defend against and elimination of demon-assisted rabid forces as God leads us. Because Marco Marino cannot tolerate any group operating on their own, he will put down or destroy many of the anti-social groups that are not giving him loyal service."

She shook her head. "In this strange time, the antichrist is working on our side to reduce our workload. Unless there are demons entering our dimension on their own business or to work with the terroristic groups we will not be tasked to stop or eliminate these forces. This arrangement will continue until the midpoint of the seven years. When Marco Marino is killed, Satan brings him back to life after three days and the whole game changes. Satan will require complete worship and devotion from everyone as he invests himself into the being of the antichrist. According to God's Angel at that time the entire Crossfire Team that opted out to stay and fight for God will be Raptured."

Jack looked at Carol. "All right. Carol, what do you see in the matrix for us to concentrate on?"

Carol sat up and nodded. "I have many aspects of demonic invasion but the one that God put on my heart for us to help with involves a small group of left-behind Christian youths in Britain. There are about sixteen kids between fifteen and twenty-two who are now attempting to provide true Christian help to the homeless in London. Ever since they realized that they had not been taken in the Rapture they have banded together and tried to emulate Christ and continue to work towards their salvation regardless of the removal of God's church from the Earth."

"But with their prayer support gone and most of their church leadership no longer available they are vulnerable to the enemy. Satan has requested the opportunity to have his demons destroy this group to discourage others from following suit. I know God wants us to help them but I haven't gotten a leading for that as yet."

Jack asked, "Are there any other situations involving demon incursion that could need our capabilities at this time?"

Carol shook her head.

Mark smiled, "Why don't you get us the particulars on this group and unless God blocks us from helping them we should see what we can do."

Laura laughed. "Mark, you know that the best way to get God to laugh is to tell Him your plans, right? I suggest we take this effort to the Father in prayer in Yahshua's name and see what He wants before we attempt to "play" God ourselves. That could be a serious sin."

Mark grinned, "Yes Ma'am."

CHAPTER TWENTY-ONE

As Jack, Mark, and Laura started to worship God they were interrupted by a phone call from within the base. Laura sighed and punched the appropriate button on her console. "Laura Malone, how can I help you?"

"General. Malone, this is Eli Horbin, I'm with the Mossad protection detail for your group. I have a young man here at entry six who is asking to speak to you or to your husband General Jack Malone. How do you want us to handle this?"

Laura thought for a few seconds. "Eli, could you show me a video of the man?"

"Yes Ma'am." A picture flashed up on her console and she analyzed the visitor. He was probably in his twenties, his build was very much like Mark's and although he might be, or have been a soldier, he showed modesty in the way he turned without being asked to help two men struggling with a heavy crate, which was tipping over. He caught the crate and lifted it back onto the cart by himself and then waved off their thanks as he had been glad to help them.

Laura was praying and asked the Lord in her mind if this visitor was on their side or the enemy's side. She got a leading that he favored the side of the Lord Yahshua.

"Okay, Eli, We'll be up there in a few minutes. Could you escort him to the visitor's lounge for us?"

"Consider it done General."

Laura captured the image and asked her husband and Mark to evaluate the man. Sarah came over also and looked at the image. Jack said to Laura, "He looks unarmed and friendly, did you pray about him?"

Laura nodded, "Yes I did and I got a leading that he was on our side. I told the Mossad security guard, Eli, that we would be up there to talk to him in a few minutes."

Sarah continued to study the image. She turned to Laura and said, "I would like to go along if that is all right with you and Mark."

Mark looked at his wife. "Sure, any particular reason?"

Sarah laughed, "Yeah, I think I've seen him in combat before. But then, he had a sword and wore white. He was an angel battling demons with us."

Laura's left eyebrow went up a notch. "Then this should prove interesting."

Jack eyed the image for a few more seconds. "Or, this could be an answer to the prayer we were about to pray." The four team members got a transit cart and went to entry six, sub level 34 and transferred to an elevator.

Two minutes later they walked into the visitor's lounge as the visitor stood up to greet them.

Laura put out her hand and introduced herself. "Hello, I'm Laura Malone, how can we help you?"

The man smiled a beautiful smile and when he spoke his voice was a deep bass that carried a ton of command tones embedded in it. "Actually, I am here to help you." He sobered a bit, "My assignment is to assist you in your current operation." He took a piece of paper out of his right pocket and handed it to Laura.

Laura looked at it and tipped her head to one side while she handed the paper to Jack.

Jack looked at the paper and read to himself. "Take Raquel with you. He is very, very good. Listen to his advice. Blessings, Hugo"

As Jack turned to Raquel to test him, he saw two men in his peripheral vision as they entered the lounge from behind Laura. Jack had a hitch in his spirit but, he felt that he had to concentrate on this new man.

Laura had already tested Raquel by silent prayer herself and nodded to him in acceptance.

One of the two new men suddenly changed direction and lunged at Laura from behind. He had a hypodermic in his right hand as he reached for Laura's neck with his left. Jack calculated the distance and knew he couldn't reach her in time to stop the man from injecting something into her neck.

The sudden combat stress made Jack see everything in slow motion because the adrenaline made his autonomic systems and senses to accelerate, Jack still tried to move the required distance to intercept the attack. He sent a heartfelt prayer for God's protection for Laura as he moved. He was still a foot away when he saw Raquel reach past Laura's shoulder with his left hand and lock onto the man's right hand which was holding the syringe.

It seemed as if the attacker had no strength as Raquel redirected the hand with the needle away from Laura and toward the attacker. As Raquel drove the needle into the man's throat, the fluid in the syringe was injected by the pressure of Raquel's hand over the attacker's hand on the syringe. The attacker's eyes grew very big and he ceased to move.

At that point, the way Jack saw the action it seemed that Raquel either stepped through Laura or disappeared from in front of Laura and reappeared behind her. He shoved the man with a needle in his throat to the left and faced the second man who was in the process of pulling a long, slim dagger out of his belt with his left hand as he approached; Raquel seemed to reach out into thin air and produced a full length sword. He then ran the sword through the second man directly through his heart.

Raquel pulled his sword back out of the man's body and stepped back and sideward so as not to hit Laura. The startled attacker dropped his dagger and collapsed to his knees with a stunned look on his face. He let out a large sigh and then fell over dead. Raquel made his sword disappear and turned back to the four astounded team members. He smiled, "Hugo says I am very good and that may be true, but, I give all glory to God for my ability to protect you."

Jack estimated that the entire event took less than five seconds from beginning to end. Laura was still turning around to see where Raquel went and Jack was attempting to stop his lunge without knocking her over. As he came to a halt he noticed that both Sarah and Mark had their handguns out and pointed toward the attackers. The action had happened so quickly they didn't have time to fire.

Jack straightened up and said, "Welcome to the team Raquel".

The man with a needle in his neck was lying on the floor quite dead and foaming at the mouth.

The Israeli team assigned to protect the base rushed into the lounge and checked the two dead men.

Jack told Eli to remove the bodies. After explaining the events they were released pending additional investigation which wouldn't take too long since the entire event was recorded on a DVD from the camera watching the room.

Jack knew there would be serious questions about how the newest member of their team managed to do what he did. In their life these days that was "situation normal".

Jack stepped over to Raquel and shook his hand. "Thank you for saving my wife."

Raquel looked intently at Jack and said, "You're welcome Mr. Malone, I was glad I could help although, I really didn't do very much."

Mark thought to himself, "This is going to be an interesting addition to the team." Sarah looked right at her husband and nodded as if she had heard his thoughts and totally agreed with him.

Laura shook her head as she thought about the last few minutes. She looked at Raquel and asked, "If you are an angel, how come you are visible to the cameras?"

Raquel seemed confused by the question for a few seconds and then nodded his head. "This interface I have with the human dimension was authorized by the Most High. I believe the answer you are looking for is that it is His desire that I appear on your electronic and film systems while I am here. It is a small thing."

Jack nodded and took out his cell phone and took a picture of Raquel and Laura. They both appeared in the retained image. "Okay then, shall we go back to the base?"

CHAPTER TWENTY-TWO

After they returned to their undersea base, Mark took Raquel for a tour of the facilities and to introduce him to the other team members.

Laura was praying about Raquel to the Lord and got some shocking news. She looked up to see Jack entering the scant information he had on Raquel into the computer system.

Laura walked over and put her hand on his shoulder. "I just had a talk with the Lord about Raquel. The description of his activities is the angel that oversees the good behavior of other angels, his name means "friend of God." He is also an angel of Earth, a guardian of the third heaven, and he was the one who brought Enoch to the heavens.

Jack stopped typing and looked at her. "That's a lot of responsibility for an angel."

Laura nodded her head and quietly said with awe, "Raquel isn't just an ordinary angel, he falls more into the category of Michael and Gabriel."

Those comments made Jack sit up and consider the ramifications. He slowly shook his head. "This mission is definitely going to be more dangerous and involved than any one we've had up till now. I'm sure of that because God would not have added an Archangel to the team unless a lot of heavenly firepower is going to be needed."

Laura realized that Jack was right. To need the power represented by that caliber of support meant that everything was far more important than it had been before and more would be required of the people on the team.

Jack asked, "How do we treat an angel of his capability?"

Laura had inquired of the Lord about that. "Just like we would any ordinary angel, respect, love, and support, and give him a lot of room if he is filled with holy anger."

Jack smiled. "Okay, since we were praying for wisdom and guidance from God then maybe we need to see if Raquel has a direction for us to follow."

Jack called Carol Moffet and asked her to join them in the war room. Carol had been anointed by Yahveh God to be the intersect between heaven and the team. When the Lord called her, or the team asked her to interpret the planned events by the enemy concerning the team's activities, she was allowed to see the heavenly matrix of eleven dimensions and the soon-to-be time lines of threats to the team. Activities which had to be approved by the Father and major events that would affect team activities. Jack shook his head as he thought about the burden on the young woman. There were literally millions of events shown on the matrix at any given moment and they were all in motion or flux continuously. The reason she could function so well was her training by Hugo. Hugo was an angel who had trained other angels for millennia and had recently trained some of the Crossfire Team. He had spent several years in heavenly time with Carol training her to do what God asked her to do. Jack felt she should be here if Raquel had information for them.

They continued to work on the project and relevant news updating until Carol arrived. A few minutes later Mark brought Raquel back to the war room. Raquel greeted Laura and Carol and then turned to face Jack.

Jack asked, "What do you think of our base?"

Raquel turned his piercing blue eyes on Jack. "You have done well considering the amount of attention the enemy and their human slaves are focusing on your operations. I am honored to be working with you and this team. What would you have me to do?"

Jack smiled and coolly returned the angel's gaze. "At the moment we need guidance and wisdom about the assignment that the Lord has for us in this time. Have you been given the information that we were starting to pray for this morning?"

Raquel nodded, "I do have the information you need to prepare for this on-going demonic attack on children on the Island of Britain, in the town of Norwich. The reason for these attacks is two-fold. First it is to eliminate one of the youngsters, a girl named Abigale Berton-Smythe. She is sixteen years old and is destined to become the next-in-line to the throne of England by her marriage to the remaining Prince in line of secession five years from now.

Second, Satan wants to send a graphic signal to other remaining Christian believers not to try and represent Yahveh or Yahshua anymore."

Raquel looked at the other people assembled in the war room. "God has ordained Abigale's future and Satan has determined to prevent it because the matrix shows that "Abby", as she wants to be known, will become the driving force in the British Isles for obedience and true worship of the Most High and His Son. Her path will be the electrifying catalyst for the races in those Isles to turn to honest worship and prayer to Yahveh. That is even though the people on Earth will be suffering through God's tribulations at that time. Because of her future, Satan will do everything he can to stop her. She has already given her life to Yahshua and knows Him as Lord. The heavenly host can defeat Satan's direct efforts. Since Satan has to get permission to kill or disable the girl makes us aware of his efforts."

Mark asked, "With all that heavenly defense, why are we being tasked to this mission? It would seem our efforts would be inconsequential to yours."

Raquel looked through Mark for a few seconds. Then he frowned, "Do you not realize that your team's anointing is needed to stop the enemy's demonic efforts to destroy Abby?"

Jack spoke up. "Raquel, are you telling us that we are the point-of-the-spear concerning Satan's illegal, and therefore not planned on the matrix, demonic entrances into our dimension?"

Raquel nodded, "You have spoken correctly. Your team, and others, have been specifically created to counter the enemy's illegal incursions into this dimension. There is great spiritual damage that can be done by the evil spiritual agents of Satan when they enter this dimension. These are not things God's messenger/warriors are allowed to prevent or combat as a heavenly force."

Mark spoke up again. "But, God knows everything that is going to happen in the entire universe. Why can't he just assign angels to be there when the demons appear in our dimension? Since it is illegal by God's rules. I would think you would be able to counter them more efficiently than we could."

Raquel smiled a thin smile. "But, then God would have to break his own rules to do that. He cannot do that without denying Himself, which He will not do."

Carol spoke up, "Hugo taught me that one portion of God's holiness is based on His absolute honor based on His Word. He won't allow Satan's demons to enter the human dimension but, at the same time He is honor-bound by His word not to use heaven to stop the incursions. Satan can illegally violate God's agreements but God will not do the same thing to stop him. That is why we have been selected, trained, and given this mission."

Jack nodded, "Okay, then we know what we have to do. Let's do it."

CHAPTER TWENTY-THREE

As the team winged its way across the Atlantic toward Britain, Jack read up on the town their mission was taking them to today.

Norwich was a rare blend of historic interest and modern sophistication. Its skyline is dominated by its magnificent Norman cathedral, boasting the largest cloisters in England, the second tallest spire in the country and an amazing 1,200 carved stone roof bosses – one of the greatest art treasures of medieval Europe. Norwich's ancient buildings and city wall remains make it the most complete medieval city in Britain. In medieval times Norwich had been one of the greatest cities in England, and today, as East Anglican's capital city, it remains so.

There are over 30 medieval churches within the Norwich city walls alone. Until the Rapture many had still functioned as parish churches, the city also houses the impressive 20th century St. John's Roman Catholic Cathedral, standing imposingly at the top of Grapes Hill.

The meeting place of the teenagers was a Pentecostal Church just west of the A147 loop. That is where the kids would meet tomorrow night around six p.m., local time, according to the information that Carol got from the matrix.

Jack got up and went back to where Raquel sat looking out of the window of the "Shrew1" one of the team's two Mach-2 fighter planes disguised as corporate jets. Jack asked, "May I sit here and talk with you?"

Raquel smiled and replied. "Of course you can. Please, don't treat me so gently. We are warriors on the same side contending with the same enemies. We should be more casual between ourselves."

Jack sat down. "That is very gracious of you. I appreciate it coming from a being that is accustomed to directly serving Yahveh all the time."

Raquel smiled even broader. "All the more reason we two should be friends. I already have a good report about you from Caleb. And, Rose said that I should enjoy being around you. It seems that they were right. How can I help you?"

Jack relaxed at the names of two of their obviously, guardian angels, that they had interacted with for quite a while. "I assume that the teenagers will meet at the Pentecostal Church tomorrow night for their regular meeting and that is when the demons will attack. Does that seem right to you?"

Raquel seemed to be looking at something Jack couldn't see. "Possibly, there are several other things going on in that vicinity at the same time and those things could interfere with the demon's schedules."

Raquel studied Jack for a few seconds. "If certain events happen during our mission I may have to be absent for an indeterminate amount of time to handle the other situation. But, I will return as quickly as I can. Do you understand?"

Jack nodded his head as he contemplated that possibility.

Mark walked up and sat down on the armrest of the chair across the aisle from them. Jack noted that Mark was at ease with Raquel as a simple matter of fact.

Mark shook his head slightly. "Is there any way we can get some layout plans or construction blueprints so that we can get a feel for the inside of the church before we go to war?"

Raquel looked at him for a few seconds. Suddenly, Mark, Jack, and Raquel were inside the Pentecostal Church. Raquel looked at him and asked, "Will this work?"

Mark was not used to travel in the spirit other than the times he went to heaven and it threw him off somewhat. There were ten or twelve people in the church around them. "Doesn't our suddenly appearing bother them?"

Raquel shook his head. They don't perceive us because we are in the spirit not in our bodies. There are those anointed humans that can sense our presence but I sense none of them here. Also, other angels and, of course, the demons can detect us.

The three of them moved around the sanctuary and the rooms beyond it. Jack noticed that the people in the church were praying most earnestly and then getting up and leaving the church. He reasoned that they were some of the church membership that didn't go with Christ in the rapture and had no leadership. All they could do is pray at this point.

Suddenly, they were all back in the Shrew as it bored its way through the skies in supercruise.

Mark thought for a few seconds. "I think we should approach the area of the meeting from several different directions to prevent having to battle with the kids in the middle."

Raquel smiled, "That is a very good strategy Mark. The demons normally appear near the area of their attack and are grouped together. If they sense an attack from several different directions, they will split up and become more vulnerable. Plus, they will not focus on their target so that they can defend themselves."

The three continued to plan their best guess defense for the children and called Laura and Sarah in to collaborate with them. Eventually, Laura and Sarah decided that they would not actively attack the demons but would defend the children, especially Abigale Berton-Smythe. Jack, Mark, Alexis, and Su Li would attack the demons on sight. David would provide live-fire capability in the event they sent in any illegal demons along with the ones that had permission to enter the human dimension. Raquel would standby and provide any backup that was needed while providing council on the developing situation.

Jack coordinated a private hanger and landing permission through the private charter service based at Norwich Airport for a private and secure location for the Shrew during their stay. Su Li brought the aircraft down lightly just after three a.m. Norwich local time. There were very few people around to see them as they taxied to their hanger. A manager of the charter service was there to open the hanger for them and to accept payment. He showed them the alarm controls, door controls, and handed them the keys.

Jack was glad they came in twenty hours before the meeting time. It gave them time to survey the area, locate the church, and get some good sleep so that everyone would be fresh and ready.

Hooked up to local power and air conditioning, with the window shades lowered for darkness, and the seats turned into full length beds it was easy to sleep during the day. Raquel stood watch as he didn't need sleep or rest.

CHAPTER TWENTY-FOUR

By six in the afternoon everyone knew their part in the defense against the demons and had loaded their weapons and other gear into a rented SUV. They headed to the area of the church to be in position for the 6:45 deployment.

Jack saw a middle-aged man wearing a trench coat against the evening chill headed for the SUV. Jack stepped out of the passenger side front seat and met the man several yards away from the van.

The balding, ruddy-faced man with the stocky build of a soccer player slightly past his prime stuck out his hand in greeting. Jack shook his hand. "Sergeant Norris?"

"At your service." The sergeant spoke with a definite British accent. "I suspect that you are General Jack Malone?"

Jack grinned at the use of his military rank appointed to him by the previous President of the United States. "Just Jack is fine. Yes sir. Has Scotland Yard approved our action here tonight?"

"Yes they have Jack, and just call me Bill. Your previous actions saving considerable numbers of agents of the Yard, not to mention hundreds of civilians and Police Officers are well remembered. There is one condition on the Action Approval. I must accompany you during this mission."

Jack sobered up somewhat. "That's perfectly fine as far as we are concerned but remember, it didn't work out too well the last time for our Scotland Yard representative."

Bill nodded his head, "I know, but orders are orders and I am the lucky duck that they assigned to go with you."

Jack smiled again, "Okay, but I want you to stay near Raquel" Jack pointed at the archangel as the others exited the SUV. "He is the tall one with blue jeans on. He will protect you if any demons get near you. Speaking of demons, where do you stand as far as God goes?"

Bill stared at Jack for a few seconds. "I'm a believer in Jesus Christ and I attend church services as often as my duties allow."

Jack probed a little deeper. "Do you believe in angels and demons?"

Bill shrugged his shoulders. "I've never met any so far. But, I understand that being around you and your team that may change. I am interested in what will happen tonight. I will let you in on a little secret though; the Yard has installed several cameras to record tonight's activities."

Jack laughed, "Okay, they won't see things that won't record so you keep a sharp eye on things and know right now that they won't believe you, at first."

Mark walked up and handed Jack his armor and web harness with his holstered handgun, grenades, and knives on it. "We need to go if we want to attend this party on time."

Jack introduced Bill and Mark and explained Bill's requirement to attend the festivities to Mark. He ended with "I want Bill to stay with Raquel if possible."

Mark nodded, shook hands with the Scotland Yard agent. After he left, Mark asked Jack, "Does he have any idea what he has gotten himself into?"

Jack shook his head as he strapped on his harness over his armor. "He says he's a believer in Jesus but he didn't go in the Rapture.

Mark grinned and slapped Jack on the shoulder. "Okay, let's see what we can do to widen his horizons tonight." Jack smiled, "That's a given."

The team gathered near the church and prayed for protection, strength, and guidance in the upcoming combat. Then they moved into position at three of the entrances to the church which led to the sanctuary.

Teenagers had been going into the church in ones and twos for the last fifteen minutes and it was three minutes of seven when Mark pushed the "go" button on his battle harness.

Jack went in first from the west side and slowly entered the sanctuary. The teenagers were lighting candles as the power had been cut off to the church when there was no one to pay the bill after the Rapture.

Several small groups of young people and some adults had come into the seating area and sat there watching the kids set up the area so that they to speak with the attendees.

Laura nudged Jack and pointed out Abby to him. She was simply one of the teens working to help with the session. Jack saw the other team members who remained on the edges of the sanctuary in the dark shadows so as to not disturb the people there.

Raquel stood next to Jack and Bill. Jack asked him quietly, "Are the demons near?"

Raquel nodded his head. "Any second now. They will focus their attack on Abby but will terrorize the other kids while they attempt to accomplish their mission."

Mark growled in a low bass. "Not on my watch they won't!"

An older teen stood up to address the people and it seemed to be the trigger for the demonic attack.

A dozen demons appeared out of thin air as they stepped into the human dimension. Jack noted that they were some of the ugliest creatures he had seen. Most had more parts than needed, arms, legs, eyes, and in one case three mouths full of pointed black teeth.

Since they appeared closer to the center of the sanctuary they were immediately seen by everyone. Many people started screaming and trying to flee only to find their path blocked by the demons.

Mark hit the attack button on his vest and started praying. His silver armor appeared as he ran toward the demons with holy anger in his eyes. The rest of the team matched him and came in at the demons from behind. The demons realized they were caught in a trap and turned to do battle.

Mark met the first demon in a rush and overpowered the demon's sword with his glowing blade which flowed with the power of Yahveh. He continued moving forward and ran the sword through the demon. He turned to find his next target only to be battered backward by a massive smash to the front of his armor by a black blade. Mark went into high speed and sliced and diced the second demon before it could recover its blade.

Laura ran and jumped up onto the platform and found Abby and four of the other teens facing a pair of demons. She began to pray and her golden armor exploded into sight along with her chrome sword with power of Yahveh flowing off of it in all directions.

Both of the demons forgot about the kids to concentrate on this new threat. One mumbled a deep bass voice as it spoke to the other demon. "Oh, look at this worthless female thinking she can attack us."

The demons moved apart and came at Laura at the same time. Laura danced to one side to limit her exposure to the second demon. Since she was outnumbered she went into high speed and went under the slowly slashing blade of the first demon. She literally cut him in half with her sword and swung back to her right to attack the second one. This one was much more capable and had also gone to high speed. He had already moved up to Laura's right and was swinging his sword so that it would strike her in the face where she had no armor. Laura knew in that instant that she couldn't block the black blade before it stuck her.

CHAPTER TWENTY-FIVE

There were demons and humans fighting everywhere in the sanctuary as the black blade raced at Laura's face.

A resounding crash shattered the black blade which tumbled to the ground as it broke in half. Sarah's glowing blade reversed back upward and decapitated the demon which collapsed into red malodorous smoke.

Laura took a breath she thought she'd never get to take and said, "Thank you Sarah."

Sarah nodded as she intercepted another demon headed for the kids on the platform. She blocked the demon's blade in low position and then in high but couldn't disengage to strike the creature due to the speed of the combat. Laura's blade cut that demon into two pieces at the waist.

Both women looked around and saw that the few remaining demons were in combat with Mark, Jack, and Su Li. Alexis entered the battle with Su Li and helped dispatch the demon she was fighting. Mark and Jack finished off their respective demons and everything seemed to come to a halt.

Mark looked around and asked, "Did we get them all?"

Jack kept scanning the darkness around them as he said, "No, our armor is still active."

A large demon appeared suddenly between Jack and Laura. This one was arrogant and confident. Jack attacked him but he sidestepped the attack and smashed Jack into the air with his black sword. Mark went into high speed and went after the demon. The demon held up his left hand and Mark dropped back into normal speed. The demon tried to run Mark through with his sword but it struck Mark's silver armor and deflected. The demon struck Mark with a backhand blow with its left hand and Mark was knocked three isles back into the seating area just missing two people sitting there in fear.

Laura ducked under the demon's sword swing and drove her sword directly into the demon's side. Her sword stopped as it impacted the demon and it spun around and side kicked Laura off of the platform. It straightened up and made for Abby and the other kids.

Su Li and Alexis took up defensive positions between the demon and the kids to try and stop its forward motion. The demon raised its sword to a high guard position over its right shoulder in preparation to remove one or both of the women.

Suddenly Raquel appeared in front of the two team members facing the large demon. He was clad in armor of white with his sword also at high guard position. "Halt Sama'el, in the name of Yahveh!"

Sama'el stopped and stared at Raquel. He roared, "Raquel, you have no right here, be gone now!"

Raquel replied, "It is you that has no right here in this dimension. You specifically have been banned by God from directly interfering with humans. Go now or face destruction."

Sama'el considered his options and decided he was the stronger of the two. He stepped into the space between himself and Raquel and attacked the angel in white. Raquel countered the demon's swing and cut down at the demon's legs. Sama'el jumped over the attack and attempted to drive his sword through Raquel. The angel rotated and the sword slid by without hitting him.

As the two archangel-level beings fought. Laura clicked on her microphone. "Everyone, pray for God's power and strength for Raquel now!"

The entire team began to beseech the Father in Yahshua's name for power and strength for Raquel. As they continued to pray and worship Yahveh, the battle definitely shifted in Raquel's favor. Sama'el was back pedaling and on the defensive. Raquel suddenly feinted a stab causing Sama'el to chop his sword downward to deflect Raquel's sword. Instead of stabbing, Raquel spun around very quickly to his left and decapitated the demon in a mighty blow to its neck.

With a choked-off snarl, Sama'el's body collapsed and dissolved into black, greasy smoke.

Raquel dropped to one knee and thanked the Most High for the victory and gave all credit for that victory to God.

Raquel changed back to jeans and shirt and the team's armor also disappeared as they gathered together on the platform. Laura, Mark, and Jack hobbled up with Jack favoring his left leg. Mark was still shaking off pieces of the seats he had demolished when he was slammed into them.

As they met in the middle of the platform, Jack asked Raquel, "Who was that?"

Raquel shook his head. "He was a very old enemy. You might know him from Jewish mythology as a fallen Archangel. For millennia he has ruled over seven habitations called Sheba Ha-Yechaloth, infernal realms of the Earth. Thousands of your years ago he was forbidden to directly interfere with humanity or enter this dimension. Thanks be to God he has been cast into the pit to await God's judgment at the end of time."

Laura laid her hand on Raquel's arm. "Thank God you were here. We had no way to stop him from getting to Abby and the others."

Raquel stared at Laura for several seconds. He then smiled and put his hands on Laura's shoulders. "In the name of Yahveh, you are healed of your wounds." He looked up and said, "That goes for all of you humans who battled Sama'el. He was not supposed to be here and considering his powers you are all fortunate to still be alive."

Laura made a small face. "Fortune had nothing to do with it. It was the grace and mercy of God that kept us alive."

He looked at Laura, "I was here because God foresaw Sama'el's interference and flagrant violation of God's rulings. I will go now and return when you need me on future missions for God." He faded out of sight.

Taking a large breath, Laura sighed. "I'm going to miss that angel." She looked over where Su Li and Alexis were talking to Abby and her friends. Walking over to them she smiled a warm smile at the future ruler of the British Isles.

A bright young girl at fourteen, Abby shook Laura's hand with a huge smile on her face. "Thank you, thank you all. Our faith has been confirmed and your bravery in fighting those demons will always be in my mind." Then as young girls are lent to do, Abby grabbed Laura in a hug. "I love you all for saving my friends and me."

Abby stepped back and studied Laura for a few seconds. "Where does your armor and sword come from?"

Laura smiled in return, "From God as an anointing to battle demons."

Abby grinned, "Then someday I want to have armor like that."

Laura put her hand up to the teenager's cheek. "Maybe you will."

The team talked to everyone and assured them that the demons would not be coming back, at least not for a while, probably years.

Jack looked at Bill and asked Mark, "Think we should wake him up?"

Mark grinned, "Yeah, I think he passed out when the demons appeared."

Laura laughed, "A whole lot of good he is going to do in describing the action tonight."

CHAPTER TWENTY-SIX

Jack brought the Scotland Yard detective back to consciousness with some smelling salts from their first aid kit. Bill was pretty groggy for the first few minutes but finally came back to his normal self. "Whot 'Appened?" He asked Jack.

Jack straightened the man's jacket and tie and summed up the action. "The demons came to attack the kids and we stopped them." He watched as the man got nervous and peered around Jack to see if there were any more of the vile creatures left. Relieved, he shook his head. "I made a bloody big mess of this business, didn't I?"

Jack laughed, "Don't forget that your agency has multiple video cameras to show them some of what happened. Unfortunately, they will probably see your decision to take a nap during the action."

Bill shook his head, "Great, that should give the lads at the Yard a great deal of ammunition to tease me with for the next few months."

Jack had an idea. "Hang on a minute Bill. He keyed his combat mic and talked to Charlie back at their undersea fortress. Charlie agreed and Jack broke the connection. "I just had our computer guru forward a data file to your boss. We put this together for a congressman who saw a demonic battle and wanted to show something to his fellow politicians. Since demons, like angels, are spiritual beings they don't show up on film or video. This file will give them a summary as to why their cameras would not record the demons and what they look like. It should shock anyone who wants to fault you for passing out."

Bill pumped Jack's hand, "Great Gov'ner, thanks a Mill."

After Bill had left, Jack joined Laura and made sure that Abby and her friends had a number to call if they had any more demon problems or needed to talk. The crew left the church after they prayed a prayer of thanks to the Lord for their success and for allowing Raquel to accompany them on the raid.

As they drove back to the airport hangar Laura asked Jack, "Do you think that we are going to suffer more attacks because of tonight's combat?"

Jack thought about that. "Maybe, maybe not. There is the factor that they have lost a major player going against us and that may make softer targets more tempting. We'll have to wait and see."

Jack made sure everything was complete as they boarded the aircraft and Su Li pushed the start switch. Within a minute the plane was powered up and combat ready for the trip back to their base.

Jack and all of the team members dictated their action reports and went through a debriefing by Charlie, long distance. Su Li complained about having to describe all the various demons but Charlie insisted.

Then Jack sat back in the comfortable seat to pray and seek the Lord on their continuing mission.

Eight hours later he was awakened by the thump of the landing gear as the Shrew landed back at the undersea base. He got up and stretched. He saw Su Li as she exited the cockpit and apologized, "I'm sorry that I fell asleep. I didn't mean for you to have to fight all night and fly all the way back while we slept."

Su Li smiled a small smile. "No problem, I had plenty of help and got to sleep for five hours myself."

Seeing Jack's raised eyebrow, she smiled and pointed to the cockpit door. Jack walked over and found Alexis finishing the logging of the flight and shutting down the other systems. He said, "Are you now the official co-pilot for this aircraft?"

Alexis smiled up at him, "Unofficial. I've now have over sixteen hours flying with Su Li, ten of them while she slept. I'm a quick learner and had already been qualified on the F-22 Raptor. This isn't too much different, at least in the combat mode. Since I am also licensed on the Citation X, I'm technically qualified for this version of that aircraft."

Jack nodded his approval. "Keep it up, officially. We've got Su Li and we now have Mike White, who trained Su Li. It would be great to have a backup for either of them if things get real busy. Has Su Li explained the fighting capabilities of the Shrew for you?"

Alexis grinned, "Several times. She can't shut up about the wonderful fighting ability of this craft. I am very impressed by its clandestine capabilities, especially the armament and sensor interfaces."

Laura came up behind Jack and poked her head around his broad shoulders. "Hi Alex, how's the pilot training going?"

At a thumb up from the other pretty blonde team member she turned to Jack. "A heads up. You've got a call coming in a few minutes that you need to take. Get this. It's the White House administration and they're seeking our help."

Jack thought about that for a few minutes. "Why would an administration that was hunting us down to put us out of business twenty days ago want our help, or expect us to give it to them?"

Laura shrugged, "It's probably demon related. At least that's my guess."

Ten minutes later, Jack was on the phone with the Secretary of Defense.

Jason Helmuth was an appointee, a dyed-in-the-wool liberal, and definitely not a fan of any military-capable unit not under his command. But, he was trying to be civilized in his conversation with Jack Malone in this specific case. "Mr. Malone, may I speak candidly?" Jack replied "The truth is always a good choice."

Helmuth let out a big sigh. "Yes, of course. It seems we have been on opposite sides of the debate on citizen-controlled military and I am ashamed to have to admit, in your team's case, that I was wrong."

Jack's eyebrows went up at this admission. "How can we help you Secretary Helmuth?"

The Secretary huffed and coughed a bit, which was not unusual for a man over three hundred pounds with a chronic smoking habit. "Regardless of the President's view of independent combat teams we have uncovered an on-going terror attack, here in Washington that we simply can't handle. I'm relying on the advice of the Premier of Russia and the President of Israel as to your team's expertise. I understand that you have the ability to deal with other worldly creatures that are undermining the government of the United States. Is this correct?"

"Yes, it is true that we battle against the enemy of mankind whenever his demons enter our dimension to work against humanity. But, we only do that when God directs us to do it."

That took the Secretary a few seconds to digest. "Yes, yes, I have had a lot of input from my people and I now believe that is the problem we've run into here."

Jack thought about that for a few seconds. "Mr. Secretary, I assume that you will ensure our freedom to solve your problem the way we want to do it and that there will be no complaints if we defend your freedom in unorthodox ways that don't cross criminal laws?"

The administration man agreed with a caveat. "I need to have one of our people working with you."

Jack agreed with the stipulation that it would be the FBI's Assistant Director Gary Rhodes who would be the man involved. "I ask for him for three reasons, one, you can trust him, two, I can trust him, and three, he's gone up against demons with us before."

The Secretary sighed again, something he seemed prone to do a lot. "He was one of the people that suggested your team in this case. Alright, I will assign him to your team for the duration. How soon can you get here?"

Jack smiled, "We have to see what God wants us to do in this case. Most likely we wouldn't be having this conversation if God didn't want us to get involved. I think we need a lot more information before jumping into your problem. One thing about demons is that they tend to know what you're doing by listening to you, like right now on the phone, and they are fairly smart about what they're planning. Why don't you have Gary Rhodes send us the particulars in this case by email. Then I can get you a time-line for our arrival. Also, there is a fee involved with this work. I assume you have been granted license to purchase our services?"

"That will be no problem, I assure you. Thank you Mr. Malone. I expect to hear from you very soon or we may not be here for you to help."

Jack hung up and thought out the situation. This probably wouldn't be an easy operation because of the level of attack against the power of the world's largest democracy.

CHAPTER TWENTY-SEVEN

The next morning, back at their undersea base, Jack called the core team together in the living room. Besides himself this functional unit included, Laura, Mark and Sarah Connelly, David Zahavy, Alexis Hutton, Su Li, Mike White, and Carol Moffet. Charlie Wu and his wife Linda were attending remotely from the Comm/Sec office.

Jack played the digital recording of his conversation with the Secretary of Defense and asked for inputs. Several people voiced their distrust of the administration or at least their less-than-enthusiastic interest of solving the government's problems with the possibility of being thrown in jail for their efforts.

Jack privately agreed but reminded them that their mission was to defend humans from invading demons as assigned by the Lord. Mark grinned, "The problem here is determining which side is the more demonic?" That generated laughter by everyone.

Jack grinned and suggested that they seek the Father's will in this matter.

Laura led the prayer for enlightenment. "Heavenly Father, we worship you and your kingdom and praise You for Your loving care and favor You give to us every day. In the name of Yahshua we pray that everyone will turn aside from sin and seek your face Father. We also pray that we are walking in your will every day."

As she prayed Jack could feel the heaviness he associated with the presence of the Holy Spirit. His spirit rose in joy and contentment as he drew nearer to God.

Laura continued, "Farther Yahveh, as your children and your servants, we seek your guidance and wisdom as to dealing with the challenge being presented by the Secretary of Defense of the United States. We know you took us out of the U.S. because this self-same administration was seeking to disband us and prevent us from doing your will. We are concerned that regardless of their intentions and needs this may be too great of an opportunity for them to do just that."

Jack waited and felt comforted by the nearness of God but didn't get any real answer to the prayer so he quietly prayed "Thank you Father, we pray all things in Yahshua's name.

He opened his eyes and beheld an older man sitting in a previously empty seat among the group. Jack silently prayed, "Father Yahveh is this messenger from you?"

He sensed a confirmation and pleasure that he was willing and obedient to ask the Lord for this information.

As the others in the group finished their praying they became aware of the old man but didn't say anything because they saw Jack smiling at him.

Jack thought for a few seconds and checked his spirit. There was a familiarity about the man and it clicked in Jack's mind that he had sat with this spirit before. "Hello Caleb."

Caleb was an angel of the Lord that had worked with Jack before when the Master Prophets had attempted to force the world into making their religion the only one in the world through nuclear blackmail. He had also been with them other times in Russia and Israel.

Caleb smiled at the assembled group. "Jack, you and your team have grown greatly in the service and spirit of the Most High. I commend you on your perseverance and tenacity. You all prayed about an assignment from God to help the present government in the United States. I was sent to bring you the word of the Lord concerning that action. God said, *"Go forth and be bold and courageous for I have seen your victory over the demonic. Out of what the enemy of mankind means for evil I will make good. My sons and daughters, use your anointing to conquer the demonic forces and leave the powers to me. I will judge them; they will not judge you. Only beware of temptation and pride. Remember, I will never leave you or forsake you because you are my children. The enemy has his believers in positions of power to contend with you as well as his demons. They too must fall."*

Caleb stood up and put his hand on the hilt of his sword, "Remember also, we will be with you as you have need." He faded out of sight.

Jack shrugged his shoulders, "Well, I think that pretty well answers the prayer, don't you?"

Laura smiled, "We have a big job ahead of us and we just got back from action in Britain. I think we need to let Mike fly us to Washington and give Su Li a break."

Charlie broke into their conversation from the ComSec floor. "I just got the input from the FBI. I'll send it to the Video Store on the big screen in there."

A few minutes later Jack used the remote to select the new E-mailed report. They began to study it.

The first thing Jack noted was that the military, all branches, plus the FBI, CIA, NSA, and a host of other alphabet agencies had taken a whack at resolving the problem with no success. The scientific community had also failed to stop the incursions and that included a very entire elite group of scientists and engineers. The problem was elevated to the Department of Homeland Security who professed an inability to handle the situation and dumped it back onto the Secretary of Defense, Jason Helmuth. He did his due diligence and decided that they needed outside help. After inquiring of all of his sources he decided that he needed to eat some crow and contact the Crossfire Team. Jack was somewhat impressed by the fact that the man decided to do this himself and not delegate the contact to an underling.

Jack moved onto the problem portion of the report. It seems that various members of Congress and the administration were visited and occasionally "roughed up" by a group of unknown intruders. These intruders seem to be able to get around, or through, every known form of defense, including armed guards and walls.

On the occasion there was a run-in with a guard, the intruders were impervious to bullets and were too powerful in the several physical battles that had occurred. A number of security personnel and guards had been killed. The incursions were somewhat political in that the intruders threatened their targets with horrible consequences if they didn't vote for or promote a seemingly polyglot of political causes, laws, and proposed legislation. An analysis of the threats indicated that the intruders wanted complete capitulation with the upcoming One World Government and all of its policies.

Jack shut off the TV and started a brain-storming session with the core group and also Charlie and Linda Wu by remote communication.

The agreed upon consensus was that Marco Marino, the Anti-Christ was using Satan's demons to ensure America's submission to the one-world government.

Mark added, "The problem for us is not just how do we protect the entire Congress and the administration, several hundred people, but why is it so bleating obvious what's going on? This is unlike normal demonic activity which is obscure, odd, and usually hidden from view. Is this a function of the Anti-Christ being imposed by Satan on their activities or is something else going on?"

Laura asked Carol what she had seen in the Matrix the last time she had a chance to look at it.

Carol shook her head. "I would not have been looking for anything in this area because I specialize in the future events involving the team and the team wasn't involved until just now."

Jack noted the incongruence and asked Carol, "But, the Matrix is the future events of the team. Wouldn't it show up even though you didn't know about it until now? After all, the future would include whatever we may be doing, right?"

Carol thought about that and cocked her head to one side. "Yes, that's true. This would imply that we aren't going to be involved or the enemy is deliberately hiding our involvement by not placing anything against us in the Matrix. I will have to scrutinize the Matrix more thoroughly. She got up and went to a couch removed from the group so as to not disturb their work.

She got down on her knees and worshiped God and praised Him and His Kingdom. Then the diamonds glowed white at her throat and forehead as she moved into her anointing.

Carol never ceased to marvel at the transition from reality of kneeling in prayer to suddenly be flying, or floating over the Matrix. It took her breath away every time. She mentally sang praises to God for the pleasure, excitement, and gratitude she felt to be allowed to do this.

Now that she had experienced this activity for over a year and had made several hundred trips to the eleven-dimensional Matrix she was sure of her capability and started to home into the dates in question. Then she analyzed the vertical section of that date range. Several tens of thousands of predicted, authorized, and probable time lines and happenings were displayed before her vision. She mentally chose the ones that affected the team the most and, this time, the government of the United States.

She still did not see anything that reflected any interaction between the two. She realized that something new was happening and she did not know how to handle it. She prayed that she could talk to Hugo, the angel that had trained her in how to correctly analyze the information in the Matrix.

CHAPTER TWENTY-EIGHT

While Carol went back to the Matrix to determine which administration or Congressional members were next in the incursion timeline, Jack called the Secretary of Defense and requested he give Gary Rhodes the authority to contact the upcoming attackees and confer access to one or more of the Crossfire Team to counter the attacks. Secretary Helmuth agreed to both conditions and asked what the team was going to do.

Jack laughed, "We're going to be on hand when a demon comes calling and persuade him to leave the people alone."

The Secretary asked, "But, how are you going to know when, and who, is going to be attacked?"

"The enemy has to request permission from God before they can interfere with our dimension, otherwise they are vulnerable to guns and bombs and the security forces already attacked would have probably stopped the illegal entries. Since they have to be here with permission we can see their plans. We are just going to read their mail and attend the meeting. Please understand, that this is not a precise science and there will be timing foul-ups, usually not caused by our people, but stressful none the less. Also the enemy will detect our pattern of interference and will try to circumvent our operations."

Jack sighed, "With several hundred possible targets the enemy can field a bigger force than what we have available. Once they detect the limits to our interference they could "flood" the attacks to overwhelm our ability to meet them. If they do this, then we will need some form of prioritization from you as to who we protect and who we have to abandon. Also, you are aware that they aren't trying to injure your people? They just want to scare everyone into voting for or backing the one-world-government. When they detect any opposition to their plan, such as our operations, then the demons might get nastier and more demanding and we will have to step up our efforts."

The Secretary asked, "Can we supplement your people with FBI agents?"

"Non-spiritual defenses have failed up till now, what makes you think they'll work in the future?"

That caused the Secretary to consider the parameters to the problem. "I see. Well, we'll just have to start your operations and see where it goes."

Jack agreed, "Thank you Mr. Secretary, we'll be in touch and I'll see that you get a daily update as to who was attacked, our response, and who we think will be the next day's targets."

Carol came into the war room and gave Jack a list. "Here's what I could get off of the Matrix. Since the enemy isn't attacking an organization, says the Congress, they have to list each person they are going to affect. The date is clear; the time of day can be somewhat vague, like, morning, lunch time, etc."

Jack looked at tomorrow's list which would be the first attacks they could interdict due to the distance. There were eight names on the list. Six Congressional members and two special ones. The minority leader and the Vice President.

The times ranged from early morning for four of them, midday for two and evening for the last two. Jack wasn't surprised that the team had eight swords people. He knew that God had been aware that this time was coming when he had Hugo train the last five to complement Laura and Sarah.

Charlie called him and told him that the others were ready and on the way to the second Shrew which was on the apron in front of their hanger. Jack picked up his final paperwork including the list and headed for the aircraft.

Mike White was completing his flight plans and E-mailing them to the FAA since their destination was Washington. He gave Jack the OK sign when Jack boarded and counted heads.

Mike closed the door and taxied out to the flight line. Five minutes later he released control of the aircraft to the tunnel computer and played passenger for the time it took for the plane to exit the massive doors in the base of the island off of the Israeli coast. He then headed up to the military air corridors and went into supercruise for the east coast of the United States.

Jack gave the particulars of each assignment to the team. He gave the Vice President to Laura and the Minority Leader to Mark. Then he assigned one to the Congressional members to himself, the others to; Sarah, Su Li, and Alexis. This covered the morning attacks and the two noontime attacks. He reassigned himself and added Mark for each of the evening attacks.

They landed at Ronald Reagan Airport and were transported to the FBI headquarters. Their equipment and weapons were transported in a separate van. David decided to remain with the van while everyone else went into the building.

Jack shook hands with Gary Rhodes and asked him, "Are we completely set up with the probable attackees?"

Gary smiled, "Yes Sir. You will be working with the Secret Service, Military Security or CID, FBI, Washington Police, and probably, Maryland Highway Patrol personnel depending on who you are protecting and where you are providing the protection."

Jack nodded, "We need to have four of us in position by seven a.m. tomorrow." He showed Gary the list of assignments.

Gary put his finger on the list. "How can you identify the people that are going to be attacked?"

Jack shrugged, "We read their mail. They have to get permission from the Lord and we can review their approved incursions."

Gary smiled, "That's great, and they have to tell you where they're going to strike. Of course it could be a trap for you."

Jack nodded his head, "That's always true, plus, the indicators we get are not always right, time, place, etc. It is just a minor help but if it is right, then we get the jump on the bad guys."

They left and stayed at an FBI safe house for what was left of the night.

The next morning, FBI strike teams got each of the six team member to their targets.

Laura walked up to the Secret Service agent at the gate to the Vice President's residence and her FBI accompaniment showed his badge to the agent and requested entrance for him and Laura. The agent checked his approved list and opened the gate. He directed them to the back patio where the Vice President and his family were having a leisurely breakfast.

They had to clear their presence with two more Secret Service agents before they were allowed to approach the VP. Laura had no weapons on her and the FBI agent had already surrendered his gun to the first agent at the gate.

As they walked up to the table where the VP and his family were just having their dishes cleared from the table, the FBI agent put up his hand to have Laura wait several steps away while he cleared her with the VP.

Laura looked around and admired the genteel setting and the serene countryside as seen from the VP's back yard. She noted four more Secret Service agents scattered around the property. They were on high alert due to the incursions on other politicos recently.

FBI agent Tim Sever stepped back to Laura and motioned her forward. She walked up to the Vice President and shook hands with him and his wife. The VP looked her over and slightly shook his head.

Laura asked him if he understood why she was there.

The VP sat back and threw his cloth napkin on the table. "Agent Sever, I was under the impression that this Crossfire Team was sending us special help with this terror problem. Why did you bring me a secretary? This is worthless."

Laura spoke up before the agent could respond. "Mr. Vice President, I'm sorry that your expectations don't meet reality. I assure you that my capabilities are presently beyond your ability to understand them. Also, I would appreciate it if you address me directly rather than through Agent Sever. My name is Laura Malone and I am one of the leaders of the Crossfire Team and our job is to prevent you, or your family from being threatened or harmed."

The VP's family included a seventeen-year-old son who laughed at Laura. "Gee dad, don't get the lady upset, she might hurt you."

The VP obviously agreed with his son and as the second most powerful man in the nation he wasn't going to have Laura give him any sass. "Now, you listen to me young lady. I don't care who you are or what you think of yourself. I am going to have some serious words with the Secretary of Defense for wasting my time. Your little charade is over!"

Laura watched the man as he pushed back from the table and stood up to reprimand her properly.

Just then one of the Secret Service agents stepped up to the VP and whispered in his ear. The VP looked out across his back yard and saw a commotion with two of the Secret Service agents out there. Suddenly there were three gunshots and one of the agents was knocked into the air and the second one disappeared below a low wall.

Before anyone could move a particularly evil looking, scale covered demon which was shaped like a human but ran on all four limbs crept over the wall and dashed toward the VP. The other three Secret Service agents came together between the demon and the VP. The three children were frightened out of their wits and couldn't even run away.

All three of the agents fired all of their rounds at the demon with no effect. The demon ran up and jumped on the middle agent, knocking him to the ground. It lashed out with a leg and kicked the agent to its left into the air. It reared up and grabbed the third agent and smashed him to the ground.

With the way clear to the VP it started forward with drool running out between its sharp teeth. Its red eyes were focused on the VP and it started to run at him.

CHAPTER TWENTY-NINE

The Vice President screamed and wanted to back towards his house with fear in his eyes and face. When he saw that his children weren't running, he moved to put himself between the demon and the kids. It was a brave act for a man who faced real terror for the first time in a long time.

A hideous roar came from the throat of the demon as it bounded over the steps leading to the table. Agent Sever stepped between the demon and the VP and got smashed completely off of the steps into the ground by the hand of the demon.

All three kids were so frightened they couldn't utter a sound. One of the fallen Secret Service agents staggered to his feet and not finding his gun ran at the demon from behind. The demon sensed the attack and whirled around grabbed the agent so quickly it was hard to see the motion of the demon's arms. The demon lifted the agent and slammed him to the brick steps and his body rolled limply down the stairs to the ground.

Uttering an evil, gloating laughter, the monster slowly turned back to move closer to the VP. Suddenly, it appeared to feel threatened and whirled around again. The only thing near it was Laura. It decided to eliminate the woman before it talked to the Vice President. It pulled out a slim black sword and charged at the woman. Then the strangest thing happened. With a glare of light, the woman walking toward the demon was encased in golden armor. Her heavenly appearance created such fear in the demon it didn't know what to do. It moved as to slash its sword downward and cut the woman down. The demon suddenly looked powerless and weak as Laura approached with a glowing sword that had the power of Yahveh flowing off of the blade in waves.

Laura continued to pray the twenty-third Psalm as she came at the demon." *Yea though I walk through the valley of the shadow of death I fear no evil for thy are with me . . ."*When the demon attempted to knock Laura to the ground her blade flashed and the demon lost its left arm as the sword removed the limb without a problem.

The demon obviously wanted to make its way back to its dimension but the sword flashed again and the head of the demon was severed from its neck and fell to the ground next to its collapsed body. All the parts of the demon rapidly vaporized into ugly gray smoke.

Laura stopped praying and her armor and sword disappeared. She walked up to the trembling VP and said. "I'm glad I was able to resolve your problem; you have a nice day Mr. Vice President.

She stepped over to the FBI agent who was trying to get up and put her hand on his right arm. As Laura's anointing flowed into the man he felt the weakness lighten and then disappear. Laura helped him up and he went with her as they stopped at each of the damaged Secret Service Agents and prayed for them. Then the two of them walked together back toward the front gate. The VP and his children stared soberly after her and the, still smoking, ugly gray smudge on the ground

Meanwhile, six miles away, Mark Connelly introduced himself to the Minority Leader of the Senate and explained why he was there. The man had seen the videos and the animations that Senator Powers had presented to the members of that August body and had decided that he didn't want to meet one of those things without one of the Crossfire Team with him.

They were talking in the man's den when, without warning of any kind, a massive demon stepped into the human dimension and slapped Mark into a wall with enough force to render a normal man unconscious. It turned its evil face to look at the minority Leader and started to tell him what he needed to do when it lost its voice.

Mark was massively muscled and used to frequent combat and daily exercises to keep himself in shape. While the blow winded him it didn't knock him out. He started to pray to God as "*his strong tower of refuge*" and his silver armor and the sword of Yahveh appeared. Taking one step backward with his left foot he whirled around to his right and used his sword to cut the demon in half with one massive swing. The demon grunted and evaporated in a rather oily smoke that smelled like garbage.

Mark stopped praying and his armor and the sword disappeared. He shook his head and went back to talking to the Minority Leader who hadn't had time to move or even go into shock before the demon was dispatched.

The Minority Leader looked at Mark and asked quietly, "How can you possibly fight those evil things without it causing you some form of mental distress?"

Mark shrugged his shoulders, "God told me to fight them and to destroy them and that's what I do. I have developed more of a caviler attitude about them because I'm more familiar with them and their commitment to kill, steal, and destroy everything that belongs to God."

Mark shook the man's hand and left for the team's temporary headquarters.

The other four team members had similar encounters with demons and dispatched them.

As everyone gathered back at the hotel room Jack took the detailed action reports and congratulated each and every one. Then he looked at the two evening attacks. "I want two people on each of these attacks. I believe that the enemy will have learned from today's action that there is a significant problem and will probably send more demons to these two last assignments."

Mark added, "Yeah, and since the additional demons are not on the Matrix you can bet they'll be illegally in our dimension."

David laughed, "That rather gives a new slant to "Illegal alien", doesn't it?

Thirty minutes later, Jack Malone and Mark Connelly presented themselves to the Congresswoman's home just around six p.m. Mark looked at the name on the nameplate, "Senator Joan Caldwell" and elbowed Jack. When Jack looked at him Mark pointed at the nameplate. "Think we should let this one eat her?"

Jack smiled a large smile at his friend. This was the liberal committee head that tried, unsuccessfully, to make him and Mark the bad guys in a Senate committee hearing eighteen months ago when they were testifying how the Crossfire Team had saved Denver, Colorado from a nuclear holocaust. The Congress was interested how they had accomplished that despite government interference because the FBI and the White House didn't believe their warning about the strike. She had lost her bid to crucify them and probably still disliked the team. Jack said, "I would buddy, but these demons are only here to talk this time. She'd probably agree with them so I doubt that they'll eat her, yet."

A Colorado Highway Patrolman opened the door and asked for their identifications. This man was built like a football player and had a really flinty look in his eyes. Obviously not a man to cross or to try to joke around with while he was on duty.

Their FBI agent leaned around Jack and showed his badge to the officer. The patrolman nodded and admitted the three of them into the elegant entrance hall. A spiral staircase led to the upstairs and there were costly, glass front bookcases around the hall. Books, china, and collectables were displayed with some elegance and flair. The subdued lighting in each case highlighted the items inside and drew the viewer's attention.

The three of them waited for a good ten minutes before the patrolman came back and ushered them into a good sized home office. The congresswoman was sitting at her desk looking at what seemed to be important paperwork.

She laid down the paperwork and took off her reading glasses. She looked at the three men in front of her with very thinly veiled dislike or possibly even repulsion. Her voice was pitched slightly higher than most women and it cut through the air like an arrow seeking a target. "What in the Sam hell are you two doing in my house?"

The FBI agent stepped into the meat grinder and offered an explanation that neither was totally necessary nor wanted by the congresswoman. "Congresswoman Caldwell, you agreed to this protection detail yesterday."

If looks could kill the FBI agent would have died right there on the spot. "YOU keep out of this. You hear me? Not another word!"

Jack studied the woman while he prayed that the Holy Spirit would give him the tolerance and love Christ had shown for people while He was on Earth. "Congresswoman Caldwell, you deny the existence of angels and demons but, they are real and they are assaulting members of Congress and the White House. Normal weapons have no effect on the demons that are in our dimension legally. We have the ability to protect you unlike the normal policeman, or soldier."

The Congresswoman slammed her hand on her desk. "Don't you dare come into my house and spread those lies. There are no such things as demons. You make them up to insure you get your share of the pie as "black operations". You can fool a lot of people but you can't fool me. You and your team are frauds and you've been defrauding America for long enough! I will not stand for this..."

She stopped speaking when there was a flurry of gunshots outside the office. A second later the body of a very dead highway patrolman smashed the door to the office down as his body was flung furiously through the closed door. His body was slashed to ribbons and both of his hands had been cut off.

With a tread that vibrated everything in the room a large and very ugly demon crouched and smashed his way into the office. The Congresswoman screamed and tried to back away from the vile look of evil the demon gave her. The hatred and evil radiated out of the demon at such a level that the Congresswoman realized that the worst fit she ever had was no more than a little girl's tantrum. For the first time in her life she realized she had never known the real truth. This "thing" scared her more than anything she had ever seen or heard of in her entire life.

Mark saw the FBI agent start to draw his sidearm and pushed him out of the way. Jack then calmly asked, "Congresswoman, would you like us to take care of this lie or do you want continue to ignore it?"

Her eyes were huge in her pale face and she nodded her head while making little pushing motions with her hands like she was trying to sweep the whole problem away from her. Jack decided that she had given them the authority to resolve the problem.

During this time the demon had stood fully upright and its head brushed the nine-foot ceiling in the room. Mark saw three smaller demons crowding in behind the big one and told the FBI agent, "Them you can kill."

The big demon let out a roar that made the Congresswoman's hair literally stand on end and vibrated everything else in the room as it moved toward Jack and Mark.

CHAPTER THIRTY

Mark and Jack began to pray and their silver armor blazed into view, lighting up the room. Along with their armor their chrome swords appeared with the esteem of Yahveh flowing off the blade in waves.

The huge demon brought both arms up to the ceiling and smashed his big fists down directly toward the two men in armor. Both warriors executed a high circle cut and severed the fists from the arms. The demon let out a frustrated scream that was twice as loud as his first roar. Jack remembered later that the volume of breath behind that scream was so strong that he slid backward by several feet.

Gunshots resounded off of the office walls as the FBI agent eliminated the three smaller demons with multiple head shots.

Greenish-black smoke was filling up the room as the smaller demons evaporated and the larger demon waved its fistless arms around. Jack stepped into the space in front of the demon and shoved his sword directly into the stomach of the beast and out the back. He then turned to his left and sliced his way out of the demon's right side. Mark stepped in and cut straight down and out of the demon. The demon lost its right leg and tipped over to toward the missing leg side. Mark ran backward so as to miss being crushed. The demon's mass was so great that when he hit the floor, everything else was bounced upward into the air.

Since Mark was on that side he finished off the demon with an overhead cut that severed the beast's neck. The room was temporarily dark as the evaporation of the huge demon let off so much dark smoke it smothered the normal light. Everybody tried not to breathe until it cleared.

When the air cleared there was nothing on the floor except the body of the highway patrolman and a large stain.

Jack and Mark stopped praying as their armor and shields disappeared. They both dropped to one knee and prayed together their thankfulness to God and gave Him all the credit for the victory.

Jack stood up and looked with pity at the Congresswoman. She had collapsed onto her desk and was wailing inconsolably. Jack walked over and lifted her up and held her in his arms as he consoled her and told her everything would be all right. She clung to him like he was a life jacket in a storm-driven sea.

The only sounds in the room were the FBI Agent reloading his gun and the crying.

Eventually the woman ceased her crying but continued to cling to Jack. Jack finally scooped her up in his arms and took her out of the room to a relatively undamaged sitting room. He laid her down on a settee and told the FBI agent to get her some psychological and emotional support from the large number of federal agents that were arriving.

Ten minutes later, after dictating their action reports to the police, Jack and Mark walked out of the house through a large hole where the front door used to be. The FBI agent was waiting for them and drove them back to their hotel. As they were getting out the agent asked them. "How can I continue to live knowing that there are those things that hate me and live to destroy me?"

Jack squatted down so he could face the agent who was still sitting in the car. He looked at the man with honesty and told him that he needed to find Jesus. That was the only power in the universe that can save him from the types of creatures he saw tonight. "Remember always, God loves you more than you can imagine. He wants the best in this life for you and wants you to live after this life in heaven with him. Until several years ago I didn't even think about Yahveh God. Now He is my every thought and what I do, I do for Him, thanking Him for sacrificing His only son on the cross. Jesus Christ said, "The greatest thing a person can do is to give up his life to save his friends." Christ did just that. He called us His Friends and even knowing what was coming, He sacrificed His life so that we could have life everlasting. If you want to fill that God-sized hole in your heart and being, see a Pastor, a Christian friend, or call me. Jesus has the answer to the question all men ask, "Why am I here?" You're here to decide to live for the God that created you or you can continue to live for yourself and suffer the consequences. Just ask yourself one question. "When I die, can I save myself from eternal damnation? Or do I need a savior." Jack took out a card with a telephone number that could reach him and handed it to the man. He smiled at the agent. "I'm betting that what you saw today will give you the reason to know that if supernatural evil can exist then so can supernatural goodness and love. Thank you for your help today."

After the agent left, Jack called Carol back at their base to see what tomorrow's schedule was. Carol responded with, "There is no schedule for tomorrow. All of those time lines have vanished. The enemy is changing tactics because of two things. First, your interference with their bullying techniques and, two, they don't need to do that anymore. The demonic efforts have accomplished their goal. The present administration in Washington has caved in and signed an agreement to join the world community. In other words, they have conceded the control of the United States to the Anti-Christ. You should all come home now. Do it quickly because the Anti-Christ is now in control of America and new time lines indicate that he will attempt to stop you and imprison you on false charges. And, he will use the full might of the U.S. military to do that."

Jack sighed a large sigh at the capitulation of America's sovereignty to the enemy by a weak and, essentially anti-American, government. Worse yet, their own country would be after them now.

He hurriedly explained things to Mark and added. "I honestly don't know if our efforts had any impact on the demonic incursions because they just got what they wanted."

Mark shook his head. "Well, I can tell you we made an impact on a half dozen demons and the legislators they were coming at."

Quickly assembling the team, they packed up and raced to the airport.

Su Li ran into the hanger and remotely unlocked and opened the Shrew as she ran toward the aircraft. The rest of the team hauled their luggage and weapons into the hanger and stowed them in the cargo hold. Everyone climbed on board and Su Li rolled out of the hanger directly onto the small airport's main runway. She had already gotten clearance to take off and she wasted no time in doing just that.

They had lifted off and rolled east as they quickly climbed toward the military air lanes when the tower called them and asked them to return immediately to the airport. Su Li snorted, "Not likely."

Mark slid into the copilot's seat next to Su Li. "They will demand you land at any base on the East Coast of the U.S. Ignore those calls and get out beyond the three-mile limit."

As Su Li made the transition of the Shrew from normal flight to Supercruise she asked Mark. "Why the three-mile limit?

Mark recalled his training concerning territorial boundaries for the military. "According to the Montego Bay convention, which has emerged as the international standard even for those states not party to it, the U.S. has uncontested sovereignty over the sea and the air above the nation including a three nautical mile distance from the coastline. They can shoot down aircraft in that domain if they have a legal reason to do so. Failing to submit to an FAA authorized tower or air traffic control center, as you just did, is grounds for military action against our aircraft."

An alert sounded on the panel and Su Li pushed the control to switch the Shrew from its Corporate Jet personae to that of a fighter. The panels all changed, the weapons came on line, the engines reconfigured to combat mode and the heads up displays in their helmets became active. Mark was still amazed by the amount of data displayed and the ability to control the weapons by cortical inputs from these helmets.

Su Li frowned, "There is a flight of four F-16s out of the DC Air National Guard from Andrews Air Force base at Camp Springs, Maryland. They are on an intercept course that is quickly becoming a tail chase. They are in full afterburner and are actively seeking our aircraft with attack radar."

Mark sighed, "We don't want to destroy four Air Force pilots and their aircraft. Can you avoid conflict with them?"

Su Li noted that Mark had no doubt she would win a conflict with the air national guard pilots and she appreciated that. "Their top speed with afterburner when their planes were new and in perfect condition is around 1500 MPH at 35,000 feet of altitude. Our top speed at that altitude in supercruise is closer to 1650 MPH. That converts to roughly 2.5 miles of more distance between us every minute. I'm pretty sure those ANG aircraft aren't new and may not be in perfect condition so I know we can run with them and even out run them. We may have to take evasive action if they launch their missiles at long range."

She checked to ensure that the throttles were all the way to the stops.

Mark chuckled, "Those afterburners eat a ton of fuel and I doubt that they have any auxiliary tanks on those birds."

At 1650 MPH the Shrew was covering roughly three miles a minute and had exited the three-mile limit in the first minute into the flight.

Su Li was monitoring the ANG channels and heard some plane-to-plane chatter. "What type of corporate jet is that? I'm maxed out in AB and they're still running away from us."

The flight commander realized the futility in continuing to chase the Shrew because his planes were rapidly depleting their fuel stores. "Break off pursuit and return to base. Let the Navy take care of them."

CHAPTER THIRTY-ONE

Once free of the pursuit Jack contacted the SecDef and explained that the administration had waited too long before seeking help. "You know, the government has capitulated to the government of Marco Marino and even though the Crossfire Team did manage to defeat the demonic forces we came up against, it was too late to affect the outcome. Also Mr. Secretary, I am upset with the efforts to keep us in the U.S. by military force. That is a direct violation of our agreement."

The Secretary coughed a few times. "I'm sorry Jack. The people over at the White House circumvented me and directed the Air Force to try and stop you. I didn't know about that until the chase was ended and the aircraft were returning to base. I would raise hell about that whole action but it won't go anywhere. I was just told that government of Marco Marino will be taking command of the Defense Department next week."

"A word of warning. I'm pretty sure that the administration is going to trump up some charges against all of your team, including you and your wife. They will then seek extradition for all of you from Israel. Since you are all American citizens they have the right to demand Israel return you to the U.S. to stand trial."

"Again, I accept the responsibility for bringing you back to help us and putting you into harm's way. The new government will use our attempt to help their politicians against you. I'm afraid that they have, earlier this hour, deliberately cut me out of the loop as far as your team is involved. But, I've already seen to a triple payment for the work you did. It was forwarded to your account an hour ago from an account the new leadership doesn't know about and may never find. So, I can fulfill that part of the bargain we made."

"I doubt that I will have any control from now on. The rumor mill has it that the new leadership will demand that the entire U.S. Military be placed under full One World Government control by next week. This is a terrible time to be a patriot working for the people. Therefore, I am resigning my position effective tonight. I want to thank you for your efforts. Several of the Congressional members you saved have highly praised your team's efforts. That includes the Vice President. Stay away from here and stay safe, Goodbye."

As the Shrew headed towards the East, Su Li gradually increased the altitude until they were above 14 miles of altitude. That was above 75,000 feet and beyond most ground-to-air missile ranges. She prayed to Yahveh that He would provide a fuel refill to get them to Israel because they weren't going to make it otherwise. She knew that the U.S. Air Force would not be allowed to help them.

Jack turned to and asked Mark, "What are the rules for extradition?"

Mark thought about it, "Well, it depends on the citizenship of the person in question. Some nations refuse to extradite their own citizens, holding trials for the persons themselves. If the originating country finds them guilty, then that country tends to sentence them in abstensia which bars them from returning to that country because they would have to serve whatever sentence they had been given."

"Most countries require themselves to deny extradition requests if, in the government's opinion, the suspect is sought for a political crime or reason. Many countries and areas, such as Australia, Canada, Mexico, and most European nations, will not allow extradition if the death penalty may be imposed on the suspect. Parties to the European Convention also cannot extradite people where they would be at significant risk of being tortured inhumanely or degradingly treated or punished."

"These restrictions are normally clearly spelled out in the extradition treaties that their governments have agreed upon. Our concern is that the U.S. has often persuaded countries to change or even break relevant laws to acquire suspects they are after."

"Countries with a rule of law typically make extradition subject to review by that country's courts. These courts may impose certain restrictions on extradition, or prevent it altogether, if for instance they deem the accusations to be based on dubious evidence, or if they believe that the defendant will not be granted a fair trial, which could be the case in our favor."

Jack called Laura and David into their meeting. He explained what the SecDef had warned him about and what Mark had told him. "It seems that they can demand Israel return our core team for trial because we are U.S. citizens. How could we avoid that?"

Laura said, "Let's ask God what to do."

The four of them praised the God of the Universe and then prayed for guidance.

CHAPTER THIRTY-TWO

As Jack sat quietly God's voice came to him. *"My son, I am the one that arranged things so that you and your people would live in the land of My chosen ones. In these last days of the Gentiles I am bringing believers in my son together with open-minded believers of the Hebrew faith. Remember, My Son, Yahshua, was a faithful believer in the Jewish faith during his life on Earth. It was never meant for believers from the Jewish faith and the Christian faith to be separated and hate each other. This is the work of the enemy. You are all my children and I love each and every one of you. It pleases me when you both worship together. Join with the people of Israel and I will bless you all."*

Jack sat up and contemplated the approval of the God.

Laura was the first to speak. "I feel as if the Father wants us to become one with his people to avoid extradition."

All four of them agreed and Jack told them what the Father had said to him. Then he said, "Okay, how do we do that?"

David thought for a few seconds. "Let me make some phone calls."

David talked first to the Mossad and then to the "HaMateh HaKlali "Supreme Commander (Chief of the General Staff) of the IDF. He explained what the Crossfire Team had been doing in the U.S. and the change of attitude after the capitulation of the government. He asked if the Israeli government could provide Israeli citizenship for all of the Crossfire Team immediately to prevent Marco Marino from attempting to eliminate the team by extraditing them as American citizens and imprisoning them. Being citizens of Israel would prevent the, now, puppet government of the U.S. from insisting on deportation of them as American citizens.

The Mossad leadership agreed with the concept and the Commander in Chief of the Israeli Defense Force insisted on it. They would take it up with the Knesset to make it legal and get it done in compensation for the team's consistent efforts against Israel's enemies.

Haim Levy who was the Chief of the General Staff asked David to let him talk to Jack. The General told Jack that the whole country and especially the Mossad and the IDF owed the team more than could ever be repaid. He added jokingly, "You know you all will have to learn to speak Hebrew and learn our ways, especially celebrating Shabbat, don't you?"

Jack laughed, "Yes Sir, I don't think that will be a problem for this crew. Thank you General Levy, and thank all those Israelis who have aided us in these efforts. We especially could not have managed without the help of people like David Zahavy and Sarah Cohen nee Connelly."

After the phone calls were over, Jack explained to the team members on the plane what they were doing to prevent the Anti-Christ from using their American citizenship against them and asked for conflicting views. There were none. Alexis summed up their situation. "Even if we continued being American citizens the "Mark of the Beast" requirements would take away our property, our rights, and eventually, our lives because as Christians we would never worship the Anti-Christ or take his mark."

Mark added, "What America has become is not the same country I swore allegiance to and, essentially, they have joined forces with the enemy."

Laura added, "When gentiles are grafted into the Jewish Faith they, and we, became citizens of God's body of believers. We can now make ourselves citizens of His chosen land."

Jack told them of General Levy's comment that they would need to learn the Hebrew language and customs, especially Shabbat. Alexis said, "I already know Hebrew and I'm sure David and Sarah will help the rest of us to learn. But, what about the hatred the Jews have for Christians?"

Jack told them what Father Yahveh had told him.

Jack then made a call to their base and had everyone assemble in the training hall. He explained their need to change citizenships to the SOG soldiers and the rest of the team, such as Charlie and Linda Wu. He gave them time, at least until the Shrew got back to think about it and make their decisions. He reminded the SOG soldiers that it would require them to invalidate their oaths to serve America and the U.S. military.

One of the women from the U.S. Air Force psychological group brought up the fact that those oaths had already been broken by the new administration when they ceded control of the country and the U.S. Military to the one-world government.

CHAPTER THIRTY-THREE

Su Li watched carefully as Alexis flew the Shrew with Mark as co-pilot. She was pretty sure either one of them could handle it. She just wanted to be available if things got dicey. Her experience in combat with the Shrew was way beyond the conditions of normal flight and might be required. Mark White had spelled Su Li for a couple of hours and was back talking with the rest of the team.

Even though the entire flight time in supercruise was only six hours for the 5700-mile trip, the communications board lit up with a second demand from the U.S. Navy. Pursuant to the government's effort to capture the Crossfire Team the Navy demanded they descend to sea level and land on the carrier that was part of the task force headed to the Middle East. Su Li chuckled to herself, "That's not going to happen." On request from the government of Israel, they didn't respond to these challenges.

The Navy Task Force ships had the new Sea Sparrow VI surface-to-air missile with sufficient altitude to reach their aircraft but they didn't launch their missiles because the indictment for the team wasn't clear and it could cause an international incident even if they didn't hit the aircraft. Su Li found out later that Israel had also demanded the U.S. government not to move militarily on the aircraft as they had two Israel citizens on board.

As their fuel tanks were reaching a dangerously low level and Su Li was beginning to consider a water landing, the comm board received a message from the Israeli Defense Force. The IDF vectored the Shrew into a lower altitude and slower speed to link up with an Israeli tanker aircraft. Since it was a KC-46A American-made tanker it was compatible with the concealed air-to-air refueling system of the Shrew.

While they were refueling Mark talked to Jack. "You know the CIA is going to ask for the Shrews back because the government's change in attitude about us and the agreements we signed with the CIA when we got these birds. What will we do for transportation then?"

Jack laughed, "Don't fret about that. The government isn't going to renege on that agreement anytime soon. They would have to give us back over four hundred and fifty million dollars, in advance. Remember? We paid for these birds."

Mark brightened up, "That's right, and the thoughts of parting with a half billion dollars will probably prevent that from happening."

Jack smiled, "At least until we get to heaven."

Laura added, "You know you are giving up your company too."

Jack smiled, "Since I haven't been there the last three or four years, my not being President and CEO won't make any difference for the next three. I can't own it if I become an Israeli, but, things won't change until the end. That means especially my inputs to the new product development department."

It was after midnight, Tel Aviv time, when the Shrew touched down on the airfield of the hidden base. Jack had everyone turn in their action reports, stow their gear, and get some sleep. Their bodies needed to reset their Circadian Rhythms and reacclimatize to the Tel Aviv time zone.

The next morning Jack talked to the other twenty-eight members of the team and got a unanimous agreement to switch allegiance to Israel from the U.S. caused by the U.S. giving their allegiance to Marco Marino's One World Government.

Jack passed this information on David who communicated it to the Israeli government. An hour later an immigration officer showed up and took the necessary personal information from all thirty-seven team members. He checked the information as he entered it into the computer he had brought with him. After confirmation of the information he told everyone to show up at the immigration office tomorrow morning at ten o'clock in the morning.

The day was spent sorting out all the things that went on while they were away, resting, praying, and exercising, gun range certifications, sword training, and for Jack and

Laura a quiet lunch on the green grass of the park above their offices and residences.

Jack was thoughtful and quiet for a while. Laura let him be because she was pretty sure he was concerned about the remaining family he left in the states. There weren't too many because his immediate family had all been called up to heaven by Yahshua in the Rapture. But, still there were one or two that had gone their own way and remained on the Earth to face the Tribulations.

Jack turned to Laura and drank in her beauty again. He smiled at her, "You know, I love you more now than I have ever before and you're more beautiful too. Thank you for being my wife and my best friend."

Laura smiled at that and lay down on her back on the ground. "Jack, you know I love you and always will. But, as a retrained housewife I am definitely beginning to look forward to heaven. No more tears, no more pain, no combat, no demons, no doldrums. I know you look forward to that also. Yahshua will call us to heaven when we've completed our mission at the three-and-a-half-year mark of the last week of Daniel. So, I've decided to live the remaining months of our life to the fullest. How do you feel about that?"

Jack nodded his agreement. "I couldn't agree with you more. I like the idea of being the best we can be for God's Kingdom on a rising note. I think I'll ask the Sensei to become a consultant to the Team if I can get him out of the Martial Arts movement here in Israel."

Laura wondered, Did the Sensei get an offer to stay or does he walk in the fullness of God and Yahshua.

Jack laughed, "Actually, he did get the offer. I think it was because God was just glad that Sensei's legendary hardheadedness finally bowed to the truth. Also, because God knows he was needed by the team in the remaining years of our service."

The day went by quickly and the next morning at 10 a.m. Tel Aviv time, Jack and the other team members walked into the immigration office in downtown Tel Aviv. The official from the Ministry of the Interior called them to attention and explained what was to occur. "I have been asked by the Knesset and the IDF to confer Israeli citizenship on each of you. You can become citizens of

Israel even though you are not Jewish because of your ability to earn your livelihood. In your cases, this is *definitely* not a problem!

The official looked around at the obviously combat-ready warriors. "I would highly recommend that you learn Hebrew as most of this country, not including the tourist businesses tend to speak Hebrew. I have been given a brief review of the service your group and each one of you that has given service to our country. I am more than amazed at the events and battles you have endured for Israel's sake. I understand that you will be registered as Jewish Christians. I think you know the bias against most non-Jewish citizens and hopefully, you understand the rationale for this attitude, which we are attempting to correct.

"Regardless of the governmental and military pressure to allow you all to become citizens, the reason you are being adopted by Israel is because the religious leaders in this country have heard from YHVH G-d himself on your behalf. Their desire to incorporate your group into our country is far greater than any other pressure applied to us."

"You are hereby given the authority to settle and are entitled to reside in Israel permanently because you have already settled at your place of work in Israel but, you will have to renounce your American citizenship so that you will cease to be foreign nationals upon becoming Israeli citizens."

"Please raise your hands if each one of you intends to renounce your American citizenship today and become an Israeli citizen."

Jack and Laura raised their hands along with the rest of the Crossfire Team except for Sarah and David who were still legally Israeli citizens.

The actual ceremony and paperwork time only took thirty more minutes. As the team headed back to the base Mark remarked as he looked at his Israel citizenship certificate, "It's funny, but I don't feel any different."

Laura chuckled, "That's because you are not part of this world, and you're just passing through. Your treasure is all stored up somewhere beyond the blue. You belong to Yahshua just as you did yesterday and because of that you were already grafted into Israel and the Jewish faith. But, today you've made a positive statement to Yahveh God that you support His chosen people."

Mark nodded in agreement with Laura's comment.

As the majority of the SOG and some of the Core Team left to return to the Sea Base, Jack asked David to explain what Shabbat was because he had promised the General he'd start celebrating it.

David asked for a vacant room so that the remaining team members could discuss some new business. One of the clerks took them to large classroom that was empty at the moment.

David looked at the others in the room. "You asked me to explain what Shabbat is. It is a celebration that every observant Jew attends each week.

You need to understand that it is a commandment you have not been obeying. The reason you haven't followed it is because it is a misunderstood Commandment that receives little or no attention in most Christian Churches. Understand that the teachers today can only pass on what they have been taught. They were not taught the Fourth of the Ten Commandments that Moses brought down from Mount Sinai."

The fourth Commandment is explained in Exodus Chapter20, verses 8 through 11. It is "mitzvoth" (a commandment) that commands us to celebrate the beginning of the weekly Shabbat, holidays, or other sacred times. In my youth I learned it well.

"Remember the Sabbath day to keep it holy.⁹ Six days you shall labor and do all your work,¹⁰ but the seventh day is a Sabbath to the LORD your God. On it you shall not do any work, neither you, nor your son or daughter, nor your male or female servant, nor your animals, nor any foreigner residing in your towns.¹¹ For in six days the LORD made the heavens and the earth, the sea, and all that is in them, but he rested on the seventh day. Therefore, the LORD blessed the Sabbath day and made it holy."

"Remember, all Hebrew days start at sundown instead of midnight."Sabbath" is the day of the week that God commanded to be set aside for worship and observance of religious duties in Judaism. In Israel the Sabbath begins at sunset on Friday and lasts 25 hours until after sunset the next day, Saturday. During this time no ordinary work or act of labor is performed."

"The key here is that the God of the Universe told His faithful, which you are now part of, to keep the Sabbath Holy throughout all ages. Because of your upbringing you have probably never celebrated the Sabbath as Shabbat and not kept the commandment as God instructed all of us to do. This was not your fault, because you did not know about it. But, now that you know the truth, it is your responsibility to keep it faithfully for God."

Laura laughed and asked, "What do we have to do to celebrate Shabbat each week?"

David sat back and lifted his hands in the air. I can teach you, or you can visit almost any home or Messianic Synagogue in the area. There are several parts to the celebration and then you have to observe the commandment not to work during Shabbat. That may be a little hard to do in our line of business, but, anything that might involve life-threatening situations or even involve preventing life-threatening situations may be done on Shabbat. And that is our calling by Yahveh's intention.

Jack asked, "What is involved in the celebration of Shabbat and when do we start this celebration each week?"

David nodded his head. "The celebration that ushers in the Sabbath is simple and involves prayer and supplication to Yahveh for those we love and for His love and to thank Him for the Sabbath. I'll teach all of you about Shabbat this Friday evening at sundown, if Yahveh's requirements don't require our time."

David thought for a few minutes. "To comprehend the excitement of Shabbat you have to amend your cultural thinking so that you look forward with joy in the Lord to Shabbat as the day of rest and celebration in the Lord each week."

Alexis asked, "How do the Jews, excuse me, how do we, as adopted Judeo-Christians, learn to live a constant life of joy? I know the people that follow the Jewish faith have had a very hard life for thousands of years, yet the people keep their joy in spite of their circumstances. How do we do that?"

Sarah smiled and spoke up. "You enroll in a life of joy by asking the Father Yahveh in the name of Yahshua to fill your heart with His joy for the rest of your life."

"Jews are taught from the time they are born about God and His love for them as a people, a race, and an individual. Our understanding encompasses a loving God who is so much greater than this life that we look for our ultimate salvation in life with Him after this one. As you say, persecution can be a daily toil and possibly fatal, but, for God. Once you learn that your life is nothing without Yahveh, whose joy is your strength, you incorporate that joy into everything you do or look forward to. You wake up with joy; you spread that joy to others, and celebrate that joy constantly. That is why the Jew looks forward to the Sabbath with joy. It is always a wonderful day of rest after six days of labor as to the Lord. The Jewish week revolves around the Shabbat, not the other way around."

"Essentially, Yahveh becomes your focus in everything you do and everything you are. Then you can endure this life and its hardships. Ancient Jewish Wisdom says, one of the tenets of learning about God requires joy in your life because if you have joy in your learning you will learn more in one hour than a person without joy can learn in two weeks."

"I think the most important thing here is this. Observing the Sabbath is not a mechanical, religious ritual, but a joyous celebration of a spiritual revelation. The intent of the heart is as important, if not more so, than doing the act. When a person chooses to celebrate the Sabbath through Shabbat, he/she is partnering with the will of God."

"Yahshua taught His disciples, saying, "The Sabbath was made for man, and not man for the Sabbath" in Mark 2:27. By His words we understand that the Sabbath is a gift from God, to us, His children."

David stood up. "All right, then it is agreed that I will lead you through your first celebration of Shabbat, and then we will want to do it every Friday if we can." On Saturday night at the end of Shabbat I will also teach you how to celebrate Havdalah, which marks the end of each Shabbat and some other Festival holidays."

David thought for a few seconds and then held up his right hand. "To understand the why of these celebrations we need to study Torah. The Torah is the first five books of the Old Testament. Many Rabbis and scholars study Torah their entire lives and every day they are learning new things as God shows them Revelation from His word. So, I think we need to have a Torah knowledgeable study leader. While we're at it we need to create, in the Sea Base, a Judeo-Christian prayer and faith center."

Jack nodded, "I can see that and we can host a Messianic-Jewish Rabbi as our teacher and to handle the corporate spiritual matters."

David grinned, "You'd better find one that can handle the very active spiritual life for this group, especially demonic events."

Jack agreed with that thought.

CHAPTER THIRTY-FOUR

After learning about Shabbat from David they left the classroom. Since the rest of the Team had already gone back to the Sea Base it was quiet at the Immigration Office. An official came up to Jack and requested that he, Laura, Mark, Sarah, David, and Alexis attend another short meeting. They were escorted to a plush Immigration side office and were surprised to find the Israeli Prime Minister waiting on them.

After the introductions were completed the Prime Minister welcomed the six warriors as new citizens of the nation of Israel. Having spent some years in the U. S. the PM was very fluent in English. He studied the six people before him. He had read all of the data on the Crossfire Team and the many times they had risked their lives to preserve Israel. He actually knew much more about them than the American government.

He smiled, "Mr. and Mrs. Malone, Mr. and Mrs. Connelly, Mr. Zahavy, and Miss Taggert. I am pleased to meet you all. I authorized your citizenship as members of Israel because of the many times you all have put yourselves and your team in harm's way for our country. I applaud your courage and dedication for Israel and I have a question. I know that Sarah and David were Jewish and through a miraculous event have become Christians. The rest of your team, including the Malones have been strong Christians all along. My question is, why? Why did you throw yourselves into such danger, and why do you continue to fight for what is now your country, a small Jewish country that is less than tolerant of Christians?"

Jack smiled back. "Mr. Prime Minister, you label us as strong Christians and I suppose that is the way most of the world sees us. In actuality we are children of Yahveh and brothers and sisters of Yahshua. We are in submission to God and our Savior which means we do what God wants."

Laura continued with Jack's comments. "We love the Lord Yahshua and Father Yahveh. God anointed us to defend humanity from demonic attacks. You of all people know that Satan wants to destroy Israel and all Jews more than any other group on Earth. He knows that you are God's chosen people and he will do anything to harm, cheat, and kill Jews. We defend God's people and as His chosen race you attract the most violent efforts the enemy can generate. Naturally then, many of our efforts have been to defend and protect Israel. That is why God removed us from the U.S. and based our efforts here."

Mark took up the discussion. "We understand that as God brings the time of the Gentiles to an end and focuses back on Israel, the enemy will also focus on this country. Our mission is our lives and we are now in the best place possible to defeat efforts to destroy what is now our country and our people. Also we love the people here, I married one."

Sarah smiled at that. "Mr. Prime Minister, our team has been placed here to defend God's people and therefore we are at your disposal concerning those efforts. You have stood for fairness and equality for all peoples but your love and support for Israel is legendary throughout the world. Please consider us and our efforts one of God's blessings for our people."

Jack added, "Mr. Prime Minister, the Lord also wants us to tear down the wall that separates Jew and Gentile. The Lord told me personally that the distrust and dislike between the two was generated by Satan to destroy God's people. Yahveh rejoices when we worship Him together rather than apart. It's not a concept that is widely embraced by either religion but that is beginning to change in Christianity. As the Jewish people start to see the change in relationship by Christians, they will also follow God's will."

The most powerful leader in Israel smiled at them. "I endorse that movement and agree that our two worlds were never meant to be antagonistic." The Prime Minister was thoughtful for a few seconds. "It hasn't been mentioned to your team, but all new citizens are normally required to put two years' mandatory service in the IDF, as do all citizens born here. I waived that requirement in lieu of services rendered. That is considering Mr. Zahavy's and the Mossad's descriptions of the war you've been in our behalf over the last few years."

The PM nodded and stood up. He shook everyone's hands and said "If I and my office can be of help, call me. Shalom."

"Shalom" was echoed by the team members.

Back on Hemered Street Jack decided they should get something to eat and see some of the city they now called home.

Mark reminded him of the travel restrictions and warnings about terrorism and crime on the Tel Aviv streets. He also mentioned the bias against, Christians and people that seem to be Americans. Laura added that the threat of kidnapping of executives and especially Americans was very high everywhere in the Middle East.

Jack frowned, "All true, so I suggest we maintain a low profile and ask our Mossad bodyguards to do the same."

Laura had noted the four-man team that she had seen at the checkpoints recently, casually orbiting around them on the streets. She knew the team's real protection was in the Lord but it always helped to have a few Israel hard guys around to convince the locals to leave them alone.

CHAPTER THIRTY-FIVE

Sarah located a mid-scale restaurant and she and David ordered for all six of them to keep the language problem to a minimum. During the meal, Laura got an urge to pray quietly in her prayer language. As she prayed she had a vision.

In the vision Laura saw many people standing around her and waving their fists at her. She had a memory of the time on the South Sea Island where the natives attacked her with knives because of the cross she was wearing. In the vision, the crowd was angry and threatening, but she didn't feel they were the enemy. Suddenly demons appeared everywhere and her armor and sword appeared. She began to defend herself from the demons and . . . the vision ended. She thought about that for a few seconds and had the feeling it was an urgent warning.

Laura rudely broke into a joke that Mark was telling. At the glance of irritation, he showed she shook her head. "Sorry Mark, this is urgent." Mark's attitude visibly changed.

She explained the vision she had just had and the urgency it evoked in her spirit. She looked around for comments.

Jack sighed, "Let's pay the bill and get out of the diner here. If we're going into demonic battle let's get some combat stretch out in the street."

The six of them walked out of the restaurant and spread slightly apart. One of a group of five young men going down the sidewalk had to stop and split up with his group to go around them. As they passed by one of the men made a rude comment, calling the four of them "idiot pig off-springs". Jack, Mark, and Laura knew it was a derisive comment but didn't understand it. Sarah, David, and Alexis did understand the slur.

Sarah, angered by the rudeness told the insulting man that he was rude and should go back to lie down with the pigs he associated with on a daily basis. Needless to say this was not received well. Sarah apologized to the Lord for speaking rudely and asked for forgiveness.

The five young men stopped and looked ready to fight. It was obvious that Jack, Mark, Laura and Alexis were Americans and the young men began swearing in Hebrew at the Americans for their insensitivity. The Mossad crew moved in to prevent a battle.

Laura had a flashback to her vision as the men shook their fists at her and the others. So she ignored the young men and concentrated all of her senses to detecting any demonic activity. Sarah picked up on something first. She suddenly turned toward the street and brought her hands up in an attitude of defense.

As the crowd began to gather and add their comments and insults to the five young men all hell, literally, broke loose.

All at once at least fifteen demons charged through a portal into the human dimension. They rushed through the people on the street which resulted in a great deal of screaming and frenetic scrambling away by the crowd. The demons roared, snarled, and grunted as they started smashing and slashing the people to get them out of the way so they could attack the Crossfire Team members. The Mossad protection detail started shooting at the demons. At the same time Jack and Mark drew their side arms and started shooting every demon they could hit. Five or six of the demons began to leak smoke and disappear but that left nine or ten that, apparently, had a legal right to be in the human dimension.

Laura, Sarah, and Alexis started to pray and their golden armor appeared in a flash of light along with their chrome swords flowing with the esteem of Yahveh. They started to battle with the closest demons as Jack and Mark joined in praying which generated the appearance of their silver armor and swords. Most of the crowd, including the five young men that had started the confrontation, stood in awe of the combat armor and swords of the Team.

Sarah grinned to herself at the look on the faces of the five men that had been cursing them recently. It was a mixture of fear, awe, and surprise.

Jack cut one demon down and got slammed two different ways by two more demons. One cross-cut Jack's back with his black blade but the armor deflected the blow while the other demon smashed the front of Jack's legs. Propelled from above and tripped below, Jack fell toward the pavement. Using his marital arts training he increased his speed by folding at the waist and diving toward the pavement. Tucking into a ball he managed to do a forward roll that brought him back up to his feet. He had seen another demon in the direction he was headed and as he came to his feet he drove his sword through that demon.

Mark was attacked simultaneously by two demons and blocked both blades with his one. Both of the black blades broke into pieces when they struck Mark's bright blade. Mark quickly stepped between the two creatures and rotated rapidly to his right. As he came around he slashed first one, and then the other demon, taking them both out of the fight.

Sarah and Laura had realized these new tactics by the demons were meant to overwhelm them so they started double-teaming each demon for superiority in each brief battle.

Alexis was dodging and floating through the attacking demons and cutting down most of them on her first pass. David joined her and they stood back-to-back as they defended themselves from the horde of the enemy.

Jack went into the time-compression, high-speed mode that the angel Hugo had trained them in and took out four more demons in short order.

But two dozen more demons flooded out of the major portal in the middle of the street. At least no more civilians remained in the battle zone as the uninjured ones had scattered quickly to get away from the battles. The Mossad team was trying to tend to and defend the injured and still not get killed themselves.

With the new group of armed demons added to the battle the team members were being overcome by sheer numbers. Even with their time-shaping capabilities there were more demons attacking them than they could possibly handle. Jack used his sword to slash two more demons but there was no effect. He stepped back and turned to take on another demon and he couldn't hurt it either. He realized that most of the core team might well be destroyed, especially since they couldn't defeat the demons. He prayed that almighty God would send His angels to help.

As four demons attacked her, Laura realized she would be unable to stop all of them. In her distress she also prayed for God's help. Instantly, some information came to mind that she had been given by Hugo months ago, but that God had hidden it from her mind until it was needed.

Laura physically slammed into and shoved three demons away. She raised her sword, hilt first, into the air. She slammed the sword into the pavement with a vengeance and shouted a word with all the passion she had.

There is no equivalent to that word in any Earthly language. For the word she pronounced was a heavenly power word. But the power it generated was enormous, way off the scale for everyone there. As the word radiated outward, every demon it touched disintegrated. As the wave front of the word expanded and surged through the battle zone it grew stronger, not weaker. All the demons were fragmented by the power in the word. It knocked down everybody but Laura, who was standing in the center of the outwardly radiating power. The team's armor protected the team members from the power in the word.

Buildings nearby lost windows, and in some cases, brick facades crumbled, light poles were knocked down and several cars exploded. Laura looked with awe at the destruction, especially that of the demons.

Still, the demonic army wasn't going to quit without destroying the Crossfire Team members. A hundred more demons started to pour out of the portal. Now this really angered Laura. She was filled with a holy anger that fortified her with a heady power and she concentrated on the portal and said that word again. This time, she shouted it with even more concentrated energy than the first time. As the new demons crumbled and disappeared the increasing power of the word slammed through the portal and started destroying everything beyond it in the demon spirit realm. Red-lit mountains fell, the terrain itself disintegrated and the air boiled. Suddenly, the portal disappeared and in that silence, a relative calm returned to the area.

Jack drew in a big breath as the team's armor faded from view. He prayed his thanks to the Lord for their survival.

Mark limped over having been smashed in the left leg hard enough to stagger him and numb his leg. Every one of the team had sustained some injuries or damage. As the six team members came together they did a group hug. Laura shook her head. "I didn't know that I had that word until we were almost destroyed."

Jack looked around at the twenty people that had been injured badly or killed by the demons. Bodies lay crumpled in the street and on the sidewalk. He was filled with regret and anger. "This is unacceptable! In an attempt to kill us they killed dozens of innocent people."

Mark was still breathing heavily, "We need to get back to the base and find out why Carol didn't warn us about this attack. Most of those demons were here legally and that had to be in the matrix."

Jack nodded to Mark's comment, "Right after we attempt to explain this to the Israeli Police. Plus, we've got another problem we need to seek the Lord's wisdom about. I struck three demons but, they weren't affected. Laura's word destroyed them but my sword had become ineffective."

Laura felt the Lord's heart about the fallen people and she walked over and knelt down and prayed over several to no avail. As she cried out to the Lord she felt a peace come over her. She didn't hear anything, but felt that these people were beyond prayer and in God's hands.

Sarah stepped back and found her cell phone. She called the Mossad and explained their situation and location. She hung up just as the first two Israeli Police cars slid to a halt near them. She interpreted the commands the police yelled at them in Hebrew. "They want us to raise our hands and kneel down, immediately."

The team did as ordered and the police quickly descended on the four of them and shoved them face first down to the ground. They were handcuffed with their hands behind them and searched for weapons. Finding their handguns, the police confiscated the guns and hauled the four of them upright. One of the officers started screaming at them while others checked the bodies in the street. Sarah shook her head and answered in Hebrew. The officer looked at her like he thought she was lying. Sarah translated, "They are demanding we show them our knives. They think we killed these people." She smiled as another police car stopped and the local Chief of Police and a Mossad agent disembarked. "This should be interesting." she said quietly.

CHAPTER THIRTY-SIX

The Police Chief called the Officer in Charge of the situation over to him. He spoke authoritatively to the Officer who shook his head and was arguing with the Chief when, ten feet in front of that officer, one of the police officers surrounding the Crossfire Team transformed into a large and violent demon. He brandished a large black sword and charged through the officers, knocking them down as he made a bee-line for the six, handcuffed team members.

Instinctively the four began to pray to God. But, their armor and swords did not appear. Jack and Mark threw themselves in front of Laura and Sarah to protect them and face the demon. The demon took a mighty swing at Jack with its sword. Jack jumped back and the blade whistled by his middle with almost nothing to spare. Even though he was handcuffed, Mark ran at the demon like a demented football linebacker and literally knocked it down by running into it. He rolled away as the demon tried to swing its sword to hit him while they were both on the ground.

Jack was looking for an opening to kick the brute as it climbed back to its feet. Even though Mark's hands were still handcuffed behind his back, he arched his back, tucked his legs under him, and brought his hands under his feet. He jumped up to his feet to face the demon. The demon stalked Mark as the police officers fired their handguns at it. The demon ignored the shots because they didn't affect it.

Catching Mark off-guard the demon jumped suddenly and landed next to him and started to swing its sword when the angel Caleb appeared between the two. Caleb was in his youthful body and armor and stood a foot taller than the demon. His sword blocked the black blade of the demon and Caleb drove his blade through the black blade to behead the demon. Caleb's fiery eyes looked up as he sheathed his sword. He winked at Mark and faded from view.

Jack looked back at the assembled police officers. What he saw was looks of people stunned out of their wits or in complete unbelief. The only one that moved was the Mossad agent who quickly trotted over to them and undid their handcuffs. He looked at Jack and told him, "You need to get back to the base quickly." He had one of the police officers return the handguns to the six Team members. He then indicated a Mossad vehicle and escorted them to it. As they were getting into the vehicle the man said, "Something bad is going on in your side of the base right now." The Mossad man told the driver, "Get them back to the inlet port as fast as you can." He barely got the door closed before the large Chevy Tahoe roared away from the curb and raced down the street with red lights flashing and the siren blaring.

Jack pulled out his cell phone. He called Charlie Wu and got a busy signal, then called Linda Wu and got the same result.

Jack's phone chirped and Jack answered it. Charlie Wu responded, "Jack, the team side of the base is locked down as tight as a drum. Where are you?" Jack told Charlie, "We are on the way there right now. What's going on?"

Charlie summed up the events. "About an hour ago we got an emergency evacuation alarm. I got everybody out and locked down the ComSec section before leaving. I just got out when the base went into automatic lock down. We've been trying to find a way back in but there doesn't seem to be any. My backdoor authorization is not effective and the entrance panels don't respond to anybody's hand, eye, or voice prints. The major concern is that Carol Moffet isn't out here with us and just as I was leaving I heard the DAS go off."

Jack didn't recognize the initials. "What's the DAS?"

Charlie replied, "That's the new Demonic Alert System I created to protect the base. I think Carol is in there with one or more demons."

Jack thought for a second. "All right, you keep looking for a way in. We'll be there in ten minutes or less."

Actually, the Mossad driver had shaved extra minutes off the drive and they were sliding to a halt at the ground level portal as Jack broke the connection.

All six members ran through the portal to an elevator and dropped the 236 floors to the subterranean base level in record time. Grabbing two shuttle carts they raced across the airfield to the main entrance of the base. Jack noticed that the SOG and the other team members were diligently probing the 500-foot-long, armor plated wall that defended the base from the airfield side. At the top, bottom, and both ends the wall was implanted in the wall of the tectonic plate that surrounded the rest of the base. Jack appreciated that while there was an intense search for a way to gain access and find out what happened to Carol, there was no panic or high drama as they pulled up and disembarked from the carts.

Su Li, and Charlie trotted over and Charlie briefed them as to the situation. "I have covered every inch of the wall we can find and there doesn't seem to be any way to get into the base. I don't know anyone that has an answer on how to get into the base."

David smiled. "I know someone that can probably get us into the base and he should be here in a few minutes. If anybody knows a secret way in it will be Hiram."

Jack frowned, "Hiram?"

David grinned at him. "I know the Mossad very well. I can ensure you that they would have definitely built a secret entrance into such a powerful base on their soil." David waved his hand. "Here he comes. Hiram is the best technician I have ever met."

Hiram was a forceful looking Israeli as he hopped out of another cart and walked over to David. Hiram looked to be in his forties but still had the broad chest and muscular arms of a twenties-something body builder. His mostly bald head and firm stride reminded Jack of a U.S. Marine just without the uniform and weapons. Hiram made several demands in Hebrew and David answered them. Hiram thought for a few seconds and nodded. He led David and the others over to the main entrance and then paced off fifty feet to the left. He leaned over and carefully ran his hands over the surface of the wall until he found a slight depression. He pushed sharply in on the depression and a small panel popped out disclosing a key lock.

Taking a key from his pocket Hiram inserted the key into the opening behind the depression and turned it to the left, back to center, to the left again, and finally, to the right. There was a low grinding noise and an eight-foot-long, four-foot-wide rectangle of the ground to their right tilted up to expose a large, dark opening. Inside the opening was the top of a staircase that led downward.

Hiram descended the stairs with David and Jack behind him. The staircase seemed to lead nowhere. The man held up his hand to stop David and Jack several steps above him. He then stepped off of the last stair and waited several seconds. He then stepped back onto the last stair and off of it again.

A light panel lit up and a display screen began to glow in the wall. The Israeli put his hand on the display screen and waited. Another panel above the first one lit up. Hiram put his right eye close to the screen and his retina was scanned by a laser. A few seconds later a green light glowed on the panel and, with a hiss of escaping air, a large section of the wall to the right of the display screen opened up by sliding upward into the ceiling. The Israeli spoke in Hebrew to David who translated it for Jack. "He says this passageway will lead us directly into the exercise room. Let's go."

Jack said, "Wait." He tapped his cell phone and spoke to Mark. In less than five minutes Charlie and Linda Wu, Mark, Sarah, Laura, Su Li and the entire SOG lined up on the stairs. Jack nodded to David, "Lead the way."

The soft echoes from the crowd's footfalls heightened the suspense as they reached the end of the tunnel. There was a single green LED lit up on the wall to the right side of the tunnel. David pushed it and a large section of the exercise room wall slid up into the ceiling.

As soon as everyone was in the large exercise room, Jack told them. "There is at least one demon here in the base somewhere. I want three, fully armed SOG warriors with each of the seven Core Team members. If you run into the demon, shoot it. If it doesn't die, let the sword-trained Core Team member handle it. Keep your eyes out for Carol Moffet. She was trapped in here with whatever got in here. Be quick, search everywhere, but be careful."

CHAPTER THIRTY-SEVEN

Charlie and Linda Wu accompanied Mark and their three SOG warriors to the armory in deep darkness lit only by pools of emergency lighting and the Night fighter LED lights the team members carried. They rapidly outfitted themselves with body armor, night-vision goggles, and M8 rifles with grenade launchers. One group at a time, the other groups followed them and outfitted themselves with the same equipment. As a group was ready they headed out to separate sections of the base.

Mark carefully led his crew to the ComSec center and let Charlie use a portable power source to activate the main entrance. Charlie walked over to the command console and powered up one computer. From that he powered up the entire base. While Mark and the SOG kept guard over them Charlie and Linda immediately started a computer search for any demonic signatures and for Carol's locator medallion. Backed by the immense computing power of twenty-five of the latest CRAY computers it took only seconds to find Carol's medallion but no sign of demonic activity was detected anywhere in the base.

Mark relayed the location of Carol's medallion to Jack and his team. He mentioned, "The medallion is stationary."

Jack's team and Laura's team quickly moved to the remote section of the base on the third level down. This was the floor where they kept dry goods and non-perishable food stuffs. As they neared the spot where the computers said Carol might be everyone tensed up as they watched for anything out of the ordinary.

Laura posed a question for Jack. "Why would Carol be here?"

Jack had been wondering the same thing. "She probably came here because she was trying to elude something that was after her. The timing on this raid was designed to stop her from seeing the downtown attack in the matrix and alerting us to the danger."

Jack spotted a dark shape lying on the floor in one of the side hallways about ten feet from the main room. Laura held up her hand and then pointed both ways with her hands, arms out. The two teams moved into a defensive grouping which watched in all directions as they checked out the area and quickly reached the fallen form. It was Carol lying on her back and not moving. Squatting down, Jack found a thready and weak pulse. Carol was unconscious with a large bruise and lump on the right side of her face. Her handgun was still in her right hand. Jack eased it out of her grip and smelled the barrel. "It's been fired."

Laura walked several steps back toward the main room. She stopped and used her Night fighter LED flashlight to illuminate the concrete floor. The brilliant light illuminated a large ugly black stain that reeked with the stench of rotting flesh. The stain stood out vividly from the white concrete. Laura looked at Jack, "I think we've also found our demon."

Jack handed his rifle to one of the SOG women and gently scooped the girl off of the floor. He carried her up to the small medical area on the second floor near the SOG quarters, where he placed her on an examination table. Meanwhile. Mark was coordinating the rest of the teams in a detailed sweep of the rest of the base; the medical tech examined the young woman.

Actually, a fully trained and licensed doctor, Lisa Dawson had opted to go into the service as a medical technician after her residency rather than sign on to a medical facility. After she finished the examination, she spoke to Jack and Laura, "She has a concussion and multiple fractures of her cheek and jaw. She took a very hard hit to her head and is in a trauma-induced coma. There is probably internal hemorrhaging in her brain. Her color is pale indicating a massive effort by her heart and blood flow system to fight the damage to her head. I recommend that we get her to the nearest Israeli hospital on the surface as quickly as possible."

Jack had been praying for Carol and was about to order Carol's evacuation when he clearly heard God's voice speak to him. *"Assemble the elders, anoint her with oil, and pray for her. Then I will heal her."*

Jack shook his head and told Lisa, "No, the Lord says we are to pray for her healing."

Lisa debated what her training, common sense, and medical experience told her to do against Jack's decision. But, Lisa trusted God completely and knew that Jack was highly anointed by God, therefore she deferred to Jack's decision.

Jack asked Laura, "Would you please get my Bible and the anointing oil from our room? I will call the core team to come here and we will pray for her."

After the ten other people of the core team had joined them, Jack told them what God had said to him. "We are to pray the word of God which are His promises of healing. We must pray in faith and have no doubt that God will heal Carol. I know you're all true believers in Yahshua and know He can do anything. So, pray with your heart for the complete healing of our sister."

After he anointed Carol and himself with the oil, he anointed everyone there. Jack then had everyone lay hands on Carol and began to praise Yahveh and Yahshua. Jack then opened his Bible to James 5:14-15 and read,

"Is any sick among you? Let him call for the elders of the church; and let them pray over him, anointing him with oil in the name of the Lord: And the prayer of faith shall save the sick, and the Lord shall raise him up; and if he has committed sins, they shall be forgiven him.",

As the praying continued Jack felt the heaviness that he always felt when he was in the presence of Holiness. Jack reread the promises of God over Carol and everyone there stood firm in their faith that God would perform what He had promised in His word. Jack felt the electrical tingling over his body that he felt when the Holy Spirit of God was operating through him. He felt the power flow through his hands and into Carol. He'd felt that same feeling when David was saved and healed in Tel Aviv after being killed by an assassin.

They ended the prayer with a heartfelt "Amen". Jack then dismissed the rest of the core team and told them to get some rest if they needed it. He stood next to the young woman and prayed his thanks to God for her healing. He impulsively reached out and moved some of Carol's hair out of her face.

Lisa took Carol's pulse and blood pressure and smiled. "She's got most of her color back in her face and her pulse is strong and steady. Also, the bruising has already lost its angry color. I think all her system needs now, is rest. I'll check back on her later this afternoon."

Laura looked at Carol and took Jack's bigger hand in hers. "I think we should take her to our room and watch her tonight."

A pleasant voice in the doorway said. "You guys have enough on your plates right now. Let me watch her tonight." Alexis stood there with David next to her. Jack nodded, "Okay, thanks, guys."

Alexis came in and looked down on Carol. She looked up and smiled at them. "I think after the donnybrook we went through on the street in Tel Aviv you could use a little quiet time."

After David carried Carol to Alexis' room he returned to talk to Jack and Laura. "After we cleared the entire base, I went outside to thank Hiram. He was gone and everything was closed up like it never existed."

Jack shook his head. "I watched him and how he got us in here. But, I can almost guarantee that if anyone else tried that they would be very dead right now."

David smiled a grim smile. "You have no idea of the tightrope he walked to help us get in here so quickly. It would take me two weeks' worth of study to even attempt it. And even after that I wouldn't do it." David waved goodbye and headed back towards Alexis' rooms.

Jack considered all that had happened this day. Looking at his wife he said, "I think we need to ask God how to counter these new mass attack techniques by the demons, why I wasn't able to cut down those last three demons with my sword, and how a demon got in here to attack Carol."

Laura added, "And why our armor and swords didn't work while we were handcuffed and that demon appeared and charged us."

CHAPTER THIRTY-EIGHT

Jack and Laura entered their apartment and walked into the living area to find an angel sitting on the couch. Jack smiled at the angel who was dressed in a pure white gown. "Hello and welcome."

The angel nodded his head, "Thank you Jack Malone. My name is Orion and I have been given the mission to clarify the demonic efforts concerning your team. As you suspected, Satan has clearly defined you and your team as primary targets due to your successes against his forces."

Laura sat down across from the angel and asked him her primary question. "How can we prevent being swarmed by an unlimited number of demons resulting in our being overwhelmed?"

Orion smiled, "That type of attack will never happen again against your team. Your use of the Word of Power has crippled the power of hell far more than you could imagine. Nor was it one that they could afford. You destroyed an entire substructure of hell's domain along with thousands of demons. Worse yet, the rampaging power you directed into the open portal was not discriminate in its affect. To sum it up, you personally have completely eliminated two entire levels of demonic control over this area of your world. Satan is very powerful and cunning but he is not stupid. Too late he realized his error in upping the volume of the attacks against your team. He sorely underestimated the Most High's equipping of your team in the terms of supernatural power. He will never do that again. But, it has multiplied his anger against your team"

Jack felt uneasy and didn't know why. He sat down and studied the angel. The angel floated into a sitting position on the couch across from them and gazed at the two humans.

Orion smiled a small smile. "Jack, you and Laura have become something of a conversation item in hell. Needless to say that causes a lot of attention to be paid to you."

Orion continued, "I will attempt to describe things in human terms, so you can understand what is going on. It seems that the enemy of your soul has complained to God that you are both fakes. That you are specially trained and talented mortals that disrupt hell's plans and are so protected by the Lord that it is an unfair advantage against him." Orion sat back and let that sink in.

Laura thought it over as said, "So? That's essentially true."

Orion smiled again. "It seems that Satan is pressing charges against the two of you and is demanding that you prove you are both only human He wants you both to defend yourselves in a special test against two of his demons without Heaven butting in your favor."

Jack began to understand what was happening. "Is this going to be a fair fight? You know Satan will cheat and put specially prepared demons against us while he does everything he can to prevent us from winning. I can't believe that God would agree to such a challenge."

Orion almost grinned as he spoke up. "Actually, God has to agree because of the rules He established eons ago. If He didn't agree then He wouldn't be God."

Laura shook her head. "I can understand that, but demons are normally fallen angels, aren't they? That makes them more powerful than human beings if you don't bring God's protection into it, what chance do we have?"

Orion frowned slightly. "It isn't fair. But, to level the playing field the contest will be on Earth, where God can referee and prevent any special tricks that Satan will attempt to give his side the win."

Jack stood up and looked at Orion, "That still doesn't make two humans and one a female, against two stupid, ignorant, and sexless demons a reasonable contest."

Laura asked, "How long do we have before this "contest" is scheduled to begin?"

Orion said, "Less than two hours your time."

Jack eyes had turned icy green, "Then we'd bettered get started." Jack started to pace and his return walk veered behind Orion. Jack started to pray in the spirit and his armor and sword appeared. He quickly struck the angel from the rear and severed his head from his body.

Laura could not understand Jack's actions. His attack on the angel scared her and she began to pray. Her armor appeared and then disappeared. Jack's armor faded from view as the beheaded angel dissolved in a cloud of black smoke.

Comprehension flooded over Laura as she stared at the spot where the "angel" had fallen. "He wasn't an angel was he?"

Jack was praying for the protection of the entire base and the removal of any demonic spirits, activities, plots, plans, or strongholds. He thanked God for the success they had in detecting this effort of the enemy to eliminate them. He looked up at his wife. "No, he wasn't an angel. He was just a demon impersonating an angel."

CHAPTER THIRTY-NINE

Laura was shaken that she hadn't sensed the disguised demon. "When did you know?"

Jack sighed, "When he said that God had to allow us to do one-on-ones with demons and that God could not interfere. Plus, he said it would be on the Earth for fairness sake. Satan is the lord of the Earth. I know that God said in his word, "*I will never leave you I will never forsake you.*" That didn't add up with the arrangements for this battle. I also realized Orion was commenting about Satan as if he was the ultimate power in the universe. I decided to test my theory knowing that if Orion wasn't a demon, my armor and sword would not appear. When they did appear I was sure he was a demon."

Laura came over and put her head on Jack's chest as she hugged him. "I'm glad one of us wasn't deceived."

The override tone sounded for their front door and Mark, Sarah, and Alexis charged into the living area with their guns out. When they only saw Jack and Laura they lowered the weapons and stared at them. Mark holstered his .40 caliber XD autoloader and smiled. "Sorry, but Charlie's new demon tagger device identified a demon in your apartment. I guess it still has bugs."

Jack and Laura parted and the black stain on the couch and floor was clearly visible. Jack smiled at Mark. "Actually, I think it works pretty well."

Jack explained what had happened. Then Jack asked Mark if he could get everyone, including the SOG to a meeting in the living area in about an hour. Mark nodded and after the three left. Laura asked, "Why so long?"

Jack smiled at her, "Gives us some time to pray before we meet. Laura nodded and then called to have the Maintenance crew to remove the stained sofa and see what they could do with the stain on the floor. She told them to pray for cleansing for themselves before tackling either job and not come into physical contact with the stains. Then Jack and Laura prayed for Yahveh's cleansing of the room and their apartment.

The couple left their apartment, walked down the hall, and then down the stairs to the living area. They were about to pray when Raquel appeared before them.

Jack smiled at the angel and asked him who he served. Raquel said, "I serve the eternal God Yahveh and His Son, Yahshua. And before you ask, Yes, I know that Yahshua was crucified, died, and rose again three days later. I was there."

Jack looked at Laura, "I guess we can trust him to really be an angel."

Raquel frowned and asked, "What has happened?"

Jack related the attempt to kidnap them by the bogus angel Orion.

Raquel frowned, "How did he get past us? The Most High has us guarding your base constantly."

Jack sighed and sat down. "I don't know how he got in but that is only one of a lot of weird things recently. He and Laura filled the angel in on the original break-in that injured Carol, the mass attack on the street in Tel Aviv, and his inability to kill the last three demons he struck with his sword.

Raquel listened and nodded. He asked them to wait for a few minutes. He disappeared only to return in less than a minute. "There should be no more intrusions into your base. Your descriptions of what has occurred allowed me to resolve that problem."

Laura cocked her head to one side, "What did you do?"

The angel looked through her with his blue eyes focused on actions beyond the human dimension. "I determined that there was a defect in our protection which allowed me to uncover three demons posing as angels that Satan had inserted on the team protecting you."

Jack shook his head. "How can demons fool you and the other angels?"

Raquel still frowned. "It is complex, multidimensional, and it would be very complicated to explain. But, it should never happen again." The angel continued. "The demon Orion did tell you the truth about the damage you did to the region of hell above Israel. He was doing that to convince you to go with him. Neither of you would have returned from that trip."

"Now, concerning your armor and sword. Like all things in this universe with the exception of Yahveh and His Son Yahshua, the armor and weapons supplied to you from Heaven are limited in their capability. While that limitation is very high, there is a limit. Due to the number of the enemy you fought in that short battle and your weak prayers you reached that limit. You were saved by Laura's use of the Power Word, otherwise, you, and the others would have all been destroyed."

Raquel stared at Jack's dismay for several seconds and then nodded his head. "Let me explain. The power in the sword is directly from the Lord. When you use the sword the power God gives it is dependent on your prayers. Because of familiarity you have begun to treat God's gift of your armor and the sword without the respect Yahveh deserves. You assume that any prayer will activate your armor and sword. While this is true, your prayers during combat need to a fervent, passionate, beseeching of God for power, in other words, you need to become more effective in your praying during battle."

Raquel looked at Laura. "Laura prays passionately when she is in battle which may be a by-product of the fact that she is female and not as confident in her physical ability as a man would be. Remember, your strength or skill is a very small component of your combat. For your struggle is not against flesh and blood, but against the rulers, against the authorities, against the powers of this dark world and against the spiritual forces of evil in the heavenly realms. That is why you need to pray in the Spirit at all times as you face the forces of evil. Again, it is not by your power but by the power of God's Spirit that you can overcome the enemy."

As he heard Ephesians 6:10-18 spoken in truth by the angel, Jack realized he had again been guilty of pride because of his abilities. He silently prayed that Yahshua would forgive him this sin as he repented from any belief that he was the power that defeated even one demon. He smiled ruefully at the angel. "I have asked Yahshua to forgive me for my pride in this matter Raquel, and I will warn the other team members about this."

Raquel studied them both. "I am glad that you understand and are willing to humble yourself. You and your team continually amaze me. I can't comprehend how you can live in a world controlled by Satan, sin, and evil strongholds yet give God all the credit and stay humble. I know that you will stand strong and defeat the enemy as directed by the Lord. We angels will stand with you in your battles." He faded from sight.

Jack smiled at Laura. "Well, there goes what I was going to tell everyone. I've just been given a whole new direction."

CHAPTER FORTY

When everyone was present and seated in the living area, Jack stood up and got their attention. Smiling he addressed the group.

"Yahveh is right all the time. As humans we are not right all the time. I was just schooled by an angel because of my pride, and rightly so. Being human I have to deal with the "old man" that I had been before I was born again into Christ. One pitfall for me is that I didn't know that from the day of my birth Yahveh was helping me to become who I am today. He didn't do that so that I could impress myself or others, he did it so that I would become a usable servant for His glory to flow through."

Jack looked around and saw understanding and compassion on the faces of everyone there. "I am heavily convicted in that, once again, I had begun to believe that I was the force that defeated demons and helped save populations. The truth is I can't do any of that without your help and none of it can be done unless the Father does the battle. I was beginning to fall back onto pride in my abilities. I have been given a loud wake-up call and have humbly repented to the Lord and I am confessing to everyone here that I can do nothing the Lord doesn't help me do. I am also giving each of you a wake-up call to examine your actions and see if you're becoming prideful. It is very easy to do with the victories we've had. Don't assume it's your capabilities. Know that it is Yahveh in you as the Holy Spirit that fights, wins, and deserves the credit. Oh, you have to battle mightily and you have to do everything you can to win the victory because He needs to flow through a human connection in this battle. That's our role, to be obedient servants and children of the Most High Elohim."

"I can honestly say that I know and love everyone here. You each have dedicated your lives and abilities to God. Keep up the good work. As a team I believe, yet again, that we are about to face our greatest test."

Surprisingly, and as if on cue, Carol Moffet walked down the staircase and into the living area. She signaled Jack that she needed to talk to him. He waved her up to the front next to him.

Jack smiled at her. "Welcome back, and thank you. How are you feeling?"

Carol looked down, "I feel fine, now. I remember getting a shot off at the demon that was chasing me and then everything went black. I remember feeling chaotic and confused for some time."

She looked back up and smiled at Jack. "Then everything became peaceful and quiet. A warm love enveloped me and I rested for a long time in it until I woke up several hours ago. I don't have any pain or injuries and I would like to know what occurred while I was "resting".

Jack hugged her gently and told her quietly that they would talk about her experience right after the meeting.

Jack let her go and asked, "What do you have for us?"

Carol blinked and looked at the entire group, and then looked back at Jack as if to say, "Tell you here, in front of everybody?"

When Jack just nodded, Carol took a deep breath and started talking. "The Crossfire Team appears to have been centrally targeted in the matrix of events over the next two weeks, but in a most unusual way. I would term it a soft but wide attack by demonic forces that are apparently attacking someone else or something else in Israel. But, each attack includes demonic contact with us. Instead of being a single, massive event, it is dozens of little events all around the same time but, this time they are only in Israel."

Jack pointed out his seat in the front row next to Laura. He then said, "I want you to be part of the meetings from now on".

After Carol was seated, Jack addressed the entire group. "What do you think of the indications that Carol has seen in our near future?"

Mark stood up so everyone could hear him. "I think it means that no matter what the devil is planning to do using demons in Israel he now has to include a probable meeting with our team which tells me that he is concerned more about how we can mess up his agenda than how he can mess up ours."

Laura stood up as Mark sat back down. "I agree with Mark." She looked at Carol. "How many meetings in one day do you see?"

Carol promptly said, "Somewhere between six and eighteen per day."

Laura nodded, "And since these are in the matrix the demons involved will be legally in our dimension. We only have seven armor bearers and they believe they can do an end around by overloading our capabilities in that area."

Before Jack could reply the one of the SOG warriors stood up and asked to address the leaders of the team. Jack nodded his approval.

Retired U.S. Army Major Brian Owens walked up to the front of the gathering and made a surprise announcement. "General Malone, myself and the other members of the Crossfire Sensitive Operations Group have been given special training to resolve the problem posed by these demonic overload attacks. Last night, we all were transported to Heaven and met, and were trained by an angel named Hugo. Because almost none of us have ever handled a sword it took three weeks in Heaven's time to bring us all up to an acceptable level of swordsmanship. But, we accomplished it in almost no time here on Earth. So, instead of seven swords at your command you now have thirty-two."

Jack grinned at Mark and turned to the spokesman for the SOG. "Major Owens, welcome to the point of the spear." Jack turned to the other members of the SOG. "Congratulations to each and every one of you. Yahveh is increasing our capabilities to meet the attempts by Satan to overwhelm us. We will have some more sword practice this afternoon to see if there is anything our battle experience can add to your abilities. Which of you were taught the time-management, high-speed techniques?"

All twenty-five hands went up.

Mark stood up and addressed the group. "I propose that SOG now stands for Swords on Guard." He got some laughs at that. "I will confirm my decision with the core group but I think we can appoint "Colonel Owens" as the leader of the SOG at this stage of our operations. As we redefine our groups we will rely on his knowledge to set up sub-groups as needed. Right now I will assume that we will have all thirty-two Armor Bearer swords to support the personnel of the IDF as needed."

The disembodied voice of Charlie Wu from ComSec was heard. "Actually Jack, make that thirty-four swords. Linda and I also got trained by Hugo last night but it only took us two weeks. In answer to your question, yes, we also got the high-speed training. I don't think there are any such things as coincidences; therefore, I think we will probably be needed also. Anyway, I just wanted to let you know."

As Charlie finished speaking, Carol Moffet stood up and said, "Me too. That's why I didn't get here for a couple of hours after I woke up. To make the SOG people feel good, it took me almost four weeks learning swordsmanship from Hugo."

Jack shook his head and looked over at Mark, "Why don't you check and see if the cleaning crew was trained by Hugo in swords too?"

After the laughter and everyone settled down, Laura got to her feet and surveyed the people there. "As the original Armor Bearer for the Crossfire Team, I want to welcome everyone to the battle. I, for one, am very glad to have company in this endeavor as it can get tiring during the battles."

CHAPTER FORTY-ONE

Many in the meeting proposed their concept of what the enemy was plotting to do to Israel. The consensus was that the demons were going to work with the Jihadists to infiltrate Israel and most likely set off explosives against the Israelis.

Laura brought up the fact that Marco Marino had banned such activities while he attempted to seduce the world's population into believing he was creating a peaceful mankind. He was hoping that they would worship him without having to force them. He had done many things to make himself look like the savior of the world.

Mark shook his head at that thought. "You're right about him and his efforts. I believe that eventually he'll get the Jihadists to go along with his scheme or kill them off. But, they are a rebellious bunch. If they are planning mass attacks against the nation of Israel that will give Marco a black eye. The world at large isn't on the Jihadists side. Neither are the governments because they can't control them. So, the good side is against them and now they are getting the resident evil on the planet against them too. I don't see a long future for them."

David added, "True, but in the short run they can hurt and kill thousands of innocent people who did nothing to them, especially the women and children."

Jack looked at David. "All right, we need to talk to the head of the IDF and the Director of the Mossad to coordinate our efforts. They can handle the Jihadists and we will deal with any supernatural demonic efforts in our dimension. Now that we have enough Armor Bearers to meet the scheduled challenges.

Jack addressed everyone. "We need to be ready at a moment's notice anywhere the IDF needs us. I think we should wear a common uniform so they can identify us and be ready for surprises such as illegal demons which can be killed by bullets and bombs." Jack spoke to the air. "Charlie, we need rock steady comm that can't be blocked or interfered with by the earthly enemy. Can you set that up in the next six hours?"

Charlie came back right away. "No problem Jack. See me before you head out and I'll outfit everyone, even the maintenance crew if they got trained by Hugo."

The meeting broke up and Jack, Mark, and David left to coordinate with the IDF and the Mossad.

Later that day Jack surveyed himself in the full length mirror in his apartment. The new uniform fit him very nicely. The one-piece uniform was made of a soft, resilient material that felt like microfiber but was very tough. It moved with the body and would stretch or shrink as needed. There was a collar with a pattern as well as a sideline down each side and a sturdy belt, also military grade, in black with a holster on one hip or the other depending on the dominate hand of the user. The other side of the belt supported triple magazines for the handgun the user had.

The basic color of the uniform was a deep blue with the trim in gold for the women and silver for the men. There was a jacket that was stylish but functional and a matching military harness to support more ominous equipment such as knives and grenades. The uniform was completed by a military beret in matching dark blue. The only insignia on the uniform was a small white lightning bolt depending from a small red cross on the left side of the uniform just below the shoulder. Clearly lettered below that were the words, "Crossfire Team"

When they sought the government's help the first thing they ran into was doubt by both groups that there were going to be any mass attacks. The Mossad hadn't heard of anything like that and the IDF didn't believe the Jihadists were capable of such a thing.

Jack wasn't dismayed by their suspicious natures. He pointed out where the attacks would originate from the border with Syria. The IDF decided after conferring with the Prime Minister that they would set up troops at each of the eighteen points. Just a squad but that should handle the bombers if they attempted to enter Israel.

The Mossad took a wait and see attitude.

Carol contacted everyone on the "sword net" as Charlie called it. "I'm sending you a list of the approximate time for each incursion at the border."

Jack stood with the IDF squad leader in the early evening darkness as the time for their incursion approached. Levi Malaren had never had much to do with God or the devil and was about as skeptical as a man could be about the attack. Still, the Prime Minister said, "Pay attention to these people, they know what is going to happen." So against his natural inclinations Levi would prepare. Ten minutes before the appointed time he placed his soldiers where they could interdict anyone attempting to enter Israel illegally.

As the time came and passed he felt confident that there would be no attack. Suddenly, his combat radio was alive with established contacts and battles at some of the other checkpoints. He told his men to be ready.

There was a muffled blast and a twenty-foot-wide hole was blasted through the cinder blocks of the containment wall. The bricks smashed into cars and buildings. Eight men masked in head scarves rushed through the gap. Most of them wore backpacks and all were carrying rifles or pistols.

Levi pushed the switch that turned on the portable Klieg lights and lit the Jihadists up like daylight. His amplified voice over the loud speakers told the attackers to stop where they were and raise their hands or they would be fired upon. The attackers hunkered down behind the cinder blocks and started shooting at the soldiers. Levi shouted "return fire" in Hebrew. The troops started shooting for effect and quickly killed three of the attackers.

Suddenly, a seven-foot-tall, massive demon appeared behind the Jihadists and stalked forward towards the IDF troops. Jack was praying the twenty-third Psalm and his silver armor and the sword of Yahveh literally exploded into being making Levi step back in awe. Jack ran forward as the demon smashed cars and knocked one of the soldiers head over heels with his free left hand while cutting down anything in his way with a huge black blade in his right.

Six more demons crackled through the dimensional barrier into the human dimension right behind the big one. These demons charged forward to attack the soldiers. While these were smaller than the first demon they were still big, extremely vicious, ugly, and stank horribly. Jack shouted to Levi to have the soldiers shoot them. These six demons broke into two groups. Three ran directly at the IDF forces to attack them while the other three moved with the big demon to attack Jack. As some of the troops shot at the smaller demons their bullets tore holes through them everywhere they hit them. The IDF soldiers were bravely shooting while attempting to avoid the vile creature's attacks as much as possible.

The big demon pounded across the ground toward Jack. Jack told Levi, "Stop the Jihadists. I'll handle these creatures." As the three creatures began to dissolve into putrid smoke the soldiers concentrated their fire on the human attackers again.

As the four demonic creatures charged toward Jack, the big demon did something new as it neared Jack. It transitioned back out of the human dimension.

Guessing what it had in mind, Jack quickly computed speed and direction for the big demon in his head as he met the three smaller demons, Jack stepped two steps to his left as the smaller demons attacked. Jack ran the most upright of the three through with his sword. The other two veered away from the glowing sword which gave Jack time to turn to his right and swing his sword from left to right. Jack was praying fervently to Yahveh as he fought, "Yea though I walk through the valley of the shadow of death, I shall fear no evil, for thou are with me." He realized that if his sword failed this time these demons would kill him in an instant.

The bigger demon tore back into the human dimension where he expected to be able to smash Jack into the ground. But, Jack wasn't there. The demon swung a mighty blow of its sword, from overhead. The black blade struck Jack's armor and knocked him backward. Jack's sword stuck the demon's sword and the black sword shattered into pieces as the power of God struck it. Jack recovered his balance, stepped back toward the demon, he brought his sword up and over into a downward slash from shoulder height. As his sword cut through the demon's shoulder and into his chest the demon wailed and disappeared again.

The two smaller demons had split up and attacked Jack from both sides. One swung a smaller sword at Jack's legs while the other had a spear and rammed it into Jack to impale his chest. When the spear hit Jack's armor it slid off to the side as Jack jumped upward and pulled his legs up to avoid being tripped by the other demon. As he rose into air, Jack one-handedly swung his sword to his right and decapitated the spear holder. The other demon ran forward, trying to impale Jack on its sword as he came back down to the ground.

Levi fired six rounds from his Galil rifle into the smaller demon and literally blew it away. Jack ensured its death by swinging his sword through its chest as it disappeared into greasy smoke. As he landed on his feet, Jack kept praying and his armor didn't disappear. He noted that the soldiers had decimated the Jihadists leaving only one man. The terrorist realized his mission was doomed and, screaming his hatred he detonated his backpack bomb attempting to kill the IDF troops. The Jihadist disintegrated in the explosion but was too far away to do more than knock the IDF soldiers down. Jack's armor kept him safe from flying debris and then it faded out along with his sword.

Jack could feel the pain and aches from the battle already as he contacted Charlie with an update on the attack.

Levi called for additional troops to seal off the area of the hole in the wall while he checked on his soldiers. The soldier that the big demon had smashed had died immediately. Three others were injured by the smaller demons, the return fire from the Jihadists, or the final blast. Levi had the remaining six troops guard the hole in the wall while they waited for the bomb disposal team to arrive and disarm the remaining explosives in the backpacks of the dead terrorists.

Jack stood guard over the troops to prevent any additional demons from attacking them. Levi walked over to Jack and held out his hand. He had a very somber expression on his face. "I will never doubt you again." he said, as he surveyed the destruction and the large stains where the demons had expired.

Jack smiled a small smile as he shook the man's hand. "I remember the first time I saw a demon. It shook me to my core. At first, they seem too vile for humans to look at let alone try to defeat. You and your troops coped very well considering they didn't really believe that those things existed until a few minutes ago."

Levi shook his head, "I think we're all going to have nightmares for a while."

CHAPTER FORTY-TWO

After the twenty-one battles all along the Syrian border with Israel, Jack and Mark met with the leaders of the Mossad and the IDF. The reports from the squad leaders in these battles were so loaded with descriptions of unkillable demons and successful Crossfire Team responses that the Mossad agreed that they miss-read the situation and the IDF wanted to include the Crossfire Team under their military control full time.

The Prime Minister vetoed that suggestion because the Crossfire Team reported directly to God and God had the ultimate control.

Mark assigned ten of the SOG to assist the IDF as needed whenever their unique capabilities were needed.

Jack didn't interfere with Mark's assignments but did question him about it when they were alone. "Why split up the team?"

Mark sighed heavily. "Because I just got a report from Gary Rhodes that will probably take precedent over the border actions here."

Jack tried to imagine what would be more important than helping the Israelis to defend their borders. "What did Gary relay to you?"

Mark sat down on the edge of a table. "Remember RHONE, the Revived Highest Order Nazi Empire?"

Jack nodded his head as he thought back to the bombship episode. "Yes, I thought getting rid of Ms. Carlington would render that outfit powerless."

Mark shook his head. "We guessed wrong thinking that Ms. Carlington had taken over the group. Actually, her operation was just a small effort in their plans. We need to pray about this but I will bet that the Father will direct us to counter and destroy them and their efforts."

Jack considered the problem. "Won't the Anti-Christ destroy them?"

Mark shook his head again, "Hardly, they work for him. According to Gary these guys are in league with the Anti-Christ, who hates us, and they hate us now for stopping three of their premier projects. After we prevented the nuclear explosion in Washington, D.C., their destruction of the next Queen of England, we also prevented them from killing the kid they think will become the next great holy man. So, we are now their number one target for destruction. I think we really need to research this group."

Jack agreed with Mark's summation. He called Charlie Wu and requested a full-up research on RHONE and its movers and shakers. He then thought about the situation and made a decision. "Okay Mark, once again, the best defense is a good offense. Let's see if the Father wants us to take on this group and, if he does, how we bring RHONE down."

Mark thought back about their experience with RHONE. "You know; we did some research on RHONE when we were going after Ms. Carlington. I don't remember any flags about a large, possibly multinational, criminal cartel at that time. Why is that?"

Jack was about to respond when his cell phone rang. Answering he recognized Charlie Wu from the caller ID listing the phone showed him as he answered. "Yes Charlie, what do you have?"

Charlie was obviously upset. "Jack, I got nothing. I have cracked every super secure computer system on the planet but I can't get anything on RHONE. Even Google doesn't have anything on it. It's like it doesn't exist in our world."

Jack said, "Hold one while I see if I can get Gary Rhodes on a three-way." Gary was in his office and Jack hooked the three of them together. He told Gary what Charlie had run into. "How solid is your intel on this group?"

Gary looked at the information packet and told Jack. "Very good, and the reason it is so good is that we had an insider who ratted the cartel out to us because he had fallen out of favor with them and was worried that they would kill him. So he brought us a bunch of material and with that we were able to get a look at RHONE and their operations. We verified everything the insider gave us."

Mark spoke up. "Gary can you get us a copy of that Intel and even a chance to talk to your snitch?"

Gary sighed, "I can get you a copy of the intel but nothing else. Within twenty-four hours the insider was dead and everything he gave us went missing off of the FBI secure site."

Jack asked, "Then how can you get us a copy of it?"

Gary laughed, "After hanging around with you guys I learned to make a second copy of everything and keep it to myself. I want to thank you also for your strong stance for Jesus."

"Oh?" said Jack.

"I could not help but see the truth in your battles with the demons and after some soul-searching I gave my life to the Lord and got baptized and filled with the Holy Spirit. I am so glad that so guys showed up in my life back in Denver a couple of years ago. My whole family is saved now and it was just in time for me to know what to do with that "finder's fee" that you sent me. I'm helping a whole lot of people with those funds. I realized that each time I help one of the downtrodden I am doing God's work and it feels really good. Of course I do it carefully and anonymously because I couldn't do it off of my income and I don't want to send up any red flags. My entire family was taken in the Rapture, but I agreed to a request from God to stay until the midpoint of the seven-year tribulation period. According to the Angel that gave me the choice I am somehow linked to your team in the near future."

Jack, Charlie, and Mark congratulated Gary and officially designated him as a brother in Christ.

After Gary hung up, Jack asked Charlie a pointed question. "Do you think that you are getting locked out of info on this group by demonic means?"

Jack heard Charlie slap himself on the forehead. "Of course! I have been around this stuff so long I'm forgetting the basics. Hold one." Charlie came back in several minutes. "I got the stuff from Gary Rhodes. With this I will be able to work around some of their protections. I'm sure they've changed everything the insider knew so it may take a while. I'll call you when I've got some significant information."

CHAPTER FORTY-THREE

Charlie worked at the job of finding out about the RHONE group by negative/reflective data collection. He told Jack that it was like inferring information about a black hole in space. You can't get direct information because even light is sucked into the black hole and not reflected. When trying to find out information about a group protected by demonic forces you go to things they will influence and build a picture that way. It took a lot longer, but it was doable.

Jack and Mark went over Charlie's package on RHONE. An hour later, Mark closed the folder and sat back. "This is big; I mean super big. This group makes the Omicron operation look like child's play. These guys have major centers in almost every nation; they influence or buy, bully, or kill their way to their objectives. They have an efficient, standing army of over one-hundred thousand fighting men and women, which doesn't include another two hundred thousand personnel, Their annual budget for military hardware operations and salaries for everyone on their payroll is over twenty billion dollars a year. They stay out of politics but serve the Anti-Christ's One World Government as a secret enforcement arm. Yet they are more secretive than the elitist power groups and there is no knowledge of them in the free press or any other investigative group. These people have started wars and finished them too. They are so big it is astounding that there seems to be nobody that knows about them directly. There are a lot of people that have been strong armed by RHONE but still don't know who is doing the strong arming. Most people believe that they are an insurance company or a finance company."

Jack smiled, "My guess is that anyone that aggressively seeks information on their group or complains too loudly ends up dead. But, while we don't have their strength or numbers, we have God on our side. Remember David and Goliath. You know why David picked up five stones and only needed one? Because he knew Goliath had four giant brothers and he knew he might need those extra stones. I think we need to inquire of the Lord as to our part, if any, where this mega cartel is involved."

Mark agreed and called the core group together in the War Room. After explaining what they had found out the entire group started corporate prayer seeking the Lord's guidance concerning RHONE.

As they prayed and praised the Lord of the Universe Jack felt the heaviness settle down on him. He felt the world fall away as he focused just on loving God.

The feeling of freedom and peace was so overwhelming Jack began to wonder if they had been released from their life on Earth and joined Yahshua in Heaven.

This request for information was again answered in a unique manner. Jack began to see a vision of giants guarding a treasure. The giants were huge and mean and formidable in the extreme. Yet, they had weaknesses and openings in their armor that would allow a skillful warrior to conquer them. As soon as he realized their weaknesses they began to fall and disappear. He advanced past where the giants had been and realized he was now facing beings of great darkness and evil. Again, there were places where the dark beings could be beaten and as they disappeared, the scene shifted to an inner sanctum. At least that was what Jack thought it was.

Inside the central core was the most invincible force that didn't seem to have any weaknesses, but it too, could be overcome but only by the power of God. The scene expanded to show thousands and thousands of these evil beings standing forth to do battle against Jack. Jack saw himself kneeling and praying as the front row of the enemy approached him. A gentle breeze came from behind him and washed the enemy away and the Son suddenly appeared and His light eliminated all darkness from Jack's vision. That's where the vision began to fade away. Jack heard, *"Be strong and courageous, do not fear death, the enemy will be given over to you but you must be patient as this will take time, years in Earth's time."*

Jack opened his eyes to see everyone else staring at him. He looked around and asked, "What?"

Laura smiled at him and said, "Do you know that you glow with a full-body halo of soft light when you are talking with the Lord?"

Jack shook his head, "I only have eyes for Him at those times."

Carol asked softly, "What did He give you?"

Jack described his vision and the encouragement that the Lord had given him at the end of the vision.

Mark said, "Could the giants be the forces of RHONE on Earth, the evil beings, demons, and the final force, Satan?"

Jack smiled, "That's good. I like it but I'm not sure because the Bible says that Satan will be active through the entire seven years of the tribulation and we are going to leave the battlefield at the mid-point of the seven years.

David added, "Yes, but, how do you know we all won't return with the Savior to continue battles for Him in the millennium?"

Jack shook his head, "Possibilities, probabilities, who knows except the Father? I think this team needs to plan for the next battles which will be against whatever those giants represent."

Sarah spoke up. "One thing is for sure, anything that is evil hates Israel because they are God's people and His country, and Jerusalem is His city."

David coughed and got everyone's attention. "I realize we are all having fun and I for one want that to go on. We do have a previous commitment that we have to attend to. This is Friday and this evening we want to celebrate Shabbat. Since we haven't had time to set up a Synagogue yet, and haven't found a Rabbi yet, I will hold the Shabbat celebration in the War Room at 6:45 P.M. this evening."

Jack smiled, "Okay, I'll get all the troops here."

CHAPTER FORTY-FOUR

At six forty-five that evening, David put on his Tallit, or prayer shawl, and stepped up to the area at the front of the War Room where they had placed one of the small tables.

"Looking at the thirty-five SOG troops and the entire Core Team he smiled at them. "Ladies and Gentlemen, we are gathered here to hold a short celebration called Shabbat."

"There are twelve steps in the normal Shabbat Celebration. I will list them for you here and then we will do each one so that you can understand them."

"Before we start the celebration we will pass around the Tzdakah box. This is for Charity for the poor. As God says in His word, to receive a blessing one needs first to be a blessing. Everyone, even homeless beggars in Israel honor this and put something in the Charity for those with less than they have."

"Next we're going to wash our hands. In Israel the people go through the "mikveh" a ceremonial pool or tub of running water where the person is completely immersed and their connection with any failure or curses are washed away. By washing our hands, we are doing a simple version of the baptism because we don't have a mikveh at hand. It still washes our spirits of curses and connections with failure."

"Then we are going to light the candles. The woman of the house normally lights the two candles and prays a prayer of thanks to G-d for the Sabbath. An unmarried woman can light a single candle in honor of her breshet, or her future husband picked by God for her. The lighting of the candles is an important spiritual symbol that helps one to mentally make the transition from the mundane work days to the joyful holy time. Then we pray for any children we have in general, then the boys and then the girls as groups. Then the head of the household reads a scripture about his wife and prays for her".

"Then she prays for him. Next we do the Kiddush which is the blessing over the wine or juice and we drink it. Next we pray a blessing over the bread and eat a piece of it. Lastly we pray a grace over the meal we just had. Then you have entered into the day of rest."

"Here, in Israel, you will find every business except police and medical services closed while everyone celebrates Shabbat."

"I think we need to have Jack act for all of us as the head of the household, and Laura act for all of the women. Each of you can hold a group or individual Shabbat celebration like this instead of one large communal gathering."

David looked around at the happy faces and smiled. "Tomorrow night we will gather again for a much shorter celebration for "Havdalah" which closes out the Sabbath and sends everyone back to work."

CHAPTER FORTY-FIVE

The Sabbath was celebrated quietly for everyone in the Sea Base. It really was a "day of rest" for the troops. Jack got up around six a.m. and did his normal workout.

Two hours later, Carol called Jack. "Jack, I see a force coming against us in the matrix. The plan seems simple. They will come against this base and destroy it sometime tomorrow. How? I don't know but they will be using two nuclear devices."

Jack called Charlie Wu. After explaining what Carol told him he didn't need to tell the head of their computer systems what to do.

Charlie started a general search for anything that would threaten Israel in the next two days. He eliminated all the rockets and human bombs that the local, Syrian-backed Hamas or Hezbollah or the radical Muslim extremists' efforts and concentrated on an International attack with a nuclear capability.

It took Charlie's advanced computers less than four minutes to reduce the probabilities, based on current activities, to list the top three threats to the undersea base. The top probability was a ninety-eight percent probability, the next was a sixty-five percent, and the last one was only a ten percent chance.

Charlie refined the top chance as the only concern and had the system give him everything it had on that situation along with possible defenses. When he was finished he sent the information to Jack and Mark.

Jack read the data and looked at Mark who said, "We had best call the IDF right now."

Jack put a call into General Levy. The General was quick to respond to the call. "Hello Jack, I expected to hear from you but not quite this soon."

Jack laughed, "Our walk with God tends to be very active. Due to the Rapture we lost our U.S. military partners, the President of the U.S. and the Chairman of the Joint Chiefs of Staff, General Miles. Since we are now

Israeli citizens, we hope to work with you concerning threats to Israel."

General Levy chuckled a low chuckle, "I will try to be as accommodating as my old friends. How can I be of assistance?"

Jack looked at the data Charlie had sent him. "It seems that Graney-class nuclear submarine that you drove off is headed back here and this time it apparently intends to attack our base with one or more nuclear-tipped ASROC weapons. Our computers indicate a ninety-eight percent probability of that happening tomorrow. The submarine is about one hundred and twenty miles south-east of our position right now."

The General digested that information and thought about it. "We have been tracking that particular mystery ship ourselves and are already on alert in the event it enters our territorial waters. So, Charlie Wu has a ninety-eight percent probability that it will attempt a nuclear strike only a mile off of our shores. After reviewing his track record and your team's efforts I am disposed to believe his conclusions. I actually wish we had the CRAY computer complex you have, but either way, it's a real threat to us. I will present this to the administration and see if we can interdict the ship rather than simply destroy it. But, if it won't heed our efforts, then destroy it we will."

Jack nodded, "Thank you General. By the way, I have it on Heavenly authority that the mystery sub is a demonically generated device that is physically in our dimension and it is under the control of Marco Marino. What about the peace treaty that your nation signed with him?"

The General laughed, "I wouldn't worry about that. If the ship refuses to identify itself then we can't be held responsible by that treaty for defending our home land. I will keep you advised Jack."

After they broke the connection Jack suggested they pray for the Israeli Navy's effort to defend them and to see if the Father wanted them to be involved in any way.

Two hours and eight minutes later General Levy called Jack. "I don't believe it!" The man was so upset he was mixing Hebrew and English terms.

Jack said, "General Levy, calm down. Tell me what the problem is."

General Levy actually growled. "These stupid politicians! They have denied the IDF permission to interfere with the "peaceful" mission this submarine is on. They said, "If we interfere with this boat's mission it will be a violation of that demon-begotten and sorry agreement they have made with Marino! They are blind, dumb, and have no understanding of military matters. They have threatened to oust the Prime Minister, call for new elections, and clamp a heavy hand on military operations if there is any action taken in this case."

Jack's spirit sank as he heard the anger and hopelessness in the General's voice. But, Jack knew better than to let the situation dictate his life through emotions. "General Levy. I understand your concern and your frustration about this. I was counting on the Israeli Military to stop this disaster. But, I will not accept the idea that the situation is bigger than my God." He thought for a few seconds. A brilliant concept came to his mind. "General, do not worry about this incursion into Israeli waters. God will give this ship the choice of leaving without attempting to attack this island or He will let them destroy themselves."

Jack's voice was full of confidence and even jubilation. "We will keep you in the loop. That sub doesn't stand a chance."

The General asked, "How are you going to stop a submarine with nuclear missiles and air to surface nuclear torpedoes?"

Jack almost laughed, "You'll have to wait and see, Sir."

Jack broke the phone connection and since he was alone in his office in his apartment he dropped to his knees and prayed his thanksgiving to a loving Father that had given him the salvation of the undersea base and their lives. Getting up he called Mark and told him what they were going to do.

Mark was quiet for a few minutes and then said, "That just might work."

CHAPTER FORTY-SIX

As the submarine approached a distance of thirty miles from the Israeli coast, the boat's Captain checked again with the sonar operator. "You're sure there are no Israeli submarines nearby and there are not any aircraft orbiting above us."

The sonar operator nodded his head, Yes Sir!

Captain Kapustin smiled and told his executive officer, "See XO, I told you that the cowardly Jews couldn't stand up to Marco Marino's orders to not get involved."

The XO nodded his head, but he had a bad feeling about this mission. He had read the information on the Crossfire Team and their relationship with God. But, he wasn't going to lose everything by making his foreboding public knowledge. He was going to do his duty.

The XO brought the submarine's forward motion to a halt. He then brought the ship up to periscope depth and raised the main periscope. After scanning the seas and the skies around them he asked the Captain, "Are we sure that we are at a safe distance to detonate the torpedoes and are we sure that there is a base under the island?"

Captain Kapustin shrugged his shoulders. "That's the word I got from the head of the OWG. Personally I don't think that it is the Crossfire Team's base because they fly aircraft and those things don't work very well under water. But, I don't care one way or the other. We have our orders, blow this insignificant atoll away. It will make a huge point to the Israelis that the OWG can do anything it wants to regardless of national territorial limits."

He turned to a rating, "Order the ASROC torpedo doors one and two to be opened."

The rating said, "Aye Aye Sir. Opening ASROC torpedo doors one and two."

The rating near the XO asked, "Sir, what exactly is a VLA ASROC torpedo?"

The XO quietly explained, "The VLA originally was intended to provide vertical-launch-capable surface ships with a quick-reaction, standoff antisubmarine weapon. The

VLA includes a solid-propellant booster thrust vector control designed to guide the missile from a vertical orientation through a pitch-over maneuver into a ballistic trajectory intended to deliver the torpedo to an aim point on the ocean surface. This variant has been additionally modified to carry a heavier torpedo and to deliver improved performance in shallow water. In other words, because of the thirty mile distance it allows us to launch the weapon vertically as a rocket which will travel close to the island and then re-enter the sea. Then it acts just like a normal torpedo."

Suddenly a loud voice in Russian reverberated through the conning tower of the submarine. ***"If you attempt to destroy the island, you will destroy yourselves."***

The XO looked at the Captain with alarm.

The Captain got a determined and irritated look on his face. "Don't listen to their garbage! There is nothing they can do to stop us. They're just trying to scare us off. Set and Mark bearings for two ASROC torpedoes."

The XO shook his head and asked, "If their God is warning us then we should..."

The Captain took out his pistol and shot the XO through the heart, killing him instantly. He then holstered his pistol, walked over and pushed the corpse out of the way with his foot, and took the XO's position. He asked if there were any more traitors on the ship. He peered at the digital display and said, "Set and Mark bearing for ASROC torpedoes one and two"

The rating repeated the order and told the Captain the torpedoes were ready to fire.

The Captain smiled because he knew there was no God and this action would get him promoted. "Fire VLA tubes one and two."

The rating repeated the order and the Firing Officer in the torpedo room mashed down the buttons to send the two nuclear-tipped, super-cavitation torpedoes out of their vertical tubes up to the surface toward the island.

As the two torpedoes shot up their vertical launch tubes they both suddenly detonated which triggered the nuclear warheads. These warheads were not the small nuclear warheads usually used in torpedoes but had been replaced by 1-megaton warheads to thoroughly destroy the island and the base they thought might be located under the island.

The two fireballs instantly merged and superheated the sea for a half-mile radius. This huge fireball blasted out of the sea and rose toward space with a roar heard throughout Israel and Syria. People in the streets of Haifa stopped to stare out over the ocean at the huge ugly mushroom cloud with fear and trembling.

In the first six microseconds after the detonation the entire submarine and the crew of 120 were fragmented into atomic particles. No evidence was ever found that the sub was there. The sea for thousands of feet around the position of the submarine was vaporized and thrown into the sky as steam. The surface wave produced by the explosion was four feet high when it hit the beaches of Israel, but it didn't do much damage due to the thirty-five-mile distance from the undersea blast.

The sea settled down after a while and the off-shore breezes blew the cloud and the radiation away until the there was no sign the explosion.

Four hours later General Levy showed up at the undersea base headquarters for the Crossfire Team. After he got a quick tour of the base he sat down with Jack, Laura, Mark, and Sarah. He reclined in his seat and studied the foursome. "Okay, how did you do it?"

Jack returned the look calmly. "Whatever do you mean General?"

"You told me yesterday that God would take care of the submarine and today the sub exploded thirty-five miles off of our coast. So, what did you do?"

Jack smiled and looked at the other three team members. "General, we could tell you that we prayed and God took them out. But, while that is true, I want our relationship to be one of trust and honesty. The actual explanation is going to make you stretch your mind considerably to understand it. But, it is the truth and in every sense, it was God stopping the submarine."

The General looked at Jack steadily and nodded his head.

Jack took a deep breath and said, "In the simplest summation, Mark and I positioned ourselves in the path of the submarine and caused it to explode when they tried to vertically launch rocket assisted nuclear-tipped torpedoes. Now, how it was done is going to require some belief in the supernatural and in science."

The four team members stood up and Jack motioned for the General to follow them to the firing range on the next floor below the living area. They repeated an earlier demonstration for the General. This time Mark walked out onto the range and stood before a sheet of plywood. He activated a force generator that Dr. Clashire had created for the team a year before.

Jack explained, "Essentially the force generator creates a field that takes any form of force like a knife thrust, bullets, explosives, or even a nuclear explosion and absorbs the energy. It uses that energy to oppose the force itself. The scientific explanation is very complex. The operative point here is that the field works. Let me demonstrate."

Jack took one of their M-8 assault rifles and handed it to the General. He told the General to fire it at Mark. The General raised an eyebrow but fired the complete thirty round magazine of 6.8 caliber rounds at Mark who stood there and smiled during the firing. Some of the rounds missed Mark and blew holes through the plywood.

Jack continued, "That is a minor demonstration of the force generator. It allows the person wearing the force generator to be unaffected by anything we know of in this world."

The General examined the assault rifle and then took out his own sidearm, an IMI Jericho 941 known as the "Baby Eagle". He looked at Jack for permission. Jack looked at Mark who nodded his approval.

Taking careful aim the General fired six rounds at Mark with the same results. Putting away his pistol the General turned to Jack. "How can you have such a device and not use it to rule the world or to stop terrorism? This device would make war obsolete."

Jack nodded his head. "Yes Sir, it would do that with two small exceptions. First, God has to allow us to use it to contravene a demonic plot, which he has only done three times so far. Second exception, is the limitation that the device will only work for born-again believers in Yahshua."

The General got a strained look on his face. "Why?"

Jack motioned for Mark to come out of the range. "General, this device was given to us by our mutual Father in Heaven to offset some spiritually illegal actions by the enemy of all mankind, Satan. By His own laws God will not dictate man's actions in this world. He would be violating His own commandments if he stopped violence and war with this device."

Jack looked to see if the General was following the conversation. "It was provided simply to counteract specific cases of the enemy using their spiritual powers without God's permission. This permission is one of the requirements on the enemy. I can't explain it except to say that the force generator is an equalizer the Father uses to prevent illegal excesses by Satan. Our team is one of many that were created by God to balance the illegal physical entry of demons into the human dimension."

The General was very intelligent and asked, "Then why did God allow you to use it to destroy the submarine. Wasn't that violating His own terms for its use?"

Jack smiled, "Because this submarine really was destroyed by the Soviets many years ago. Satan used demonic power to, essentially, reanimate it and keep it working in this dimension through that demonic power. I am not smart enough to explain how that is done; I only know it involves using two of the eleven dimensions that exist outside of man's knowledge. Anyway, it was another illegal trick of Satan's to destroy God's people. The use of the force generator was acceptable in this case."

General Levy thought that through and then asked, "How did you and Mr. Connelly use the force generator to destroy the submarine?"

Jack gave Mark the floor. "General, we plotted the track of the submarine, which didn't deviate at all because they knew your country would not be allowed to intervene in its mission. We also computed the approximate location where it would fire from. Because of the blast radius underwater the sub had to deliver the torpedoes from a safe distance.

Jack and I were already in scuba gear in the water at that location when the submarine approached us and went to periscope depth for a launch of the vertically orientated missiles. I attached a hydrophone speaker to the casing of

189

the sub on the conning tower to allow us to warn them in Russian that if they tried to destroy the island they themselves would be destroyed."

Mark shook his head. "We were sure they would ignore the warning and fire anyway. So, we swam over to the VLA torpedo tubes were. When they opened the outer doors of two of the tubes we placed C-4 explosive charges just inside the tubes. When they fired the torpedoes up the tubes it detonated the charges which blocked the way. We knew that the blasts would trigger the torpedo nuclear warheads which would then detonate. What we didn't know was that they were much bigger than the normal nuclear tipped torpedoes. Charlie Wu estimated after the explosion that each torpedo had a one-megaton warhead instead of the tactical warhead in the two kiloton range. When the torpedoes detonated it vaporized the submarine in the first second of the explosion."

The General sighed. "Such stupidity on their part." He looked at Jack and Mark standing there with him. "And you two were within a few hundred yards of the explosion?"

Mark smiled, "Actually, we were within a few dozen feet of the explosion and I am very glad to tell you that the force generators worked perfectly."

The General considered that statement and asked, "What was it like to be at the heart of a nuclear blast of that size?"

Jack laughed, "Very unimpressive. Everything went white and then settled down after about thirty seconds as the sea rushed in to fill in the void created by the explosion. We didn't feel anything through the force generator's protection and the field is connected somehow to the Earth's gravitational field so we weren't thrown miles away or anything. We swam about a half mile toward the island when a ship, which was waiting behind the island, concealed from the submarine, picked us up. They didn't even have to decontaminate us for radiation because we didn't get any radiation through the field generated by the devices. That's the whole story. We will ask that you don't mention the field generators because it could cause a useless arms race."

The General could see that. "All right, I'll keep that out of my report. No one would believe me anyway. I want to commend your bravery regardless of the technical genius of the force generator. You couldn't have known for sure it would protect you in the heart of a nuclear reaction."

Mark smiled, "True, but God did know and told us not to be afraid."

CHAPTER FORTY-SEVEN

After General Levy left the base, Jack and Laura went to their apartment to relax.

Laura studied Jack for a few minutes and then asked him, "Weren't you the least bit scared to be right there when the atom bombs went off?"

Jack sighed, "Of course I was scared. But, I beat the fear back with the knowledge that God is supreme in all things and He had told me to do what we did. When I confessed the fear as disbelief He took the fear away and I was filled with a great peace. Mark didn't really explain the instant of the explosion to the General in full detail. Actually, there was a split second when we saw the fundamental construction of all matter in the universe within the heart of the explosion. There were instantaneous colors beyond belief and for that tiny fragment of time we were at the place like unto the heart of the Sun and all creation was evident before our eyes. It was very humbling and exciting at the same time. Of course, if we didn't have the force generators our eyes would have melted in that same instant. God bless Doctor Clashire and his conversion which led to his obedience to Yahshua and his persistence in developing the force generator units."

Laura snuggled up to Jack on the couch. "I sort of envy you and Mark but I'm not sure I could have gutted it up to do what you two did."

Jack laughed quietly, "Seeing some of the monsters you have fought I think I prefer the nuclear explosion. I gave all the glory to Yahveh and Yahshua. I have never felt more satisfaction being a child of God than I did at the instant the bombs went off; it was simply amazing. I got to see the building blocks of the universe that God created and I lived to tell you about it."

They continued to sit together there in comfort for a while when suddenly Jack's communicator started ringing.

Jack answered and heard the familiar tones of General Levy. "Jack, I need your help immediately. I'm trapped in my vehicle three blocks from your base by what appears to be a demon. It has disabled my vehicle and is attempting to get to me. If it wasn't for the armor-plating and bullet-proof glass, I wouldn't be making this call. Several of my men have been seriously wounded or killed trying to stop this thing; I don't know how many are dead. Please hurry."

Jack prayed and said, "General, you will be safe for a while. It doesn't want you. It's using you to get us to come out to fight it. We're on the way right now." Jack hung up and told Laura to call Mark.

Laura was up and pulling on her boots. "My call was from Sarah. She and Mark are already on the way to the General's location. I heard what you told the General and warned them about it being a trap."

Jack was worried about his friends but they were very capable and had their armor to protect them. Still, he hurried and ran to a transport vehicle that was waiting at the entrance to the base. They made it to the elevator nearest to the General's position and hit the Emergency/Override switch which made the elevator car race up to the surface like a missile.

They were met just outside the portal door by one of the Mossad SUVs and jumped in. They made the three blocks in less than one minute. During the entire race to get to the General Jack was communicating through Charlie Wu to the other team members and the Mossad for the backup they needed. Laura was praying that the Father would release His angels to back them up.

They exited the SUV praying and their armor and swords appeared. Jack could see Mark and Sarah battling with the large demon. This time it seemed the demon was holding his own against their swords. Jack spoke into his combat microphone. "Mark, Sarah drop back and bring it towards the General's vehicle. We'll join in the dance at that point."

Mark and Sarah started to back-pedal slowly. The demon came at them until it saw Jack and Laura boxing it in. Then it stopped moving and opened a large interdimensional rift. It tried to make one big enough it could encircle all of the combatants but started having trouble maintaining the consistency of the rift.

Jack; with Laura by his side moved slowly back from the demon and the rift. Jack was praying a deep prayer for the Father's help in preventing this spawn of Satan from capturing anyone.

The demon grew in size until it was ten feet tall and much more massive. It began to expand the rift when Jack's sword disappeared. More demons could be seen in the rift when Jack felt a familiar weight in his right hand. He looked and there was the iridescent javelin that had the diamond tip with the power of Yahveh coming off of it in waves of power.

Jack took a stance and then took two big running steps toward the demon and hurled the lance at the demon's heart. The demon put its sword in front of himself to ward off the lance. The lance went through the sword and then the demon itself. The demon began to dissipate as it died and the lance entered the rift when it exploded with a clap of thunder and a power wave that knocked everyone on the human side of the rift down including the members of the team with their armor.

The sudden clap of power snapped the rift closed with the power of God shining like the sun in the darkness inside the rift as it snapped shut.

Quiet returned to the street and with a metal wrenching sound the door to the damaged vehicle was forced open. General Levy stepped out and surveyed the scene. There were several dozen citizens cowering nearby. There were the bodies of four of his soldiers lying in the state of disarray that death leaves one in. The armor of the Crossfire Team faded away with their swords and shields. But, they were still moving with purpose. Jack and Laura grabbed the General by the arms and moved him away from his damaged vehicle and along the sidewalk to the SUV they had come in.

They got in with the General and the driver used reverse to good effect and backed up a full block's length at speed. The SUV spun around and raced forward back to the base entrance where the three passengers got out and raced into the base's surface entrance. Jack got them into an elevator and down to the base level in half the time it normally took. The General ran with them to one of the surface travel carts and hung on for dear life as Laura piloted them back to the Crossfire part of the base. They slowed down after entering the base itself.

As they stood there getting their breaths back, General Levy asked between gulps of air, "I take it that there is more about to happen?"

Jack nodded, "Yes Sir. Carol told me on the way to the scene of your attack that the whole thing was an elaborate trap and that it will continue for the next hour."

Laura picked up the story. "This base is protected by the angels of Heaven and is outside the reach of the enemy. That's why we rushed you here. Please listen to Charlie and try to relax and rest. We've got to go back and defeat this attack."

The General was about to say something when the two warriors saluted him and took off back out the entrance. Charlie Wu's voice sounded near the General. "Welcome General Levy. If you will follow the arrows on the floor, I will have you come to our Communications and Security area and you can follow the battle from here."

CHAPTER FORTY-EIGHT

Jack contacted Charlie as they hurried back to the scene of the attack. "Is everything ready?"

Charlie laughed lightly. "Oh boy is it. The Mossad got the IDF fired up full speed when they found out that General Levy was involved. You've got everything you wanted waiting for your direction."

Jack broke the connection and told Laura, "You fill in Mark and Sarah and be ready to duck. I think that fake angel Orion lied about them never using the mass attack on us again."

Laura frowned, "Didn't Raquel tell us that what Orion told us was essentially true?"

Jack thought back. "No, Orion told us, ""*That type of attack will never happen again against your team*." Raquel confirmed that the Word of Power did great damage to the demon's realm. But, Raquel did not confirm that mass attacks against us would not happen again. I think this is the way the demonic world will try to attack us today because they believe we won't be ready for another mass attack."

They reached the area of the attack and Jack checked with the IDF to see if they were ready. The IDF controller for this action confirmed that they were very ready.

As Jack and Laura walked up to Mark and Sarah they noticed that the streets were clear of bodies, civilians and anything else that could be warned away or removed from the area.

Laura was praying in the Spirit as usual when her armor suddenly appeared along with her sword. In a reflex the other team members began to pray and their armor also appeared. There were multiple, loud rumbling, crackling, and shrieking sounds as a dozen rifts opened up to the demonic world and Jack could see hundreds of demons poised to charge into the human dimension.

Jack said just three words over the comm-link to the IDF. "Do it now."

For a few seconds dozens of demons in the front ranks rushed into the world unimpeded. With a tremendous roar, twelve Israeli Delilah cruise missiles blasted by only feet over their heads and into each rift. As they flew into the rift each missile detonated so violently that the rifts were destroyed and disappeared.

Mark jumped up from where the explosions had thrown him. He found Jack and said, "What did you do?"

Jack pried himself out of a pile of debris and shook dust off of his armor which then faded as did Mark's as they quit praying. "Not much, I just wanted to send the proper message to Satan to stop trying to overwhelm us. I had the IDF and the Israeli Air Force launch twelve of their loitering cruise missiles into a tight orbit around this place until the rifts opened up. I remember how Charlie used Hellfire missiles in that canyon when we were being overwhelmed to shut three rifts. I did add one thing that required the authorization of the Prime Minister. I had them replace the warhead in each missile with a tactical nuke."

Mark was stunned. "What is with you? You like playing with nuclear weapons?" Mark couldn't hide a grin as he talked. "This is the second time in a week we've used them."

Jack shrugged; I wanted the message to be loud and clear. By the way, I got a word from the Holy Spirit that the demons would be coming at us from twelve directions that is why I had the right number of missiles waiting for them to open the rifts."

Mark looked around, "I think those blasts took care of the demons that came out first."

Jack smiled, "I haven't seen any, but I thought that there may be some demons that had permission to be here and they wouldn't be destroyed by bullets or bombs. That would probably include nuclear weapons."

Jack's comm beeped. Laura spoke to him, "Jack, please come back to the area near the General's vehicle."

Jack and Mark automatically started to pray and their armor appeared. They ran over to the vehicle to find Laura, Sarah, and David in their armor with a demon sitting on the ground between them. Jack asked Laura, "What's going on?"

Laura said, "This one wants to surrender, supposedly."

Jack prayed to Yahshua, "Heavenly Master Yahshua, what do we do with this demon?"

The answer was clear and immediate. "Destroy him."

Jack stepped between Laura and David and ran his sword through the demon's throat so violently he beheaded the demon as it sat there. It dissolved into slimy smoke and disappeared.

Laura frowned and looked at Jack. "Why did you . . ."

Jack cut her off. "Rose told me to never give a demon a break because they will use it against you. Their only goals are to kill, steal, and destroy. We are not even supposed to talk to them. I prayed for direction and Yahshua told me to destroy him immediately. Not too long ago I hesitated in destroying a demon and it took advantage of that compassion and was about to kill me and I would have died if Rose hadn't stepped in and destroyed it. "

As their armor faded along with their swords Laura nodded her head. "You're right. I was letting my human compassion override my duty. It won't happen again." Sarah and David seconded her comments.

Mark walked over to them and asked, "How do you think the demonic realm will respond to us frying them with twelve nuclear bombs?"

Jack shook his head. "I don't know, hopefully they will resist losing that many of their demons in a single attack against us."

David laughed, "I could see you trying to get the U.S. government to allow us to use nuclear weapons on such short notice."

Sarah smiled, "They would have had to form a committee to determine if they should even entertain such an idea."

Laura frowned again and asked Jack, "I'm concerned about such a major response. I hope you got God's leading before you used Israeli nuclear weapons on the demonic realm. I don't know that we had the authority to do that."

Jack thought about his wife's comment. He realized he had, again, resorted to using his ability instead of asking God what to do.

CHAPTER FORTY-NINE

After they returned to the base, Jack went to one of the private rooms on the SOG level to pray.

He praised Yahshua and asked Him to cleanse him in the Blood of the Lamb and to forgive his sins, especially the sin of pride. While he was praying he felt the heaviness in his spirit when he was in contact with the Holy Spirit. He asked Yahshua for understanding of what his pride may have caused by acting without seeking permission from Him first.

Jack recognized the voice of Yahshua, his lord. *"Jack, in your zeal to stop the enemy from attacking your group you decided in your mind to seek the correct answer. You know that the mind, governed by the flesh is hostile to God; it does not submit to God's law, nor can it do so. You should know better than to conform to the pattern of this world, but you should be transformed by the renewing of your mind. Then you will be able to test and approve what God's will is—His good, pleasing and perfect will. But, since you have humbled yourself and asked for forgiveness I have granted you that forgiveness. In this matter you are free, free indeed. I urge you to carefully consider your decisions regarding your actions in the future."*

"Your use of these weapons has changed the relationship between your team and the enemy. You achieved your goal of preventing more attacks of that kind, but at what cost? This unilateral action has made the destruction of you and your team even more important to Satan. Especially because you used his own rebellion against God when he opened the portals to allow demons God did not authorize into the human dimension. Satan, by his own actions, allowed you to profoundly damage his kingdom over Israel."

"Satan will now direct the false Christ to use the New World Order's military arm of RHONE in a directed effort to find and destroy the Crossfire Team, regardless of the costs. Be fully warned that this will be a very intensive effort. Yet, you have crippled the enemy's efforts to come

against my believers by centering his attention on you and your team. I will be with you and your team forever. I will not forsake you or abandon you."

Jack cried out, "I truly am sorry for my rashness. Eternal Holy Spirit of God, please, please help me to remember to do all things in your will not my own."

The tears fell as Jack felt the love and closeness of his Savior.

Sometime later Jack went back and walked into the War Room to return to the battle.

Laura saw him and was concerned by the look on his face. She got up from her seat and came to him and embraced him with a closeness and warmth he needed right then. He held her for a few minutes and then kissed her and stood back to look at her. He smiled and put his arm around her as they walked back to the console.

Jack asked the core team to assemble in the War Room. After they arrived, he identified Laura, Mark, Sarah, David, Alexis, Charlie Wu, Linda Wu, Su Li, and Mike White in addition to himself. Ten warriors of God and all true believers.

Jack made sure the recorders were on and addressed the group gathered at the consoles around the main desk. "Guys, I have a confession to make to you all. One of my main weaknesses is familiar to us all and especially to you Mark. It is being prideful and standing on my own understanding and capabilities instead of relying on Yahshua or Yahveh to direct my steps, again."

Jack looked at his wife. "As I said, we all fall victim to this sin. Well, I just put all of your necks on the devil's chopping block because I "figured out" what I thought was the right response to the mass attacks they were using against us. I didn't ask the Lord if this was the right thing to do. I just made a "logical" decision in my mind and then involved God's people, the nation of Israel, in my decision to use nuclear-tipped warheads to close the rifts with extreme prejudice. I assumed that the Lord would back the plan, and essentially He did by allowing the Israeli Air Force to use those weapons, which Israel tells everybody they don't have, to send a message to Satan."

Jack thought for a few seconds, "I went into prayer when we returned and I got a very stern reminder from our

Lord that our battles are not won by my strength or might but by the Spirit of God. The central topic was that I should have asked if it was the right thing to do. I can assure you that it was not the right thing to do. It apparently has accomplished my goal to stop those types of mass attacks on us but I personally have moved us to one of the top spots in Satan's hate list and have incurred the wrath of Satan in the form of an intense effort by the Anti-Christ and RHONE to eliminate each and every one of us."

He looked around the group. "I want to deeply apologize for bringing this focus on us and I also want to ask each and every one of you for forgiveness for my rash and egotistical decision."

Everyone but Mark spoke from the heart and forgave their friend and leader. Mark waited until everyone else was finished and then said, "Old buddy, I forgive you but want to remind you that our mission is to find and eliminate RHONE if possible. I can't think of a better way to find them than to have them seeking us. You did act rashly by not checking in with the Lord but in the bigger scheme you have announced our intentions by singeing the hair on Satan's tail so that he understands we're serious." Mark stood up and started clapping his hands. He was quickly joined by everyone else. When the applause died down and everyone sat down again, Jack said, "Thank you all. And a special thanks to Mark for putting the best face on my mistake. I love each one of you and you make me proud to fight alongside of you."

Laura spoke to Charlie, "You need to get this information to the SOG and to all the part-timers on our payroll. They will also be considered prime targets for RHONE because of their connection to the team."

Charlie had been typing while the conversation was going on. "Already done Laura."

Mark stood up. "Let's pray for guidance and then brainstorm our options. We're a little handicapped until we see what RHONE is up to concerning us but, let's consider bloodying their nose to get them going the way WE want them to go."

CHAPTER FIFTY

As they were praying Jack's comm unit vibrated against his arm. He stopped praying and studied the readout. Rising quietly so as to not disturb the others he padded out of the War Room and went into the living room.

He pushed the comm switch and asked, "Yes Carol, what do you need?"

Carol Moffet's voice was troubled. "Jack, I really don't like what I'm seeing in the matrix for the team. Can I meet with you for a few minutes?"

Jack agreed to meet with her in fifteen minutes. He hung up and went back into the War Room. He sat down and tapped on his console to get everyone's attention. "I think one of our answers to our prayers is about to present itself. Carol will be here in about twelve minutes to tell us what the matrix shows concerning the team. She seems very concerned about the data she is finding there. I want everyone here to listen to her report and consider the possibilities. After she is done with her report we will discuss it."

Carol walked in and Jack pointed to her position at the circular console. She seated herself and turned on the recorders. She looked at each one of the people there and then fixed her vision on Jack. "I have spent several hours trying to understand the flood of information that is appearing on the matrix concerning the team."

Carol sighed and Jack could tell she was agitated and fatigued from her efforts. She continued, "The events shown are strange because they do not include any direct contact between the demonic realm and the Crossfire Team. I believe it is directions for people on the Earth to accomplish things against the team, to locate the team, and many other operations. They appear to be centering their efforts on Israel and not the U.S. There just are no demonic efforts involved against the team. Because most things done on Earth are not shown on the matrix I can't see the efforts or their timing. I am becoming useless to warn you about attacks or efforts against the team other than to tell you that there are major efforts being demanded by Satan concerning the team. For the matrix and for my participation this is where the lines end." She seemed downcast and pretty well defeated.

Jack prayed for guidance and heard from the Lord. "Thank you Carol. We appreciate your honest evaluation of your situation as you see it. But, speaking from a more experienced standpoint I would suggest you use this time to pray for as much more training as Hugo can give you in the more advanced uses of the matrix. Also, I need to comment about your increasing role with the team. I asked the Lord about this new lack of vision on the matrix. I was told that it is only a temporary lull because Satan is giving control of our elimination to RHONE. RHONE doesn't have to ask God for permission to operate in the human dimension so none of their plans will be seen there unless a demon or an angel becomes involved with us."

Jack got up and went over to Carol. She stood up and Jack hugged her. He stepped back and smiled at her. "As soon as we have scored enough significant victories over RHONE, or they aren't able to destroy us in the time allotted by Satan then the demonic world will again be petitioning God for permission to go after us. So, this time is actually only a vacation for you. The word that God gave me is that you will be very busy, soon. That bodes well for the team because it means that RHONE will fail. Do you see the bigger picture?"

Carol was grinning. "Oh yeah, I will pray about it but what you have said rings true in my spirit and I apologize for letting my lack of work defeat my purpose that the Father gave me." She hugged Jack and waved to everyone else and left for her suite.

Mark smiled, "I see why you were the President of your own company. That was the best pep talk I've heard since I gave one to a bunch of mentally defeated Navy Seals." Mark stood up and saluted Jack. "I bow to your superior people skills."

Sarah laughed, "Yes sir, I also believe that encouraging people does come in more favorable than that of just killing someone to resolve the situation. All though, good can be achieved that way too."

David had been thinking, "I see what you meant about that being one of the answers to our prayers Jack. It confirms that Satan has given his problem of the Crossfire Team over to the Anti-Christ and RHONE. Let's plan on that to start with." Mark held up his right hand. "Keeping in mind that the demonic can jump in at any time if they want to."

Jack sat back down at the console. "Okay, first things first. Let's make this base as invisible to outsiders as possible. I recommend that we close all three auxiliary portals and elevators and only use the one that even the Israeli government believes leads only to a Mossad operation."

"Charlie, see if you can improve our satellite coverage and our ground-based defenses to prevent anyone from seeing our aircraft anywhere near the island above us.

Charlie nodded and left for the computer center.

Mark thought about RHONE for a few minutes and asked Linda Wu to see what she could find out about it through the military and clandestine information on the web.

Laura started praying for enlightenment from God concerning their opponent and their methods. David called a friend at the Mossad while Alexis did the same at the U.S. National Clandestine Service in Washington, D.C.

Jack and Mark sat at a separate table and discussed the enemy.

Mark shook his head. "RHONE is obviously capable of out-gunning us with the Anti-Christ behind them. That submarine for example is beyond our capabilities."

Jack nodded, "Yeah, they definitely have a much bigger military capability than we could manage. Therefore, we can't go head-to-head with them in that arena. We need to find another way to keep them from walking over us and to bring them down."

CHAPTER FIFTY-ONE

For the next three days everyone dug into the secret group known only as RHONE. Scheduled breaks kept them fresh as they practiced their swordsmanship, martial arts, weapons, swimming, underwater assault, and other focused activities.

On the fourth day Jack called everyone together in the War Room again for an update on RHONE.

Mark stated off first. "This is one of the best examples I've ever even heard about displaying the effects of evil in one group. They seem to have cornered the market on bigots, low-life, anti-Semites, perverts, and schemers of every kind. The sad thing is that the military arm of RHONE has a lot of really talented people. But, they are all messed up in one way or the other. How they maintain discipline is beyond me but somehow they do it. They have over a hundred thousand men and women around the world in hidden bases. All of these people are on call for anything the Anti-Christ wants them to do. That includes killing innocent men, women, and children without a thought or care."

Sarah spoke up. "I can tell you how they do it. The disciplinary control of the RHONE military is based on the carrot and the stick reward system. If the soldier does as told and is effective they get rewarded by whatever means the most to them. Money, power, control, sadism, pedophilia, murder, rape, or any other "treat" they desire. That's the carrot for good performance. There is only one stick and that is to die. Step out of line, say the wrong thing, do the wrong thing, whatever, they are killed by the elite fifteen-hundred seemingly supernatural SS troops that report only to the supreme leader of RHONE. The regular troops know that they are watched constantly and any deviation from approved conduct or action, no matter how small or well hidden, results in a quick and horrible death which serves as an example to the other troops to stay in line. My data indicates that they have eliminated over twenty-five thousand of their troops in the last eight years.

And, there are always ten new recruits waiting to fill every emptied slot."

Laura stood up. "The reason that the troops can't get away with anything, I believe, is because there are demons watching the troops all the time. As evil spirits they can be in the room with one of the troops completely undetected and see what the soldier tries to hide. This gets passed onto the SS troops and that's the end for that soldier. This is an efficient method since most of them don't believe there are such things as demons anyway."

Mark finished up the military evaluation of the troops of RHONE. "They are only mediocre as armies go. Their dedication is bought, their enthusiasm is by requirement, and their cooperation is forced. Still the commanders of these troops know how to make battle victories. Normally they do it through sheer numbers. Spy work and precise operations are routed through and accomplished by the SS division."

Linda Wu stood up and addressed the group in a clear voice that wasn't loud but commanded attention. "The short history of this RHONE group is that they formed immediately after World War II in Germany. They were vicious and very discrete so that they couldn't be brought to justice for the crimes they committed. They accomplished their anonymity by eliminating anyone that could compromise the operations or members of RHONE."

Linda looked around at the others in the War Room. "The elitist power groups which also survived the overthrow of Nazi Germany forged an alliance with the RHONE in 1950 and used them as their military arm. The RHONE became very well-funded and world-wide under this arrangement. Their basic make-up and operational capabilities were the same, hatred for Jews, Poles, Christians, Muslims, and almost every other organized group that didn't think like them. They literally worshipped Hitler until the early 2000s. That is when Satan got really involved and they became associated with the up and coming Marco Marino, the Anti-Christ. I was able to determine that the RHONE supreme commander is an Italian named Carlo Ricci. He is a personal friend of Marco Marino and was a General in the Italian army. He has operational bases in New York, London, Madrid, Rome,

Naples, as well as several in places in China, Russia, and the Middle East. He tends to keep a rolling operation and never remains in one place for long as a protection against assassination."

Mark added, "The very method of his operation can be an opening for us. If we can track him and predict where he will be at any given time, then we can prepare a site to take him out."

Laura questioned that tactic. "But, won't the Anti-Christ just replace him with another leader?"

Jack nodded, "Sure, but the uncertainty created by our being able to get to him will have ripple effects throughout the RHONE establishment that will knock it out of its normal functioning and possibly open up other cracks we can exploit. I suggest we concentrate of finding him, questioning him, and removing him from his position."

CHAPTER FIFTY-TWO

Only Jack and Mark heard the soft voice near their ears. It was Charlie Wu's voice. "Could you two get away for a few minutes and come to ComSec and see me? I have some interesting information."

Jack got up and walked out of the War Room followed by Mark while the other core team members continued to discuss the information for an assault on the leader of RHONE.

Charlie greeted them and had them sit down next to him. He brought up a man's picture on the main screen on the wall in front of his desk. "This is the latest picture of Carlo Ricci from a CIA data base. The picture showed a dynamic man probably six-foot-tall with salt and pepper colored hair. His posture, the look on his face, and his dress all said, "Leader". His skin was either well-tanned or he had an olive complexion. But, it was his eyes that grabbed the attention. He looked driven and angry. Those eyes said that the man would not accept any failure. On his part or for anyone working for him.

Mark grunted, "Yeah, I've seen this guy before. Six years ago in a joint U.S. Navy, Italian Navy exercise. He was a visiting Army General. As I recall he was a real nit-picker then. Nothing escaped his eyes and he wasn't shy about calling out officers as well as ratings for mistakes. When the U.S. Navy Seals made the Italian team look bad in one exercise General Ricci snapped his clipboard in half in anger and dissatisfaction. One of our Navy officers called Ricci a perfectionist and a real pain for anyone who didn't measure up to his standards. On a positive note, the General never asked anybody to do anything he couldn't do. At least during the joint exercises."

Jack nodded, "That's good Intel guys. Now, Charlie, can you figure a way to determine where he will be and what his vulnerabilities are which would give us an edge?

Charlie reached over and picked up a thick pad of paper which he handed to Mark. "There you go guys. Crayton put that together a few minutes ago."

Jack looked over Mark's shoulder as they paged through the report. Mark closed it and looked at Jack. "I am impressed. This Crayton plan has all the hallmarks of being a masterpiece in the spy game book of the year contest."

Jack slapped Charlie on the shoulder. "You need to give Crayton a promotion or at least a raise."

Charlie laughed, "What, like more electricity?"

After returning to the War Room Jack threw Carlo Ricci's picture up on the main screen and then explained the Crayton plan to the rest of the team. David slapped his thigh and laughed. "That has to be one for the annuals. I would never have dreamed up something that wild, yet doable."

Alexis nodded. "I like it. If we live through it, then I want a sanitized copy to give to the guys back at the Clandestine Service in D.C."

Laura smiled and told Jack, "Okay, super spies, why don't you spell this out for us that haven't lived in the black ops world."

Jack nodded, "All right. Crayton's plan uses RHONEs own operation to give us an opportunity to remove Carlo Ricci from his staff without risking our lives."

Laura smiled slightly, "How?"

Jack put his hand up to give Mark the floor.

Mark smiled, "Well, Charlie had Crayton do all the heavy lifting on this one." Charlie's voice came out of the air. "I heard that." Everyone laughed and Mark continued. "Crayton was able to study all the previous data on Ricci's movements because the FBI and CIA have been tracking his group ever since he left the Italian military. Crayton was able to discern patterns in the seemingly random movements that Ricci makes every month. I think it is because Ricci has certain functions or meetings that he needs to attend each month and that sets part of his movements consistently during a given month. "

"I figure it probably took ten microseconds for Crayton to determine all the places that Ricci is going to be and pick the place to hit him that gives us the best probability of a win. I personally think that the problem will be our getaway. We control things up until we become visible in their world. Then they will bring all the guns they can train on us and things could get dicey."

Jack spoke up, "That is the awesomeness of this plan. We are going to snatch Carlo Ricci and be completely gone without a trace before they become aware of anything happening."

Mark threw a picture up on the main screen. "Here is Ricci's plush, ultra-modern stateroom on his own private railroad passenger car that travels from Rome to Naples on the Italian Hi-Speed Rail Line. Actually, the whole car is his stateroom."

David asked, "Doesn't the train travel around 300 KPH?"

Mark grinned, "Yes it does, and with some help from the Mossad we're going to steal Carlo Ricci out of his stateroom at speed."

Alexis grinned, "Sounds like Mission Impossible. Tell us more."

Mark nodded, "Okay. The key to this snatch is that Carlo has a duplicate car in Rome in the event that the normal car has any problems. Since we are talking about Italy, this event occurs fairly frequently, like once every sixty days or so. We are going to walk in under the very noses of Ricci's troops and the railroad managers and modify the second car. Then, just before he arrives to board his car, we sabotage it. The replacement car will be substituted for the original car and we are set."

Mark displayed another picture on the main screen. "This, ladies and gentlemen, is Carlo Ricci's super zoomy toilet. Notice three things about this commode. The first is that it includes a throne-like toilet. The second thing is that the part of the bathroom that contains the toilet is circular in design so that when used it rotates closed so as to not offend anyone by just sitting there or needing a door. The third thing is that it is located directly against the outer wall of the car. We are going to modify the replacement car so that when Carlo rotates the toilet so that he can use it, we take control."

Mark added several drawings to the picture on the screen. "When Carlo enters the commode, the unit rotates to the shut position. When he is seated on his throne, a knockout gas will be administered, rendering him

210

unconscious. Four padded clamps will secure him in his seat and the outer wall will slide aside displaying Carlo for the world to see. At that precise moment the throne will catapult Carlo out of the train to be captured by us. We will have modified the seat arrangement so that it will eject Carlo and still leave the toilet essentially untouched. The seat will retract and the door will slide shut and we will leave with Carlo for a place far away. By the time his companion calls his troops because Carlo has not come out of the toilet nor responded to her knocking we will have Carlo Ricci over a hundred miles away."

David asked, "How will we know when he will be using the train or using the toilet?

Jack replied, "That is where the Mossad comes in for the second time. You see, Carlo uses the train primarily when he wants to make a conquest of a suitably desirable woman. The Mossad will make sure that their agent will be the suitably desirable woman and is selected by a lust-smitten Carlo Ricci. When she is in his love nest she will doctor his food or drink with a small bit of chemical, at the right time, which will quickly require him to use the potty."

Laura laughed, "I like it but still don't know how we are going to come alongside a train traveling roughly 160 miles per hour, catch a catapulted Carlo without killing him, and do it in plain sight of everyone on board as well as the predictable cameras covering the train from the front and the back."

Charlie's voice spoke out of thin air."The modified computer we will put in the car will use a virus to take over the cameras and run a long loop during the capture time."

Su Li tipped her head to one side, "I expect I will be the one to "catch" this Carlo who is being shot into a hundred-sixty-miles-an-hour slipstream without being seen, right?"

Mark smiled, "No, actually you're going to be the backup pilot to Mike White and see how he does this. The outside snatch will be covered by a double-edged sword, it will be pitch black and he'll only have thirty seconds or five and a half miles to drop in, get the package, and pull pitch while the train is between two tunnels."

Su Li smiled and shook her head. "This I gotta see."

CHAPTER FIFTY-THREE

Charlie Wu called Mark. "Mark I managed to get the complete detail specifications on Carlo's replacement car including the amazing spinning toilet. I am sending them to you along with Crayton's suggestions on how to put the changes we need into it the quickest way yet keep it undetectable."

Mark said "Thanks buddy" and scanned the schematics. He called for Jack and Alexis to come to the War Room and start figuring how to make these semi-major changes in less than eight hours in Italy while Carlo's goons and the Italian train people were around.

David called the Mossad and requested a senior agent to help with their "project". Two hours later Parker Abbas was led into the War Room by Laura. After greeting everyone there he settled in to talk to David and Jack.

"How can I be of assistance?" Parker was a senior field agent manager that had worked with the team to prevent a nuclear bombing in the tunnels under the Western Wall in Jerusalem just a month before.

David explained what they were doing to counteract an all-out war against the team by RHONE.

Parker sat back and considered the consequences of such an action. "You know; we don't have a real case against Carlo Ricci that would stand up in any court in the world. We know his character and we're aware of the thousands of employees he's had killed but there are no direct links to him. If you do this and get caught you will be considered as criminals and worse, terrorists."

David nodded, "We know that. The question is, will the Mossad help us in this matter? If we are detected, then Israel would get a black eye in the international media and governments."

Parker looked at his old friend, the man that had trained him years before. "David, you were with the Mossad years longer than I. You know that the worry about being caught or identified is not an operational concern. The leaders of the Mossad owe this team a tremendous debt and that won't worry them so much. I think they'll go along with it. I don't know that they will be willing to sacrifice an agent if things would go wrong on your side of the operation."

Sarah and Alexis both said, "I'll do it if they won't."

Parker looked at both of the women. "Sarah, I think you are far too much an Israeli for Carlo Ricci. He hates Israel and doesn't think highly of their women. Alexis on the other hand is probably exactly what he is always looking for in a beautiful, available woman."

While always competitive, Sarah realized the truth in Parker's words. She looked at Alexis. "Well girl, we have some work to do if you are to be the chosen one."

When Parker went back to the Mossad to pitch the idea and get a go-no go decision, Mark and Jack worked on the modifications that would work to make Crayton's plan a success. Jack quickly realized they needed professional help on the mechanical level. Mark asked, "Do you think Dr. Clashire would be able to help?"

Jack shook his head, "No, Clashire is a theoretical physicist and we need a hands-on mechanical engineer who is capable of producing a working prototype in less than two weeks."

Mark frowned, "That means bringing in an outsider who could compromise the team now or later, especially since the Anti-Christ and RHONE have bundles of money and Marino is being seen as the Messiah of peace throughout the non-Christian world."

Jack smiled, "Maybe we don't have to bring in an outsider. I seem to recall that several of the SOG candidates we interviewed were in the military mechanical fields."

Mark nodded, "I will check this out." He got up and left for the SOG area.

Alexis came over with Laura and they both sat down on the chairs near Jack.

Laura asked, "Jack have you prayed about this action and asked the Lord if this is His will?"

Jack grinned at his wife. "Oh yeah. After Charlie showed us Crayton's plan I sought permission to pursue this course. God is in agreement that Carlo Ricci needs to be destroyed for his hatred of Yahveh's chosen people."

Laura laughed, "Well, there you go."

Alexis looked thoughtful so Jack asked her, "Do you think you can do this if the Mossad isn't inclined to do so?"

Alexis focused on Jack and smiled. "Sure, actually I've done more dangerous operations with even greater potential for disaster. I'll be able to buffalo this ex-General easily and get the results you need. It's my exit plan I'm concerned about. I will be the only connection between Carlo being okay and Carlo being gone. It may not be an unrealistic projection to think that the underlings will want to "grill" me really hard. Everyone can be broken if enough pressure and drugs are used. It may be a dead end for me if we succeed."

Jack thought about that and realized she was right. "Then let's plan it so that they don't get that opportunity."

Alexis' left eyebrow went up a notch. "Just how much can you do to save me without compromising the entire snatch operation?"

Jack smiled, "Let me run this by our newest tactician, Crayton."

CHAPTER FIFTY-FOUR

Mark walked into the Sensitive Operations Group area and spoke to the "Colonel Brian Owens" who was in charge of the unit. "Hi Brian, how is it going?"

The Colonel shook Mark's hand and tipped his head to one side. "It's not easy keeping all these sharp people sharp without constant action. I would like permission to second the SOG to the IDF whenever we are in stand down mode. I realize we're on call twenty-four, seven but I could insist on that with the IDF. Also, the fact that we've had experience with demonic involvement and we're all now trained and equipped to battle demons would be a major asset to them. This could also free up the core team."

Mark grinned and nodded his head, "Thought that through didn't you?"

Bob grinned back. "Yes I did, General."

Mark stared at the man for a few seconds. "Did you also think it through that the enemy will notice these changes and decide to use demons to pick off your people one at a time?"

"Brian nodded, "Yes Sir. Our people will only go out in teams of four. They are already getting Intel from the core group as to what to watch for and what to do in attack events. Laura seems very well versed in this type of action."

Mark looked out at the troops training in close quarters combat and approved of the activity. "All right Colonel, I'll run it by the Malones and see if it flies. Personally, I think it's a good idea and will tell them so. But, I've come here for another need. Who in this SOG is the best mechanical designer and hands-on engineer in the mechanical field?"

Brian didn't even take time to consider the answer. "Megan Cole, a Marine expert, hands down."

Mark nodded, "Could you bring her here for me to talk to?"

The Colonel saluted Mark who crisply returned the salute. Mark maintained the highest level of service quality since leaving the Navy, which included saluting correctly.

As the Colonel returned with Sgt. Cole, Mark evaluated her. She was Caucasian, about five foot, six inches in height, probably a hundred and forty-five pounds, black hair, looking very fit and strong. She was attractive with an infectious smile. She stopped three steps from Mark and saluted him, "Sergeant Cole reporting as ordered."

Mark felt like he was back in the service again as he returned her salute. "At ease, Sergeant. Grab a chair; we need to talk about a mission."

Mark knew this would ease her worries about being summoned and would allow her to focus on the request. He also knew from her handshake that she wasn't awed by talking to a General, but she was courteous.

Mark studied her for a few seconds. "Megan, the core team has an urgent need for a master mechanical designer and mechanic to put together some clandestine equipment and install it within the next ten days. Would you be interested in this challenge?"

She thought about his statement for several seconds. "Yes Sir."

Mark nodded, "This will also require you to travel to a foreign land and perform installation of your design under very tight time constraints, in the enemy's camp. Are you still interested?"

She grinned, "Is there ever anything that needs to be done slowly and openly in the clandestine world? I think that is a requirement and it is what I've trained on since I joined the Marines. In fact,", she grinned," one of the best t-shirts recruiting for the Marines states, "Join the U.S. Marine Corp, visit foreign lands, meet exciting and unique people, kill them."

Mark grinned at that. He asked her, "What have you done before along these lines under urgent time constraints?"

Megan's memories of such a time filled her mind.

-----------------------******-----------------------

"As a member of the Marine Support Team, considering my skill set, I was directed to accompany three scientists flying into Iraq right after the invasion in Desert Shield. My assignment was to help the scientists in finding and disarming a possible WMD at the Iraqi Airport. It turned out that the actual location was a half mile west of the airport in a bunker that was still in contested territory. We had a squad of U.S. Marines for protection and two Humvees. We reached the site around 0100 local time and searched the bunker without finding anything."

She searched Mark's eyes to see if he had gone through similar experiences. She felt camaraderie in his expression and his nod. She realized this man may have gone through much more than she had. "The scientists thought that we had been given a bogus lead and were ready to head back to the airport. I was praying and asking the Holy Spirit if we had missed anything when I had a vision of a panel in the back wall of the small bunker. I asked one of the scientists if he would hold a flashlight for me and walked back to the back wall. I still didn't see anything so I started to run my fingers across the wall from side to side. I have some kind of sense in my fingers for mechanical things. I detected a slight vertical seam that I couldn't see even with the light. I kept checking and found a second seam three feet to the left of the first one. I asked someone to bring me a large screwdriver. I put the screwdriver against the first seam and pressed hard on it. Nothing. I was getting flack from the scientists about wasting their time and it irritated me. I stepped back and drove the screwdriver into the wall. Fortunately, I hit the seam and it split open up and down the wall. I did it on the other seam but it took me three tries before I hit it square."

Mark asked the Colonel to get them all some water which he did out of an ice chest in the office. After Megan had a drink she continued her story.

"I pried the wall apart with the screwdriver. At this point the scientists stopped heckling me and started helping me remove the panel. We were all pulling on it when it gave way and we all fell backward. The guy holding the light dropped it and then fell on it."

"We all scrambled around in the dark, got the scientist up, and recovered the light. It was still shining and I pointed it into the opening where the panel had been. What we saw scared the water out of all of us. The light showed us a large metal box about six feet long and four feet high and deep. The thing that scared us was the control panel on top of the box was lit up and the Geiger counter the scientists brought with them left no doubt that this was a nuclear weapon."

"Since that was why we were all there anyway, I decided to go in and look more closely at it. I figured if it was a bomb and it was about to go off I couldn't get far enough away to save myself so I might as well see if we could disarm it. When I got next to it I found that we had triggered the countdown timer by breaking into the room. The entire bomb and timer were encased in heavy metal and held together with inset zerts with a very strange pattern for a tool. We didn't have any heavy tools like that anyway and the timer was already down to twenty-two minutes before detonation."

"About that time there are several explosions that caused dust and dirt to drop from the ceiling and made us all fall down or bounce around. One of the Marines ran into the bunker and yelled that this place was under attack by a large force of Iraqi military and we had to evacuate immediately. The squad couldn't survive a clash with the enemy's superior forces. Knowing the military mind and having some experience with attempting to convince a Marine about anything I ran into the bunker and grabbed him by the arm and literally dragged him into the bomb room. I pointed at the timer, now at nineteen minutes and told him. "This is a nuclear bomb and if we don't stop it there will be an explosion that we can't run away from in the time remaining. Get more forces here because we can't leave."

"Seeing his stunned and frozen face I slapped him and brought him back to focus. "Get help now, Marine!" He nodded and ran back out of the bunker. Right after he left several rounds came through the open bunker door and ricocheted around the room."

She sat back and stared at her memories in her mind. "The scientist knew the drill. We had to stop the clock or we were toast. In unison the three scientists turned to me. One of them said, "We can stop it from detonating if we can get at it. Can you open it up, without setting it off?"

Megan Cole continued her story. "I considered the situation. We didn't have the tools to open it up and we didn't have anything to break the box. So, I realized I needed to come up with something really unique, very quickly. The explosions outside of the bunker were continuing, an occasional round was still coming into the bunker and I could hear Iraqis screaming somewhere outside. The rate of rifle fire was increasing from both sides."

"So, I prayed for guidance. My prayer was sincere and heartfelt. I prayed, "Jesus, I need to get this bomb case open. I can't do it by myself, I need your guidance and I need wisdom. I then thanked Him and waited. The scientists were either becoming more frantic or had resigned and then I had a thought. I don't think I generated that thought. I think God placed it into my mind. With nothing to lose since we were down to twelve minutes on the countdown timer I told all three scientists to grab hold of the metal box and try to lift it upward with me. They did as I asked and the, roughly four-hundred-pound box lifted straight up and off of the bomb and timer. You have to understand that the circumstances encouraged all of us to lift a hundred pounds each. We dumped the box into the bunker out of the way. Then I looked at them and said, "It's all yours boys." and stepped back. They stopped the countdown timer with six minutes to spare and disarmed the weapon in less than ten minutes."

She smiled, "About that time the Air Force got into the act and they had to be flying less than ten feet above the bunker. There were hundreds of explosions on the Iraqi forces outside the bunker. After that the volume of automatic weapons fire started to decrease outside and a squad of Marines with a Captain leading them rushed into the bunker. I saluted him and then held up my hand and told him, "We've disarmed the bomb, Sir. But we need some form of nuclear transport to get it out of here. You might want people in shielded suits because I don't know how "hot" the weapon is presently."

The Captain looked at me for several seconds and then walked into the small bomb room and saw for himself that the bomb had been disarmed. He walked out and started to leave when he stopped and shook all of our hands. He held my hand for bit and told me, "I really didn't think we were going to live through this after the PFC told me about the bomb. Thank you. He looked up at the Scientists and said, "Thank you all."

"He left a platoon to guard us and arranged for transport. After that we left and went to a make-shift decontamination set-up at the airport. It turned out we hadn't been exposed excessively. The shower felt good and I think I provided an interesting spectacle for the Scientists when we were scrubbed down and rinsed off."

She smiled, "Once we were finished, one of the scientists, who originally didn't expect much from a soldier, especially a woman, hugged me and kissed me on the forehead. He looked at me and told me I had given him his life back. I leaned over and whispered, "Tell Jesus, He is the one that solved the problem of the box."

-----------------------*****-----------------------

She looked at Mark as she finished the story.

Mark nodded, "You'll do fine." He stood up and she scrambled to get up with him. Mark smiled, "Yes, Jesus solved your problem, but, it was only because you humbled yourself and asked Him. One question, there was a lot of political fallout in the media because we supposedly never found WMDs in Iraq. What about this one?"

She grinned, "Politics Sir, I was given a medal for bravery and told to totally forget it ever happened. Situation normal all fouled up, SNAFU."

Mark turned to Colonel Farmington, "Colonel I am going to second Sergeant Cole to the core group for at least the next few weeks, possibly permanently. Can you get along without her?"

The Colonel saluted Mark and nodded. "Yes Sir, I expect you'll see her do great things."

Mark told her she would be billeted in the core team area and to get her things. Mark told her to report to the War Room as quickly as she could.

CHAPTER FIFTY-FIVE

When Mark walked back into the War Room he saw Jack. "I think you'll find the mechanical engineer I got will work out very well with this group."

Sergeant Cole walked into the War Room and sought out Mark. She saluted and Mark stopped her from completing her routine of stating her status. "It's all right Megan, we don't stand on rank and protocol because we normally don't have the time. Let me introduce you to everyone and then let us sit down and discuss the situation and the parameters."

After the introductions Mark and Jack told her about the mission. Mark asked Charlie to join them and took the four of them into a conference room so their conversations wouldn't interrupt the ongoing discussions in the War Room.

Charlie brought the detailed specifications for the rotating bathroom up on both the big screen and the large inset desk screen in front of them. "This is the current bathroom and the mechanisms that drive its rotating cylinder for privacy. What we need to do is create an ejection mechanism in the throne-like toilet with padded clamps to keep the "customer" in place during his short but somewhat violent trip. We also need to provide a means of introducing quick-acting knockout gas to the occupant, a sliding door in the outside wall of the car which can't be detected without a microscope and a way to eliminate all signs of any of these mechanisms after the job is done. Also we need to design it, build it, test run it, and have it ready to go to Italy in less than ten days. In addition, we now will also need some form of exit for the female agent involved, because she would possibly face violent interrogation."

Megan looked at Charlie, "Oh, is that all? I thought it was going to be a tough problem." She looked at Jack and pursed her lips. "It can be done but will take a considerable amount of money, ultra-fast shipping, and a lot of coffee."

Jack smiled a wan smile, "Done."

Megan smiled back, "Also, I wouldn't try to accomplish your mission requirements in the way you have in mind right now."

Jack, Charlie, and Mark stopped and looked at her.

She said, "I think I can see a better way to do it without the danger to your agent, your team in the helicopter, and the most of the split-second timing that that operation would require."

Mark looked at Jack, "Okay, what is your suggestion?"

She took computer control of the detailed specifications of the railcar shown on the big screen. She homed in on the side view of the floor and wheel trolleys for the high speed train car. "Take a look at the arrangement of the vehicle structure at this place. If we can design, build, test, and install a hidden, two-person escape module here under the floor. Then, your agent can apply the knockout gas directly to the target, move him to this location, underneath the car's floor, and get them both into the escape vehicle. Then we could have them leave the train far more safely than the danger of blasting him out of the side of the car, catching him in a thirty second helicopter grab and then trying to hide the agent and disguise the whole operation without being seen."

Mark nodded, "Okay, but how can this escape module leave the bottom of the railcar at roughly three hundred kilometers per hour?"

Megan smiled at Mark, "The army has some small rocket propulsion units that would fit here. Use three of them to accelerate the escape vehicle to the same speed as the train and just slip out between the wheel trolleys in the dark. The escape vehicle could immediately climb above the train and away to where it would rendezvous with the helicopter in the air. The helicopter could capture the vehicle and go to a prearranged site to transfer the people to the chopper. That way there will be no sign of how the two of them disappeared."

Jack thought about it for several seconds. "Can we do all that in the next ten days?"

Megan nodded, "I'm pretty sure we can. I designed a more complicated vehicle that was used to get a dissident out of China and it only took eight days. It will still take megabucks, a crew of efficient craftsmen, and a lot of coffee."

Mark told her to get started.

Megan needed several different sets of mechanical design software that would normally take six to eight days to acquire, not including shipping time. Charlie called down fifteen minutes later with the codes to use all three of the software packages on the computer in the conference room.

Megan's eyebrows lifted. She brought up the software and started on her designs. Jack left her to her work and went back into the War Room. Finding David talking to Mark he waited until they looked at him. "We need to know about the Mossad's involvement and we need to plant the agent where Carlo will find her and take her on a trip on the railroad."

CHAPTER FIFTY-SIX

The design of the escape vehicle, which was now called a "Pod", took only two days. At a secret location in Tel Aviv a select team of Israeli experts manufactured and built the pod in two more days. Mark worked with some friends from his old life as a Navy SEAL to acquire the three U.S. Army rocket motors. He was very satisfied when the motors locked precisely into their mounts on the pod.

Charlie designed the software that would guide the rocket powered pod out from under the railcar and to a meeting with the helicopter. He also created a software worm that would fake out the security cameras on Carlo's railcar. The program would then remove itself after the pod left the railcar.

As David had expected, the Mossad agreed to help steer Carlo into his ill-fated train trip but they would not provide an agent to lure Carlo into the trap. Alexis nodded when she heard and went ahead working with Sarah to make sure she filled the bill for what Carlo was looking for in a short-term romance.

After buying dresses she tried them on again back at the base. Looking at her reflection in the mirror she frowned at the short skirt and tight blouse Sarah had selected. She told Sarah, "I haven't looked this trashy since the last time I played the part of a prostitute."

Sarah laughed, "You still look very attractive and that is what the data says will attract Carlo Ricci."

Alexis snorted, "Ugh, that thought makes me want to take a shower."

David came into the War Room and met with Jack. "I've got the train car manufacturer to legitimize our repair to the replacement car. They have contacted both Carlo Ricci's transportation group and the Italian train people to allow us the eight hours on Wednesday next week to make our "repairs". How are we going to sneak the pod into the repair facility and onto the car without arousing suspicion?"

Jack smiled, "It will be our leading edge computer scanner and software tester. Charlie has set it up so that we can demonstrate its capabilities without showing them its real use."

David nodded, "Good, they should embrace our new technology. They'll probably want us to use it on their regular train car too."

Jack grinned, "We've got that covered. As a dedicated repair crew for railcars, we'll supposedly be on another job when the primary train car stops working. In the week before a repair crew can attend to the damaged train car we will modify the pod to do exactly what its cover says it will do. In fact, the manufacturer likes the idea so much he wants us to build him six of them. Cost is not a problem for these companies. Charlie says we will make a handsome profit off of these new "tester" pods. In fact, we may have just improved the industry's ability to test and repair high-speed train cars."

David laughed, "Since you are using Israeli technicians to build these things why doesn't Charlie improve on his design by reducing the size of the pod and make one that can be fixed to the train cars permanently and include audio, visual, and location monitoring that can be tapped into by the Mossad whenever they want to see who's doing what and if they can use the information?"

Jack shook his head, "There won't be enough time to make it usable. The OWG will be controlling everyone soon and it's less than seven years until the return of Christ to the Earth."

In Alexis' suite of rooms she sat on the bed and wistfully went over the stack of clothes, tools, weapons, and communications equipment that she couldn't take with her on this trip. Carefully putting everything away she then checked the time. She had to leave with her two small bags for the Airport in Tel Aviv for her initial meeting with Carlo Ricci in Italy in less than an hour. She took the bags and left her suite and went down to the main living area. Leaving her bags at the elevator; she checked the wall display and located David Zahavy's indicator light in the garden area.

As she entered the massive garden area she took a deep breath. She always liked this place, even more than she had liked the original one in Colorado. It spoke of peace and tranquility to her soul. She saw David reading the Bible in a restful nook. She stopped at the entrance to the area until he looked up and saw her. His smile was heartfelt; she could tell he was very happy to see her. She smiled at him, walked over to sit down next to him.

He stood up at her approach and hugged her. She pulled him close and he gave her a kiss on the cheek. She smiled again as they sat down.

She appraised him closely. "David, I wanted to spend some time with you before I go on this mission."

He nodded his head, "Thank you, I wanted you to prepare in your own way so that you will have everything you need to do clearly in mind without personal or emotional ties fogging everything up."

She took his larger hands in hers and kissed the back of both hands. "You are wise in the ways of spies. But, I couldn't leave without seeing you. You've come to mean so much to me since you joined the team." She looked in his eyes as she sensed the upcoming change in their relationship. She took a deep breath. "I love you."

There it was, a declaration of her feelings that had been unstated for months. She knew he was more than aware of the dangers of this mission for her. He smiled at her, "I love you too, Alexis. But, since I was married before and am somewhat older than you I wanted our relationship to grow until you were satisfied with me and my intentions."

Alexis relaxed, and laughed. "How long have you known how I felt towards you?"

David nodded, "Since we rescued you from that mountain top after you had been captured by the Omicron Cartel. When you woke up, your eyes spoke volumes to me."

Alexis smiled as she recalled the warmth of David's embrace in the helicopter and the feeling she was loved by him. "And how long have you been in love with me?"

David grinned, "I think I fell in love with you after watching you function in the spy world so efficiently. I had been praying about you and felt that the Father was encouraging me to take care of you, even though you obviously can take care of yourself. I knew I was in love with your spirit after the mountain rescue."

Alexis sobered up considerably. "Now that we know how we feel about each other, we have to part and make our way through the hazards of this mission."

David pulled her to him and warmly embraced her. "There will always be another mission. I'd like to think it is what we want because we're so good at what we do. But, I will miss you terribly and will be praying for you all the time you're gone."

Alexis pulled back a little and then kissed him tenderly on the mouth. She disentangled herself and stood up. "That's hello, not goodbye. I'll see you soon." She patted his hand and walked away towards the escalator to the main living area.

David was balancing his new found happiness with his concern for her safety on this mission. He prayed an earnest prayer for her safety and asked Yahshua to guard her in every way and to put his angels around her throughout the entire mission. He felt peace fill his spirit and knew she was in the best hands she could ever be.

CHAPTER FIFTY-SEVEN

Alexis disembarked the Alitalia flight at the Leonardo da Vinci-Fiumicino Airporta. She stopped at a coffee bar and got a cup of coffee. Her Mossad contact walked into the coffee bar. Pretending to be old girlfriends they chattered away as they walked toward the exit doors in Terminal 1. Alexis was using the cover name Elizabeth Conner, Countess of Avon. Her profile was that of an old money, wealthy young lady of jet-set fame who traveled the world over in search of new adventures. Charlie had created a large volume of history for her, which included supposed dalliances with semi-famous young people but not with any of the high profile types which would have already been news.

She was dressed in an Oscar de la Renta-designed outfit that clearly cost several thousand dollars. Her necklace, rings, and bracelet were worth twice that much. Her hair and makeup were impeccable and her attitude was one of calculated superiority to the common man.

Her contact told her, "Go to the Hotel Eden in Rome at the Via Ludovisi 49. Carlo Ricci would be there around noon. He's found several of his conquests there. Be careful, this one can be abusive or even violent." Her contact waved goodbye and walked away from her.

Alexis found the limousine rental booth and requested her prearranged car and driver. She gave the man behind the counter a look as if to say he was worth less than lint because he didn't immediately get her bags. The man's boss saw what was going on and moved in quickly to keep her satisfied. He took her bags and walked her to the first chauffeured Rolls Royce available. She waited in the limo as the man took her American Express Centurion credit card to fill out the paperwork. She knew that would spike interest in her because the card was backed by a six-million-dollar deposit.

Paperwork completed she gave the hotel address to the driver and told him that she wanted to be there by eleven-forty-five and no later.

The rich leather interior of the Rolls cushioned her as she rode in almost total silence into Rome. She thought, "I could get used to this level of coddling."

As she exited the limo she spoke to the driver in excellent Italian and asked him to be back at the hotel by one o'clock sharp. She strode commandingly into the lobby and saw the sign for the elevator to the rooftop restaurant, the most exclusive one in Rome. She walked into the La Terrazza dell' Eden restaurant and asked for the best table available. She slipped the Maître d' two hundred Euros as he kissed the back of her hand. This ensured she would be close to Carlo Ricci. She noted that they had secluded rooms for special guests so she asked the Maître d' why she couldn't have one of the enclosed rooms. The Maître d' smiled and said that all of the private rooms, including the room she was looking at were already in use. This room was taken by a Mr. Ricci. She said, "That is sad." She took a table close to the window yet near the private room to make sure Ricci would definitely see her. If not, she'd find a way to make him see her.

She ordered off of the menu listing items that provided savory Fabio Ciervo's haute cuisine. She chose carefully so as to not fill up. She didn't have to worry about picking expensive dishes since there were no prices on the menu.

Checking the time, she saw that it was almost noon. She asked her server for a special bottle of wine that cost close to two thousand dollars. Almost magically, the maître d' appeared next to her table and made soothing words to gloss over the fact that he had to check her credit before he could produce such a rare vintage wine.

While he was checking her credit his eyebrows rose and he motioned the wine steward to get the bottle of wine out of their reserve. Because it was so very special the Maître d' himself served the bottle to her table to have her taste it. As he was removing the cork Alexis saw Carlo Ricci and three other men approach her table on the way to the private room. Alexis totally ignored him and focused on the bottle of wine. This made Ricci also look at the ancient vintage bottle. He looked at Alexis and stopped near her table. The other three men also stopped. She made two of them as muscle and the other as a toady.

Carlo smiled at her and said in Italian, "Your taste is almost as excellent as your beauty."

Alexis let her vision move to him and she offered her hand to him. He bent and kissed the back of her hand and was rewarded by inhaling the aroma of Clive Christian Imperial Majesty Perfume for Women. 16.9 oz. of this exotic perfume cost over $435,000.00 and could tame a raging lion with one smell.

Alexis could almost see hearts in the man's eyes. He stood up and came back to normal. He inquired as to her name. She studied him for a few seconds as if deciding if he were worthy of speaking to her. She smiled at him and was rewarded with the hearts in the eyes again. "Lady Elizabeth Conner, Countess of Avon. Are you the gentleman that took the room I wanted?"

He bowed again, "My name is Carlo Ricci." He stood again and made a small smile, "Yes, I am he. But to console you in your loss I can offer to share the room with you if that would please you."

Alexis had read that this guy was oily smooth and he proved it right there. She looked at his companions. "Thank you, I appreciate the gesture but you seem to be involved in business and I don't want to intrude."

Carlo smiled a smile one would see on a shark. "These gentlemen were just making sure I arrived in time. They are leaving now." That last was not lost on the three men. They turned and left immediately.

Carlo held out his hand and Alexis took it, remembering to count the number of fingers she had after he let go. Carlo told the Maître d' to bring her wine into the private room.

After they were seated and arranged by the Maître d', Alexis looked frankly at Carlo. "I am impressed. Most of the men I know don't have three bodyguards everywhere they go. You must be a very important man."

Playing to the man's ego was the quickest way to get him to talk about his favorite subject, himself.

Alexis kept the relationship at an arm's distance to project the image that she wasn't easy and only somewhat impressed by power. She spoke Italian fluently and kept things light. The more she did this the more she intrigued him. He ignored his lunch as he attempted to make her appreciate him more. She gave small signs that she was slightly interested in him but nothing of any real substance. She wanted him to want her, desperately if possible.

Carlo bought the lunch and her bottle of wine which they both had emptied and even took care of the generous tips. She checked the time and told Carlo she had enjoyed the meal and the use of his room. She got up to leave and he asked her to stay. She smiled, "Not today Senor Ricci, I have business I have to attend to shortly. Maybe next time." She opened a small diamond encrusted case and gave him a business card with her cell phone number and some of her perfume on it. "Give me a call when you have some free time. I'll be in Italy for the next six days."

He stood up and bowed to her. "I look forward to our next visit." Then, like it was a sudden thought, "Where are you staying?"

She looked introspective for a few seconds. "I think I'll stay here. I like it. One meets such interesting people in this hotel." That brought a small smile to Carlo's face.

She stopped at the desk and arranged for one of the more expensive suites. She asked the bell hop to accompany her to her car to get her bags.

Alexis left the hotel lobby exactly at one p.m. and her Rolls pulled to the curb. The driver hurried around to open the door for her. She had the driver give her two bags to the bell hop. As she got in she noticed that one of Ricci's men was watching her from a distance. She also noticed another one of his men in a car when the first one walked quickly over to it and got in. Obviously she was going to be followed.

She went to the Bank of Italy in Rome and then led her followers on a monumental shopping spree. She acquired hats, shoes, furs, and a lot of clothes. Alexis knew that she'd have to reimburse the team for these things but it was fun and exhilarating to act like you were rich and carefree. She realized suddenly that she was rich, but not carefree. She finally returned to the Hotel Eden and played with all her new clothes. She was fairly sure that Carlo would have had her room bugged for sound and video and she played to that probable audience. She called Jack through a cutout and gave him her situation in rich girl terms. "Hi, Father! I'm in Rome at the Hotel Eden. I met an interesting man you might know. His name is Carlo Ricci and he is quite a handsome gentleman. We had lunch together and it was fun. I might see him again while I'm here. There's a good chance. How are you doing with your latest piece of technology?"

Jack played along knowing that the phone line could well be bugged. "I'm fine darling, thank for caring about my work. We've finished the trials and will put the project into use in the next couple of days. Are you going to go to see your friend Tony tomorrow?"

Alexis was trying not to overact. "I don't think so, Father, but Carlo is so much more a gentleman than Tony. He showed me I need to seriously think about the men I know."

Jack told her, "I think I would like to meet Mr. Ricci. I have heard about him from someone but I don't recall what they told me. Something about the military I believe."

Alexis said, "Okay Father I will stay in touch with you daily. I love you, "Ciao"!" and hung up.

CHAPTER FIFTY-EIGHT

After a light supper in the rooftop restaurant Alexis returned to her room or her stage as she liked to think of it. She made herself busy as she hung up her new clothes and unpacked her two suitcases. She saw many signs that someone had gone through her things but acted as if nothing happened.

In the bathroom she detected a new jewel-like decoration on the mirror that hadn't been there earlier. It was, most likely, a peeping sound and video pickup. She carefully checked the rest of the bathroom under the pretense of getting ready to take a shower. She put on her best show of getting ready to undress and then hung a suction hook above the new jewel and then hung her nightgown on the hook, effectively blinding the camera.

She made sure she walked out to the living room in a loose sleep shirt that kept her modesty while enticing the watchers. It was all an act to make Carlo even more interested in her.

She double locked her door and turned out the lights. She put on the second set of eyeglasses which she brought with her and was able to detect the infrared lights that pulsed on and off near the location of two infrared cameras. "So, they wanted to see what she did in the dark did they?"

Sitting on her bed she fiddled with her cell phone and tripped the flash part of the camera. The bright flash would have caused failure of the IR cameras for a short time. Then she climbed under the covers and went to sleep after an earnest prayer to Yahshua that He would watch over her and protect her this night.

She woke early and went through her routine of getting ready. This took a great deal longer than her normal Army routine of shower, brush your teeth, and get dressed. She had hair to do, makeup to apply, careful application of ointments and oils to give the pampered illusion to her skin. Dressed in one of her new outfits she left the room for a nice breakfast before going sightseeing.

233

She was just about finished with her meal when her cell phone rang. She made a slight smile and answered. "Elizabeth Conner".

Carlo Ricci's voice was a deep basso. "Hello Countess, this is Carlo Ricci from lunch yesterday. I hope you slept well. How are you doing this morning?"

Alexis sweetened her tone, "Yes, Carlo Ricci, I slept well and am preparing for a busy day. How are you today?"

Carlo played his cards well and carefully. "I am also busy this morning but actually wanted to see you again. Will you have any time for me today?"

"Cute" thought Alexis. "I could possibly find some time to meet you for tea or coffee today. What time would work for you?"

Carlo was hooked. "How about three this afternoon? I could send my car around and we could have tea on the patio of my home."

Alexis let the answer wait for a count of six. "Alright then Carlo. I will be out front of the Hotel Eden around two-thirty. Caio"

Carlo said "Caio Bella signora" and hung up. Translated that was "Goodbye beautiful lady". Alexis hung up and walked over to an unoccupied bench near the Tivoli Fountain. She casually put the two-way ear bud in her left ear and reached into her pocket and keyed a second cell phone that she had kept on herself all the time yesterday. Carlo's goons knew nothing about this phone. She turned to look at the fountain and quietly spoke the number for Charlie Wu in ComSec at the base in Israel.

Charlie answered immediately. "Well, hello Bella signora. What can I do for you?"

Alexis laughed, "You heard the invitation to his house. Can you get me a layout and any pertinent information about the place? I don't want him trying to score and make me miss his special train ride."

Charlie whistled over the phone. "Hey, I really like that outfit you're wearing. Anyway, I just sent the information on his estate outside of Rome to your phone. I doubt that he will make a move there, I think he just wants to let you know he isn't married."

Alexis giggled, "I doubt marriage would slow him down much."

Charlie sobered up a bit. "Be careful with this one Alex. He isn't married because his wife of twenty-three years died two years ago under suspicious circumstances. The Italian police think she was drowned and not accidently either. But, he has the connections and the money to buy his way out of any Italian investigation. Also, you'll be glad to know that there have been over sixty hits on your history and you've moved up six pages on the social Medias."

Alexis was also sobered by that revelation. "Thanks Charlie, I'll be careful." She got up from the bench and went into a hotel and used their bathroom. She carefully memorized the details of Carlo's house and then erased the inputs. If they did find this phone, there was nothing unusual in its memory or chips to incriminate her as anything but a rich girl with privacy issues.

At two-thirty she stepped out of the Hotel Eden and was met by Carlo's driver. He also had a Rolls Royce and it was a nice ride out of Rome to Carlo's estate.

The driver let her out of the car as Carlo walked out of his house to welcome her.

Tea went well with jokes and the occasional question about her past. She had memorized it and didn't have any problem answering his inquires that were obviously generated by her false history.

He offered her some Champagne and talked about world events and how the Italian government was trying to self-destruct financially. Alexis passed the financial matter off as insignificant in her world. She allowed Carlo to ogle her without her seeming to notice. He really was intrigued by her and it showed. When he passed by with the Champagne he got another whiff of her perfume and it actually stopped him in his tracks. He asked her what that beautiful scent was.

Alexis told him offhand, "Clive Christian Imperial Majesty, I like it so much I invested in two more bottles of it last time so that I would not run out of it. I think I got the last two bottles."

Alexis almost laughed at the look on his face when he realized she had casually spent almost a million dollars on "her latest" purchase of perfume.

Carlo twirled his Champagne in his glass. Making up his mind he looked up at Alexis. "How would you like to go on a special luxury train ride to Salerno? I can promise you it will be the best trip you've ever gone on."

Knowing the installation of the pod wouldn't be ready for two days she asked him when he wanted to take this fantastic train trip. He said, "Well, I have to go out of town for three days, so let's say Friday, I'll meet you at your hotel at four p.m. if that is agreeable to you."

She agreed saying, "That would be acceptable because I am tied up for the next two and a half days. How long is this trip and when will we be back in Rome?"

The trip takes about four to five hours on a bullet train and we will want to dine in Salerno. I know of a wonderful place there. It is very romantic and overlooks the city. We'll be back on Saturday afternoon."

Alexis smiled sweetly and let her eyes look eager which translated into her hunger for him in his mind. She agreed with the timing and bid him farewell as she had to get back for an important meeting that evening with a business partner.

CHAPTER FIFTY-NINE

Jack was airborne with Megan Cole, Mark, Sarah, Charlie, and David when he got a call from Alexis. "Hello, darling, how are you doing?"

Alexis kept up the act. "Fine Father. I'm meeting with Marcus Winze tonight and will be busy through Friday afternoon. Then I'm going to take a train ride Friday to Salerno and see the sights. I think my train is going to leave around six p.m. Friday and I may be out of contact during the trip. If I get a chance, I'll call you from Salerno, okay?"

Jack smiled, "Sure thing pumpkin, have a great time. See you."

Jack told the others, "Alexis has been invited on a train ride on Friday. I think we need to have the modifications to the replacement train car in place by Thursday night. And by Friday morning the primary train car needs to break down sufficiently to require a replacement."

Sergeant Conner spoke up. "If the two cars are pretty much the same then I can make the primary car break down in a way that their maintenance crew will seem to be the cause."

Jack nodded his head. "We'll make a disturbance to draw attention away from you while you mess up the primary car. How long do you need?"

She shook her head, "Don't know yet. Probably ten minutes at the most."

Mark agreed with Jack. "Okay, just give us a heads up when you need the time."

The Embraer 120 Brasilia set down on the runway of the Leonardo da Vinci-Fiumicino Airporta Tuesday morning and taxied to the cargo area. The crew was wearing the uniforms and jacket emblazoned with the railcar manufacturer "TRACARCO". They had the fork lift deliver the pod and their luggage to a prearranged Dodge Cargo van. Then they drove to a restaurant and had an early lunch. After lunch they drove to the train storage area where Carlo Ricci's two luxury train cars were held.

After their paperwork got them into the storage building and up to the two train cars they had to pass muster with Ricci's enforcers. They were inspected and the pod passed as inspection gear.

The lead security man, Peter Burros was suspicious and asked, "Why are you guys here? We didn't call you."

Jack asked to speak to Burros privately. "The company has detected a possible problem with the interline tension between the wheel trolleys. This problem has already affected two of this type of railcar. Here, let me show you what the problem is." Jack took out the computer tablet he had in his computer bag.

He brought up a view of the bottom of the railcar and the four wheel trolleys. "When you travel at high speed, anything over eighty miles per hour for long periods, a harmonic forward and back swaying motion develops in each trolley. He had the trolleys on the tablet start to move slightly back and forth. Normally this doesn't cause a problem and in fact was built into the trolleys to release tension. The problem is if two of the trolleys on the same end of the car match harmonic sways." He made that motion happen on the front of the car shown on the tablet. "Even then the motion doesn't cause concern. The problem occurs when two trolleys on one end of the car are in synchronization when the railcar enters a turn of over three degrees. Due to the sway it either lengthens or shortens the wheel center to wheel center length from one end of the car to the other. This would still not cause a problem unless the car is in the curve and going over one hundred miles per hour." He looked at Burros to see if he understood. "See the detail here. The matched sway at the speed of one hundred eighty-five kilometers per hour changes the ability of the trolleys to stay on the tracks due to the length difference. This will cause the trolleys to leave the tracks because they are forced off by the misalignment of the length between trolleys." The diagram on the tablet showed the front trolleys lifting off of the rail and derailing the car.

Burros asked Jack, "What happened with the car that derailed?"

Jack shook his head, "Two hundred-thirty-three people were killed, twenty-six cars behind our car derailed with it and over two hundred more people were critically injured or required hospitalization."

Burros nodded, "Yeah, I heard about that accident. It happened in Germany didn't it?"

Jack shook his head, "No, it was in Norway. The accident was heavily censored and played down as a track malfunction due to the politics of the government-owned train system. Actually, they didn't figure out why the car derailed at that time. Our engineers figured out the problem after three months. We have been traveling all over to fix the cars that could be affected."

Jack pulled out a sheet from TRACARCO showing a list of numbers for cars subject to this unique malfunction. He ran his finger down the list and the number on the replacement car was underlined. "We have to fix this and then go to the United Emirates three days from now. Do we have the time to fix this car? If we don't then we will go and fix the next one. Who knows, the combination of sway, speed, and curvature may not happen for a while with any car."

Burros balanced the possibility of the problem happening to this car against what would happen to him if he was wrong. He looked closely at Jack. "Why isn't the other car here on that list? And how long will it take you to make the modifications?"

Jack shrugged his shoulders. "I don't make the list; my crew just fixes the ones listed. The most time is rigging the test pod to the car and doing the calibrations. I would guess we could get it done in eight to ten hours spread over two days."

Jack could see the man vacillating in his decision so Jack tipped him over their way. "Also, the cost for this modification is entirely covered by your warranty. The owner doesn't have to pay for anything."

That was the deciding straw. Burros was relieved and told Jack, "Okay, get started. The other car needs to be ready to go on Friday. This car is a backup one anyway. Keep me up to date with your repairs and I or one of my men will be stopping by every now and then to see how it is going."

Jack nodded, "That is good. I only need to know where the bathrooms are and where we can send out to get food."

The security man pointed out the bathrooms to Jack and told him that they would get the food for the workers and that way they wouldn't break security with the repair crew having vendors going in and out."

Jack gave the high sign to the other team members and Burros went off to attend to more pressing problems like the pretty secretary he had his eye on in the next building.

CHAPTER SIXTY

The team had rehearsed the modifications and began doing many things at one time. Mark and Jack were given the job to create a liftable panel in the floor of the plush car. Megan, Sarah, and David cleared out the area where the pod was to go and set up the releasable clamps to hold it in place until the rockets fired. Charlie connected his computers into the railcar's systems and began the modifications that would provide Alexis' protection from surveillance during the gassing of Carlo and their movement into the pod. He also directed the railcar computer to give the pod electronics a precise mileage for ejection at the right place.

Mark and Jack removed the plush carpeting and cut the opening into the floor of the car. They then used Megan's measurements to replace the opening with a liftable panel exactly the size of the hole. Even if the carpet was removed the line in the floor would be unnoticeable because the framework for the liftable panel was underneath the flooring. The electronic arc cut the hole so precisely that they had to use grease to get it to move. The tension hinges at the back end of the panel, also under the floor, would allow Alexis to lift it easily and it would seat back exactly. After the pod dropped away several small thermal charges would tack weld the panel back in place permanently. The attachments under the car would drop off or melt away leaving the bottom of the car like it was before the pod was attached or the panel cut. After they connected the pod they practiced with the small remote switch to cause the panel to lift and the pod to open. Sarah lowered Mark into the pod to insure that Alexis could do that. Sarah then got into the pod with Mark and they simulated the firing of the rockets, release of the pod and closure of the panel and rug.

Megan had secured time-release glue that would seal the carpet cut completely without wrinkle.

While this was going on Megan slipped over by the edge of the replacement car and signaled Jack. Jack ignited a flare which he threw onto the cement dock behind the replacement railcar. He then yelled at the others who all got out of the railcar and proceeded to use a fire extinguisher to try and put out the flare. All the fire extinguisher did was to create a great amount of smoke and obscured everything. Eventually two of the security crew got there right after the flare died out. Jack explained that the flare had been ignited by accident and apologized for the time wasted. The smoke evaporated and the security crew looked around. Finding nothing they left. Jack returned to the car to find Megan working on the pod. She smiled at Jack and nodded.

Twice Peter Burros visited them to see how the progress was going. Jack used the video tablet to show him the calibrations emanating from the pod and how they were realigning the trolleys to prevent the sway. Then they had to recalibrate everything to ensure that the trolleys were repaired and would not cause problems.

Finally, Wednesday evening they were done. Unless you knew exactly what to look for you couldn't tell that the jet-black pod was still attached to the railcar. They used prefab parts to build another fake pod to remove with their tools.

Jack was tired but pleased. Burros showed up and looked at the car and under it. He had no training or pervious knowledge of the bottom of the vehicle and everything looked normal to him. He approved their repairs and signed off on the maintenance log.

The crew left in the same van and eventually left in the same plane from the airport.

Jack sent a text message to Alexis' phone. "New technology project was a success. Hope you enjoy your time in Rome and will see you next weekend. Love, Father.

Alexis smiled at the text and replied, "Thank you Father. See you soon. "

The next two days went by with a rush as the team got the helicopters in place and practiced the pod pickup. Then things got ragged.

Charlie rushed into the command trailer located in the hills west of the town of Latina, Italy. "Guys, I think we may have a problem. I just found out that last week Rail Italia added forward and backward looking video cameras to all of their high-speed trains. They are not under computer control and would definitely see the pod leaving the railcar and climbing upward."

Mark stared at the problem. "I think I know what we can do. It will require both helicopters. The first one will have to blanket the train track with a sticky aluminum chaff that looks like smoke just as the train arrives at the ejection point to blind the cameras and the other to pick up the pod. I think I know where we can get the smoke canisters in time. It looks like Su Li and Mike White will be doing separate missions after all."

Megan nodded, "We've scheduled the pod to leave when the train is going through a left hand turn while Carlo's car is at the apex of the turn. The smoke will reduce any possible sighting of the pod rockets as it leaves."

Jack nodded, "Get on the second helicopter and the canisters. We've only got sixteen hours until the train gets to the release point."

CHAPTER SIXTY-ONE

Alexis checked out of the hotel and sent all of her belongings to the proxy address that would get her things to the underwater base by the time she got back.

She kept a few things that were of the utmost importance to her. The list included her cell phone, the remote that triggered the hatch to the pod, and a small makeup bag.

She had a light meal and waited until four-thirty and walked out of the hotel front door. Carlo's limo was out front and she walked to it. The driver got out and opened the back door for her. She settled down in the luxurious seats as the driver threaded through the Rome rush hour traffic to the train station.

The driver let her out at the main entrance to the station and she walked to the doors and opened one and walked into the main concourse. She spotted Carlo immediately. He was telling one of his men something. The other man nodded and slipped away into the crowd. Carlo spotted her and his face lit up with a big smile. He met her half way and escorted her to one of the train tracks. A big sign above the concourse showed Salerno as the destination of the high-speed train. She smiled at him and they walked down the train until they came to his car. He ushered her into the car and she gushed over the lavish interior and the interesting bathroom.

He poured them both a five-star brandy. She sipped the drink and he went to the bathroom. She looked at the small remote and saw the pin-head LED in green telling her she was on the right railcar and the system was active. That was a major relief.

Carlo came back and they talked small talk until the train left the station. As it ramped up to its full speed it was amazing how quickly the terrain flashed by the large windows of the railcar. She was watching the passing countryside when Carlo got up and walked behind her. He put his hand on her shoulder and leaned down to whisper in her ear. "We have an hour until supper is served from the dining car. Would you like to see the bedroom?"

She knew that they had eighty minutes to go before she was supposed to render him unconscious but considered speeding up the schedule if he got too amorous. She put her hand over his and smiled at him. "Not yet Carlos, I've come down with a bit of a headache. Could you get us something to snack on first? I'm so much more fun when I don't have this pain bothering me."

Alexis could almost see the thoughts going through his mind. He could wait because she would be more cooperative and thus more fun. He still had several hours before they would be approaching Salerno and if things didn't work out he had the entire evening in Salerno and the whole trip back. "Certainly, I will call to the dining car and see what I can get for us."

While he was talking to the dining car she prayed quietly that the Father and Yahshua would give her success in her quest to capture Carlo and make a clean getaway. She fell quiet and had a one-second vision. She was battling a demon and Carlo was getting a gun. The vision ended and she realized that God had given her a warning that a demon was apparently assigned to protect Carlo and was worried about her. She thanked the Father.

They chatted for about ten minutes when the entry chime sounded. Carlo went and got the food tray and brought it in. She ate sparingly but enough to satisfy Carlo that she really needed it. She then took two headache pills and smiled weakly at the passionate Italian. "This should clear up my headache in a little bit." She got up and bent over, kissing him on the cheek. "I'll be right back"

Alexis drew out the bathroom visit as long as she could and then washed her hands and dried them. She got the vial of knock-out dust and carefully opened the vial. She put it in her left hand and rotated the bathroom wall and walked back to where Carlo was sitting. She smiled at him and said, "I'm feeling better already. Where were we?"

He began to grin when there was a familiar crackling and creaking and a demon stepped out of the demonic dimension into the human dimension inside of the railcar. It was a typically gross and deformed demon and Carlo was repulsed by it and grabbed for his handgun. The demon walked toward them and the car rocked side to side with its steps.

Alexis instantly evaluated the combat situation. Carlo was directly in front of her and the demon was coming from her right. With her left hand she threw the knock out powder at Carlo's head and said, "Relax lover, let the girl take care of this."

She began to pray and her golden armor exploded into view along with the sword of the word with the esteem of Yahveh flowing off of the chrome blade in waves. Carlo had just enough time before he passed out to see the glorious transformation. Alexis spun to her right and with one mighty swing she cut the demon's head off of its body. The demon was as surprised as the now unconscious Carlo Ricci had been. It disappeared into gray smoke with a whimper.

Alexis' armor faded away along with the sword. She checked her time and saw that she was several seconds behind schedule. She pushed the button on the remote control and the panel in the floor opened up revealing the two couch-like positions in the pod below her feet.

Alexis took Carlo's gun away from him and put it in a drawer in the small table next to the seat he was in. She used part of her dress to do that so as to not leave any fingerprints on the gun.

She did a dead lift of Carlo's sleeping body and carried him to the pod. She lowered him feet first into the pod and slid his body down until it was in the correct position. Glancing around her made sure that she didn't leave anything belonging to her in the speeding railcar. She climbed into the pod on her side face down, and smoothed down her dress. She quickly strapped Carlo into position and used the plastic riot cuffs from inside her boots to tie his hands to the strap. She lay down on her stomach and pushed the remote button for a second time. The upper cover of the pod slid into position and the two of them were closed tightly into the cushions. She had seen the floor of the car closing before her vision was cut off by the top of the pod.

She activated the small video screen in front of her position. She then pushed the comm button and heard David's voice. It felt good to hear a friendly voice. His comments concerned the countdown to release of the pod.

"Alexis, you've got six seconds until pod release. Remember everything is computer controlled so relax and enjoy the ride."

There was a heavy vibration which she interpreted as the rockets firing. There was a sudden jerk and the screen showed the rail ties flashing by terribly fast just below the pod. The pod moved to the right and suddenly they were out from under the railcar and veering to the right and climbing. There was a lot of distortion in the screen and it looked like it fogged over for several seconds. The screen cleared in time for her to see the train racing away from her to her left and then she could make out a gray on black horizon ahead of her. David's voice came back, "You are free of the train and we are about to capture the pod. This may be a bit rough, so hang on."

There was a series of bangs on the outside of the pod and she was jerked in several directions at the same time. Then the camera went blank and everything settled down. David said, "We got you! Relax for a few minutes until we can land and get you out of there."

She reviewed her mission to that point and was satisfied that it had gone according to plan. She was thinking about the next steps when Carlo groaned. He didn't wake up but thrashed about and then stopped moving.

There was another thump that she figured was the helicopter landing. More thumps and movement and then the pod top slid back and she could see David, Mark, and Sarah above her. She unclamped the two padded arms that had held her in place and was lifted out of the pod by willing hands. She took a deep breath and sighed. "Hello everyone, nice to see you again." David wrapped her up in a bear hug and kissed her on the cheek. "Welcome home Alexis." She grinned and patted him on the back. "I'm so glad to see you."

Mark said, "We were all on edge until now. Wow! What is that fantastic perfume you're wearing?" It seemed to have the same effect on men everywhere. She grinned, "I'll tell you later."

Jack and Mark unbuckled Carlo Ricci and immediately injected him with a stronger sleep agent. They then tucked him back into the pod, strapped him in and secured his hands and feet. Carefully putting the top back on the pod they then lifted the pod and slid it into a large black sleeve which was fixed under the belly of the helicopter.

David smiled at her. "You get to ride up top with the real people. He doesn't."

CHAPTER SIXTY-TWO

The two helicopters flew back to the airport and landed near their hangers. The pod was transferred to an Israeli C130 along with the team and their belongings. After settling up with the rental people Jack and Mark joined up with the other team members and dropped into the web seats on the C130 for the ride back to Tel Aviv. The team generated their after-action reports and debriefs on the trip back.

Alexis questioned the appearance of the demon on the train. Jack thought about it, prayed about it, and told her, "Apparently Satan doesn't give RHONE all the freedom they think they've got. It looks like the enemy wants to keep track of all the major players. I am so glad you were blessed with the armor of God and were able to defeat the demon."

Alexis smiled, "Me too. But, do you think Satan found out that we grabbed Carlo?"

Jack smiled, "That depends on whether or not Satan gave the demon the command to intervene with you and Carlo or if it just decided to do it on its own. Remember that Satan doesn't have the abilities like God to know everything and be everywhere."

A team of Mossad agents had taken over the care of Carlo Ricci for the trip and would deliver him to the Mossad interrogation area when they arrived back home. David's two agents that had come over from the Mossad to the Crossfire Team, Judah Maritz and Aaron Jacobson, would interrogate him on information on all RHONE operations, especially the one against the Crossfire Team.

David and Alexis were in deep conversation the entire trip back to Israel. Laura noticed and whispered to Jack. "I think someone is getting serious about their romance. Care to bet how long before the "M" word is used?"

Jack grinned and shook his head. He kissed Laura and sat back. He never bet on anything against her when it concerned romance.

Sunday after the Italian job, the entire crew that went to Italy was relaxing in the large family room located at the head of the four staircases from the first floor.

David was sitting between Alexis and Jack and Laura. David stood up and asked for everyone's attention. When it got quiet David surprised no one by announcing their plans. "Friends and fellow warriors, it is with great happiness I want to announce that I have asked Alexis to marry me and she has accepted." There were a lot of congratulations and clapping. David motioned for Alexis to join him and then held up his hands for silence. "We have decided to get married right here on base to cut down on unwanted party crashers. The wedding will be next Saturday during Shabbat. You are all invited; critical mission-related absences will be allowed."

Alexis squeezed his hand and spoke up. "I've come to love each and every one of you and we do so want to share our happiness at this wedding. Gifts are not required nor will any be rejected. I will let the ladies know about a color theme sometime tomorrow and we want to have a real blowout of a reception. Now, before any of you strain your brain, David is nineteen years older than I am and I am convinced that it was because God thought it would take an additional nineteen years for him to mature properly before marrying me."

David shook his head, "I had to wait until she was of legal age to be married."

The hearty laughter drew some of the SOG folks from the workout areas two stories down. David assured them the entire SOG would be invited as would any selected people from both of our pasts if they can get here in time.

Mark and Sarah congratulated the couple and then wandered over to where Jack and Laura were talking. Mark was grinning, "I never thought they would last so long before they took the plunge. David has been looking at Alexis with puppy dog eyes for more than a year."

Laura grinned, "Yeah, reminds me of you and Sarah in Tel Aviv."

Sarah laughed, "Look, you two are the "old" married couple and we all look up to you for guidance regarding the state of wedded bliss. How can we make their blessed event more special?"

Mark said, "You know, we should have bachelor and bachelorette parties for these two, they deserve it.

Jack nodded, "Yes we should, but, remember it needs to be on base. There are some highly paid assassins looking for us and the disappearance of Carlo Ricci will probably increase their desire to get their hands on any of us. Especially people who are celebrating and not watching for trouble. Remember what happened to the ladies in Denver on a simple shopping trip. Also, let's try and keep it above board and decent."

The colors of blue and white with silver accents in honor of their new home were selected and the women scurried to find dresses that they liked in those colors. Anyone venturing out of the base was accompanied by several of the SOG personnel and several Mossad security types. Still by Friday morning most people were ready for the big occasion the next day.

Jack contacted the Mossad and connected with Judah Moritz. "Judah, how is the interrogation of Carlo Ricci going?"

Judah laughed, "It's like peeling an onion. We've had good days and bad days. I think his capture has given him thought about his fate with the Anti-Christ. He became more talkative and started asking for a deal. We should wrap this up after today. What are your plans for him?"

Jack chuckled, "I want to release him back into the world. I personally doubt that he would last an hour but that is his choice. If he wants a deal, tell him no charges, no imprisonment. We can relocate him or just let him go."

Judah sighed, "Well he's been asking for a deal and he wants to talk to Elizabeth Conner. I have convinced him that he will be fortunate to ever get out of prison."

Jack told him, "Judah, I doubt that the ex-General has any friends at this point. Give him this deal. We will put him into a witness protection program and relocate him for his safety."

Judah thought for a few seconds. "I think he knows that won't work because the demonic connection won't be fooled by a new name and whatever distance he travels." Judah told Jack, "Hang on a minute; I'm getting news from Aaron."

Judah came back on. "He's provided ever thing he knows and even what he has speculated. He gave up resisting and spilled his guts. We'll work to make sure what he's told us is valid.

Jack asked, "Do you think he gave up too easily?"

Judah thought about that. "Are you thinking they knew we'd grab him and they filled him with misinformation?"

Jack shook his head, "I don't know. See if you can verify what he's told you so far." Jack called Carol Moffet. "Carol, can you determine from the matrix if our capture of Carlo Ricci was a set up by the enemy knowing that we would interrogate him?

She said that she would see what she could.

Ten minutes later Carol called back. "Jack, I think they were caught off guard by our grabbing him. There are numerous new requests involving Carlo's name to have demons enter our dimension since that time. They are scrambling to find Carlo and eliminate him."

Jack thought about that, "Okay. They won't find him because the angels of the Most High protect the side of the undersea base, thanks a lot."

Jack called Judah, "I want you and Aaron to come to the War Room as soon as you are able to give us a report of your findings from the interrogation. And don't forget that you have a wedding to go to tomorrow."

Judah agreed saying, "We will be over there in about an hour. We implanted some history changes for Carlo. We amplified his desire to protect women instead of just lusting after them, and we implanted the idea that "the countess of Avon" was not real. More like an unattainable dream. That way he won't be fixated on the Elizabeth Conner cover."

Jack smiled, "Good, her husband-to-be will be most grateful."

CHAPTER SIXTY-THREE

An hour later the core team met with Judah and Aaron

Judah started off by summarizing their findings. "Carlo Ricci was far more the mastermind of RHONE than any of us gave him credit for before we had a chance to interrogate him. He took over RHONE just after the first Iraqi war which RHONE helped to foment between Iraq and the United States. The previous leader of RHONE overstepped his mandate in August 1990 by inciting Saddam Hussein, the dictator of Iraq to order his army across the border into tiny Kuwait. This miscalculation actually caused the U.S-led coalition to invade Iraq. That man was never heard of again."

Judah put a chart up on the screen. "Carlo Ricci was the youngest General in the Italian army and was hand-picked to run RHONE. Carlo created the massive growth of RHONE and personally staffed the membership of their military. He probably did not know he was being guided by demonic influence but he followed Satan's leading as if they were his own thoughts to do what he has done. He created the SS troops based on Hitler's SS. They are the most violent and feared group by the pseudo-Nazi regular troops of RHONE."

"Carlo Ricci attempted to project a non-routine lifestyle in an effort to randomize his movements. He did this to prevent anyone from kidnapping him while at the same time letting him follow his own desires without limit."

"As a young man Carlo became a lifelong friend of a minor government official named Marco Marino. That friendship led to Marino's support and backing of the secret army of RHONE. We doubt that Carlo realized that Marco would soon be his boss."

"During his interrogation we have learned of hundreds of plots, plans, and operations, many of which are already in place to assist the Anti-Christ in his takeover of the entire world. These plans are being carefully presented to the leaders of the world when they impact normal society. But, our focus was to determine what RHONE had in mind for the Crossfire Team. To that end we drilled a little deeper than we normally do to confirm and detail their plans for us."

Remember, RHONE is a military and black operations group of a hundred thousand soldiers and spies. The scope of RHONE is six times larger than the U.S. intelligence services and the Russian intelligence services combined. This includes all of the black ops military units assisting their spies around the world. They have had their claws in just about every third-world war or battle and actually provide many of the mercenaries on both sides of the conflicts in the Middle East, Africa, South America, and so forth. Usually, RHONE has agenda and supplies superior forces for the side they want to win for political or military reasons. The troops that join the losing side act as agents in place and do what they can to destroy morale and provide Intel on the losing side's operations."

"RHONE has assigned a complete division of their troops, SS troops, and intelligence operatives to the task of eliminating the Crossfire Team. That is roughly ten to fifteen thousand soldiers. In most modern militaries, a division tends to be the smallest combined arms unit capable of independent operations; due to its self-sustaining role as a unit with a range of combat troops and suitable combat support forces, which can be divided into various specific combinations. As you can see, they are very serious about eliminating the Crossfire Team. Carlo Ricci cannot remember such a major force being focused on any single target so small in the history of RHONE."

"At the time of his capture, Carlo Ricci had assigned a Colonel Walhams to lead this division and to that end the Colonel has directed his elite troops to find us. The balance of the troops, most of the division, is on standby until we can be located and a suitable plan of attack is devised."

"That essentially is what this man knew of the operations against us. They are on a search and destroy mission and they will not rest until they find us and eliminate us." Judah sat down.

Jack thanked both of the young Jewish men for their expertise in Carlo's interrogation. Then he spoke to the core team.

"Well, this is what we expected but in a much bigger way than any of us thought they would employ. We can defeat a division in a variety of ways but I suggest we find a better way than toe-to-toe combat. We need to come up with a way that will deflect their interest in us. Let's work in groups and see what we can come up with over the next few days. We'll reconvene on Sunday right after the wedding."

Everyone chose up partnerships or small teams to attack the problem. But, on Saturday, during Shabbat (the original Jewish holy day, Friday at sundown until Saturday at sundown), they gathered together to celebrate Alexis and David's wedding.

The Zahavy wedding was officiated by Rabbi Hiram Greenberg, the same Messianic Jewish Rabbi that married Sarah and Mark before. Alexis was a gorgeous vision in white and David was a handsome groom in his blue tuxedo. The wedding incorporated Jewish and Christian themes and reflected the new man and woman which combine the two faiths. It was a beautiful ceremony and there wasn't a dry eye in the audience. Even though it was made up primarily of seasoned warriors tears were acceptable.

Alexis' mother was able to come to the wedding. Alexis's dad was in frail health and could only send his blessing by phone. Alexis's mother had been escorted from the U.S. by the director of the National Clandestine Service (NCS) which is one of the four main components of the Central Intelligence Agency. The director was also attending to represent Alexis' friends and co-workers from her last occupation. Several dozen Mossad leaders and coworkers attended from David's past.

The reception was exciting and the most enjoyable time anyone there could remember. While Alcohol was provided it was not used very much because most of the people involved were happy enough without stimulants.

The fun part of the reception was the fact that Alexis was still wearing her special perfume from their Italian mission. It still had a definite effect on men and women alike.

After the reception David and Alexis left on a honeymoon to an undisclosed location for two weeks. Jack knew they were on a cruise in the South Pacific and that they would be safe there. He didn't tell anyone except Laura, who was happy for them when she found out where they went.

CHAPTER SIXTY-FOUR

Two weeks later, Jack and Laura were relaxing in their apartment in the undersea base. Jack finished reviewing the global summary that Charlie Wu had created from his computer invasion of the intelligence agencies around the world. This was a totally different picture of world events than the one presented by the world news services.

Laura smiled at Jack, "How bad is it out there?"

Jack smiled back, "Dark, and getting darker. Marco Marino has consolidated his control of the majority of the world. He is being portrayed as the savior of the world. He has eliminated wars in general and brought all national militaries under his own control. Countries that have complaints can only take them to him for resolution. His spin masters always turn these things into victories for Marino and therefore the entire world.

People are no longer under pressure due to financial markets as he controls all movement of capital or resources throughout the world. While it is painted over as a new and wonderful world, the same pressures are still plaguing the globe. Hunger and death are mounting in the third world countries. Sin abounds everywhere the Anti-Christ assumes control. While gangs and riots are treated with violet control so are legitimate dissents or protests. The next phase of prophesy is coming true as the money in all countries is now under Marino's control and it is allotted to the governments or people that please him or the most newsworthy events that he can turn to his advantage."

His demand that everyone take the Mark of the Beast chip is being touted as the most wonderful thing ever created for world peace. The fact that a person cannot do business without the chip is seen as a unifying experience, not the absolute control of everyone on the planet. A person cannot buy food, gasoline, groceries, health care, or own property if they don't take the mark. To simply survive daily in life a person has to make a decision to take the mark. The believers who know that to accept the mark is a one-way ticket to hell and refuse are jailed or left to die on the streets without hope or help."

Jack shook his head, "Remember the movement to stock up supplies in remote locations so that people would be able to exist without the mark? Well, the idea was good, but most people didn't realize you can't buy a plane ticket, bus ticket, or gasoline to travel to that place after the mark was mandated. Many of them are trapped in cities where the only modes of transportation for a person without the mark are by bicycle, if they have one, or on foot. Anyone that complains is marked by computer and watched by the agents of RHONE and if they continue to complain they are arrested and either "counseled" or jailed as potential rebels.

"The One World Government, the OWG, has created large prisons outside all major cities of the world to hold the "dissidents", rebels, or the unruly. This is fed to the people as necessary "Social Control" and is necessary to preserve world peace. No one will complain about that because they would end up in the system as dissidents."

The OWG has completely taken control of the internet and all the Social Media throughout the world to prevent, "non-peaceful communications" from distorting or coming out against the government. The computer monitors are very good at detecting all non-governmental messages or keywords. Communications of every kind, telephone, radio, TV, Internet are strictly controlled as is the news. Elections are also controlled by the thugs of RHONE so that only pro-OWG candidates are elected thereby solidifying Marino's control of the world.

New court decisions have made prostitution legal, world-wide, abortion is also suggested and encouraged and legal. Women are losing their rights and positions of power and control everywhere, regardless of their capability or effectiveness. The Muslim masses are demanding Sharia Law be adopted worldwide which will completely eliminate human rights and relegate women to being chattel again."

"The only places these policies, the mark, and Marino's other controls are not being enforced are in Russia, China, and for the most part, Israel. The pressure is building in the new United Nations which is in Stockholm, to force these nations to conform. Other than that, things are rosy out there."

Laura sighed, "I feel so sorry for the people of the world. The Rapture has occurred, totalitarian control with evil in charge is running the world, and there is little or no hope left to the masses of humanity."

Jack agreed with her. "It is still in God's control. This is simply a reminder of the truth of the Gospel. People accepted other gods and other ways of living rather than what the God of the Universe offered them. Now they are paying for that isolation from God. I truly feel saddened by the billions of people that are going to have to go through the rest of the tribulations through no fault of their own except their ignorance of Yahveh and Yahshua."

The Crossfire Team will return in

"Revelation Crossfire".

If this story has awakened you or moved you to seek the love of Christ and His power for your life, whether you've never accepted Jesus as your savior or you've fallen away, repeat the following prayer and begin a most wonderful journey into eternal life with Him today.

Father God in heaven, As You said in Your Holy Word, (Romans 10:9) that if we confess the Lord our God and believe in our hearts that God raised Jesus from the dead, we shall be saved.

(The prayer on the next page is a sample prayer when asking Jesus into your heart as your Savior. You can also pray this in your own words.)

Salvation Prayer

Dear God in heaven, I come to you in the name of Jesus. I confess to You that I am a sinner, and I am sorry for my sins and the life that I have lived; I need your forgiveness. I believe that your only begotten Son Jesus Christ shed His precious blood on the cross at Calvary and died for my sins, and I am now willing to turn from my sin.

Right now I confess Jesus as the Lord of my life and my soul. With all my heart, I truly believe that your Holy Spirit raised Jesus from the dead. Today I accept Jesus Christ as my personal Savior and according to Your Word, right now I am saved.

I thank you Jesus, for your unlimited grace which has saved me from my sins. I thank you Jesus that your grace that never leads to license, but rather it always leads to repentance. Therefore Lord Jesus, transform my life so that I may bring glory and honor to you alone and not to myself.

I Thank you Lord Jesus, for dying for me at Calvary and giving me eternal life.

Amen.

If you just said this prayer and you meant it with all your heart, believe that you are now saved and have been born again.

You may ask, "Now that I am saved, what do I do next?" First of all you need to get into a spirit-filled, bible-based church that teaches the Scriptures, and you need to study God's Word.

Once you have found a church home, you will want to become water-baptized. By accepting Christ you are baptized in the spirit, but it is through water-baptism that you publically announce your obedience to the Lord Jesus. Water baptism is a symbol of your salvation from the dead. You were dead but now you live, for Jesus Christ has redeemed you for a price! The price was His atoning death on the cross. May God Bless You!

www.ingramcontent.com/pod-product-compliance
Lightning Source LLC
Chambersburg PA
CBHW070902180626
46817CB00003B/878